WITHDRAWN

PERILOUS FRONTIER

PERILOUS FRONTIER

A QUARTET OF CRIME IN THE OLD WEST

JOHN D. NESBITT
JIM JONES
PHIL MILLS, JR.
LARRY D. SWEAZY

EDITED BY HAZEL RUMNEY

THORNDIKE PRESS
A part of Gale, a Cengage Company

GALE
A Cengage Company

GALE
A Cengage Company

Copyright © 2021 by Five Star Publishing, a part of Gale, a Cengage Company.
Double Deceit © 2021 by John D. Nesbitt
Scarecrows © 2021 by Jim Jones
Cold the Bitter Heart © 2021 by Phil Mills, Jr.
Wind in His Face © 2021 by Larry D. Sweazy
Thorndike Press, a part of Gale, a Cengage Company.

ALL RIGHTS RESERVED
This novel is a work of fiction. Names, characters, places, and incidents are either the product of the author's imagination, or, if real, used fictitiously.

The publisher bears no responsibility for the quality of information provided through author or third-party Web sites and does not have any control over, nor assume any responsibility for, information contained in these sites. Providing these sites should not be construed as an endorsement or approval by the publisher of these organizations or of the positions they may take on various issues.
Thorndike Press® Large Print Hardcover Western.
The text of this Large Print edition is unabridged.
Other aspects of the book may vary from the original edition.
Set in 16 pt. Plantin.

LIBRARY OF CONGRESS CIP DATA ON FILE.
CATALOGUING IN PUBLICATION FOR THIS BOOK
IS AVAILABLE FROM THE LIBRARY OF CONGRESS.

ISBN-13: 978-1-4328-8647-9 (hardcover alk. paper)

Published in 2022 by arrangement with Cherry Weiner Literary Agency

Printed in Mexico
Print Number: 01   Print Year: 2022

TABLE OF CONTENTS

■ ■ ■ ■ ■

A DUNBAR
WESTERN MYSTERY

DOUBLE DECEIT

JOHN D. NESBITT

■ ■ ■ ■ ■

I

The man named Dunbar came to the Temple Basin country and the town of Perse in late October, when the weather was turning cold. We had just had our third snowstorm of the year. The first one was wet and rich, with large snowflakes falling from clouds that looked like folds of wet gray felt. The second was dry and powdery, and it melted in a day. Now the third snow was a daylong shower of thin, tiny flakes that came slanting in on a wind from the north and piled up about three inches deep.

I was bringing in my grandfather's horse when I saw a lone rider leading a packhorse. He came from the north, following the trail that led through the gap in the Osteen Breaks. I had lived with my grandfather long enough to know the different kinds of horses according to their colors and markings. The stranger was riding a blue roan and leading a buckskin. Small clouds of breath rose from the horses' nostrils, and their hooves threw up puffs of snow.

The sweep of land behind him, as it sloped up toward the breaks and the gap, was a vast carpet of white. For a moment I had the fancy that the man was riding out of a mass of snow, as if he had come down with the storm. I blinked and squinted, regained my sense of dimension, and saw the trail of his horses through the surface of the snow as they plucked their way down the slope into Temple Basin.

I turned my attention to the rider again. He wore a black hat and a deerskin-colored coat. As he drew closer, I saw that he had dark hair, dark eyes, and a bushy dark mustache. He sat tall in the saddle with his shoulders squared. His coat was of canvas, and his gloves, close to the same yellowish color, were of leather. He worked the reins and the lead rope, then raised a gloved hand in greeting. For as much as I had learned to be wary of strangers, I had a sense that he was a man I could trust.

His horses were huffing and blowing as he brought them to a stop a few yards away from where I sat on my horse. I wondered what he thought of me, just a girl, riding by myself with a horse in tow.

"Good afternoon," he said.

"How do you do?"

"Well enough." He pressed his hands together with his fingers interlocking, as a way of snugging his gloves. "I hope I haven't lost my way. This trail leads to Perse, doesn't it?"

"Yes, it does."

"Cold weather seems to be coming early this year."

"That's what my grandpa says."

"I'm lookin' for a place to drop my anchor before it gets dark."

I nodded. I thought it was a good idea, but I didn't think I had any authority to tell him so.

He cast a glance over at Snip, my grandfather's horse. "I wouldn't mind findin' a place where I could put up for a day or two and work for my keep."

"I don't have any say. I'm just a girl."

He smiled. "I don't mean to be that forward. I thought you might know of someone." He took off his hat with the hand that held the lead rope and rested it over the hand that held the reins. "By the way, my name is J.R. Dunbar, and I'm pleased to meet you."

"My name is Katie Moran. I live with my grandpa not too far from here." I pointed with my thumb over my right shoulder. As

11

an afterthought, I said, "His name's not Moran. It's Cooper."

"That's good to know. That is, it's good to know whose range I'm going through or by." He settled his hat on his head.

"You do ranch work, I suppose."

He nodded. "It's my trade."

"Well, I can't offer you a job. But I think it would be all right if you wanted to stop over at our place. My grandpa never has trouble finding work for someone to do, and he might be able to tell you where to look for a paying job. He knows all the outfits."

"That's kind of you." He tensed his upper body. "The air chills fast when the sun starts to slip." He adjusted his reins. "You're sure your grandfather won't mind?"

"I don't think so. He can use the help."

Grandpa was sitting in a chair by the wood-burning stove with his splinted leg stuck out straight. He tipped his head to see who was following me into the house.

"Evenin'," he said.

"And good evening to you." The visitor took off his hat.

I said, "Grandpa, this is Mr. Dunbar. I thought it would be all right if he put up for the night. He says he wants to work for his keep."

Grandpa gave a short smile as he looked Mr. Dunbar up and down. "If Katie thinks it's all right, then I guess I do, too. My name's Will Cooper." He held out his hand, and they shook.

Our guest motioned with his head as his glance fell on Grandpa's outstretched leg. "Sorry to see you've got a leg in a splint. I hope it's temporary."

"So do I. It should be. I got thrown by a horse a little while back. Slowed me down, as to what I can get around and do."

"I'll be glad to help as long as I'm here."

"That's good of you, Mr. Dunbar."

"You don't have to use the 'mister' with me. My last name is good enough."

"Same with me. Call me Will and skip the formalities." After a few seconds, he looked around at me and said, "I suppose you need to put the horses away."

"Yes, we do," I said. "I just wanted to make sure it was all right for him to stay."

Grandpa scratched the tuft of gray hair on the side of his head. "It's the custom of the country, but it's good that you ask to be sure."

Dusk was gathering in the barn as I unsaddled and brushed my horse, Baldy, and put him in the corral with Snip. I stood by and watched as Dunbar untied the lashes on his packhorse. The load relaxed, and the horse sighed. Dunbar worked with smooth, sure motions as he took down the bundles and laid them on a canvas sheet on the straw.

"I imagine I'll sleep here in the barn," he said. "I'll roll out my bed later." He smiled. "Not get so many critters in it that way."

He loosened the cinches and breeching on the packsaddle, gathered the straps, and pulled the sawbuck free. As he did so, he lifted the pad and blanket and turned them upside down to dry on top of the packsaddle. He set the gear next to his riding saddle on a plank rail.

"Here's a brush," I said, handing him the one I had used.

"Thanks." He put on his gloves and went about brushing the buckskin, laying one hand on the horse as he worked with the other. Every motion was smooth, and when he finished with the buckskin, he moved to the blue roan. Now and then he uttered a low syllable, and I sensed a closeness of spirit between him and his two horses.

"You can put them in their own corral," I said. "Each pen has a feed rack."

"Saw that. I'll pitch the hay."

Grandpa was hobbling around the kitchen

in lamplight as we went in from the dusk. A skillet was sputtering on top of the cookstove, and the smell of bacon grease hovered on the air.

I set my cap on a peg, and Dunbar hung his hat near it. The water in the washbasin was cold, but I was used to it, so I splashed my face and wrung my hands. Dunbar followed, as I imagined he had done in many a bunkhouse.

Grandpa said, "I just laid some deer meat in the frying pan."

"Good," said Dunbar.

"Katie shot a deer a little while back. Same day I broke my ankle."

"Oh." Dunbar turned to me and said, "Good for you."

I smiled. I didn't know what to say, so I gave a light shrug.

Grandpa spoke again. "I'm about to put on a second pan to fry some potatoes."

"I'll get it." I moved across the kitchen and took hold of the skillet that I had left on the sideboard that morning. I had wiped it clean, and nothing had fallen in it in the meanwhile, so I set it on the stove top.

Grandpa spooned in a couple of gobs of bacon grease and whacked the spoon on the lip of the skillet. With a sideways glance at Dunbar, he said, "What do you make of this country?"

"Looks nice enough, from what I saw. Quite a bit of it is covered with snow."

"I suppose it is. I haven't been out much. But it's good grassland. You don't see large patches of pure sagebrush, though it could come to that, over time, with too heavy grazing."

"I've seen it in other places."

"Which way did you come in?"

"From the north. Through the gap."

"Those are the Osteen Breaks along the north. On the east you've got the Meridian Hills, then the Yellow Dog Bluffs across the south, and Temple Rim curving around on the west. This whole area is called Temple Basin."

Dunbar nodded.

"Have you been here before?"

"Maybe once. Several years back."

"Well, the grease is melting. Let me put in the spuds. Have a seat if you'd like."

Dunbar took off his canvas coat, which had a blanket lining, and set it on the back of a chair. He pulled the chair away from the table and sat down.

He folded his hands above his waist and took on an unassuming air. He wore a dark, charcoal-gray wool vest with a wool shirt of lighter gray beneath it. A dark-handled revolver hung in a brown holster, and his boots of matching brown had silver-colored spurs. He did not wear conchos or beaded cuffs or any of the similar adornments I had seen on some men since I came to Wyoming. All the same, in his plainness, he seemed to have a briskness about him, a kind of energy one sensed around husky animals like deer or horses.

I set the table as Grandpa tended to the two skillets. I caught an occasional glimpse of Dunbar, his dark hair matted where his hat had been, a calm expression on his face. I wondered if he would take out tobacco and papers, as other men did when they were idle, but he did not. He was not restless or fidgety, and he did not show an urgency to break the silence.

Grandpa had lived by himself for several years, and he did not have the compulsion to talk, either. After years of chatter and hubbub at the orphanage, I was becoming used to the quiet as well.

Grandpa lifted one skillet and pivoted to set it on the wooden tabletop. The venison had been fried to a dark brown, and a rich aroma wafted up. Grandpa set the sizzling fried potatoes next to the meat. "Here's supper," he said.

Dunbar turned his chair to the table.

Grandpa sat down facing him, and I took a seat at the end of the table. We ate in silence for several minutes until Grandpa spoke.

"I don't know what your plans are, but if you wanted to stay over for a couple of days, I've got plenty of work to do. I've fallen behind since I got laid up. Katie's a good help, but she can't do everything."

"Sounds fine to me," said Dunbar.

"I thought I'd let you try the grub first."

"It's good."

"Better than refried boiled cabbage."

"I've eaten that, too."

Grandpa laughed. "I imagine you have. But if someone's workin' for board and room, I figure I'd better feed him better than that."

"No quarrel from me, Mr. Cooper."

"Will."

"Yes, sir. Will. And I'll say it again. This deer meat is first-rate."

"I agree. I'm sorry I don't have any whiskey to go along with it."

"That's all right. I enjoy a nip now and then, but I don't need it every day." Dunbar smiled at me. "You seem well adjusted to all of this. I guess you would be, if you killed the deer and you take care of your own horses."

"It was my first deer. I like it out here."

■ ■ ■ ■

Morning sunlight sparkled on the frosty grass that stuck up out of the snow. Fall roundup was a little more than a week away, and Grandpa wanted us to haze our cows toward the home range, so Dunbar and I rode out to check cattle. Dunbar had saddled the blue roan, and I was riding Baldy. I had brought Snip in the day before so I could use him if I needed, but I was leery of climbing onto him on a cold morning. He had laid his jaw across the top rail and nickered as we rode out of the yard, and I had thought of what a sweet fellow he seemed like even when he had the devil within him.

As the sun rose, I felt the warmth on my back. The frost on the blades of the dry pasture grass faded, and the snow at the base was beginning to melt. All summer long, I had gotten used to seeing grasshoppers skitter away and small, pale moths rise from the sparse flowering plants, but now it seemed as if the bugs of summer were dead.

We saw a few bunches of Lazy M Bar cattle, but we had not yet seen any of our own when Dunbar drew rein on a small rise.

"Whose brand is this we've been seeing?"

"Calvin Manke. He has two sections west of ours, and his cattle graze out from there."

"I see. And how much deeded land do you have?"

"Grandpa has one section. A quarter of it is fenced. That's where we had Snip. Grandpa calls it the calving pasture."

Dunbar nodded as he studied the land. "So Manke's place is west of the trail I came down on yesterday, and your place is to the east."

"That's right."

"Are we on his land right now?"

"We might be. Some of this is open range."

"How is he for a neighbor?"

"I hardly know him. Grandpa hasn't said much about him to me."

"We might get a chance to find out. Looks like three men coming this way." He motioned with his head, and I made out three specks about a half mile away.

"Shall we wait here?" I asked.

"Might as well. No need to take off and raise suspicions."

"I suppose."

I felt a tone of nervousness in my voice, and I thought Dunbar might have sensed it, too.

He said, "I was glad to hear you say last night that you like it out here."

20

"I do. I've been here almost a year."

"Uh-huh."

I felt that he was letting me speak, so I went on. "I was living in an orphanage in Pennsylvania. Grandpa found me there, and he asked me if I wanted to come out here and live. I thought I had been in the orphanage long enough. I didn't know what to expect, and I had heard stories about how hard the winters were out on the wheat farms, but Grandpa said, 'We're family, you know,' and that won me over. So I packed my few things and came out here with him."

"Seems as if you've learned a few of the ways."

"I have. But there's always more to learn."

"That doesn't change, though there's folks that come out here and after a year know everything."

"Grandpa says you need to learn to take the country on its own terms."

"I agree with him on that."

"When he says 'the country,' he means the land, the animals, and the people who live here. The whole thing."

"That's right. They say people are the same everywhere you go, that human nature doesn't change. But people come here for different reasons, and some of them take to curious ways that they wouldn't in the

21

places where they came from."

"I've gathered that. One thing Grandpa mentioned is that everyone out here is from somewhere else."

"All the white people, anyway."

"Well, yes. I haven't seen an Indian since I've been here."

"There's them, and if you go south, you'll meet Mexican people who have been here for generations."

"I hadn't thought of that, but of course I read something about it in school."

"In Pennsylvania."

"Yes, in the orphanage."

The three men on horses had dipped out of sight, and now they reappeared, less than a quarter of a mile away. Two of them rode side by side, and the third one followed.

"Does any one of them look like your neighbor Manke?"

"I believe so. The one on the left. The man on the right looks like his hired man."

We waited without speaking as the men drew closer. I recognized Calvin Manke by his round, shining face and dark eyebrows. He wore a sheepskin coat, thick gloves, and a medium-height, flat-topped hat with a curled brim. He was seated on a stout brown horse, and his boots stuck out.

Next to him, Hunt Crawford rode a lean

bay horse. Unlike his boss, the hired man rode slouched in the saddle. He wore a dull black wool overcoat with sleeves that almost covered his hands. A floppy-brimmed, dust-colored hat with a tall crown looked as if it had been pushed down over his ears, but as he came closer within view, I saw that the hat was pressing his straight, straw-colored hair over his ears, covering them. He lifted his head and brought his face out of shadow, and I saw his needle nose and washed-out, close-set eyes.

Saddle leather creaked and swished, spurs and bit chains jingled, and horse hooves thudded. The group of three came to a stop about ten yards away. I had a full view of our cattleman neighbor and his hired man, but I couldn't see the third rider very well, and I did not want to be staring at him.

Manke spoke first. "Good morning. I hope you know whose land you're on."

Dunbar answered. "I'm working for Mr. Cooper and his granddaughter here. We're lookin' to see if any of their cattle need to be pushed back."

"I'm Calvin Manke."

"I thought you might be. My name's Dunbar. Pleased to meet you. We've seen plenty of your cattle as we came across Mr. Cooper's land."

Hunt Crawford had been looking us over, and now he spoke up. "I don't think you'll find any of his stock over here. We push 'em out whenever we see 'em."

Dunbar nodded. "Your name?"

"I'm Hunt Crawford. Foreman for the Lazy M Bar." He sniffed, pushed his bare hand across the bottom of his nose, and drew a bag of tobacco out of his inside coat pocket. He continued talking as he began to roll a cigarette. "Even at that, some of Cooper's stuff is liable to get gathered up with ours. In another ten days or so, we'll let you know when you can come to our roundup and cut out anything of yours. Heard the old man was laid up. Didn't think the girl could do it herself." He licked the seam of his cigarette, tapped it, and stuck it in the side of his mouth. He brought a match out of nowhere, struck it in a way I did not see, and lit his cigarette with his head tipped to one side.

During this time, Manke seemed to be staring at empty space. He had not looked over our horses and our outfits, as other men had the habit of doing and as Hunt Crawford had just done. Now Manke's horse shifted, and he grabbed his saddle horn. He scowled at me as if I had caught him at something.

24

"I might be around that long," said Dunbar.

Manke's expression faded, and he brought his gaze to bear on Dunbar. I thought he was having to make an effort to face him. He said, "I hope you're not the type that has trouble following you. We all get along here. We don't have trouble."

"That's good."

Crawford tossed the dead match on the ground where the snow was giving way in the sunshine. "We'll let you know. Meanwhile, I don't think you need to ride over this way any farther. There aren't any of Cooper's cattle here." He tipped his head like before, lifted his hand, and took a drag on his cigarette.

Dunbar said, "We'll try to stay off your land and keep to the open range. I'd like to see a little more of the country while we've got good weather."

"Can't stop you from that." Crawford rolled the cigarette to the other side of his mouth without touching it, then gave a toss with his head and turned his horse to the left.

Manke followed, and the third rider came into view. The pit of my stomach lurched as I recognized the red hair, blue eyes, and upturned nose of Jeff Hayden. He was wearing a brown wool cap with the ear lugs tied up, and he had a smirk on his face.

"Hullo, Katie." He raised his hand as he turned his horse and followed the others. He was riding a speckled horse I had not seen before, so I assumed it was a Lazy M Bar mount.

My displeasure must have been plain to see. Dunbar said, "Who's the tagalong?"

"His name's Jeff Hayden, and I don't like him. The day I shot my deer, he barged in and wanted to take over. He brushed up against me in a way I didn't like, and I told him so."

"Good for you."

"This is the first time I've seen him since then, and he acts like nothing happened."

"Well, if we go to their camp on roundup, we'll stay clear of him. I don't think we can avoid Mr. Crawford, but I don't think he sees us as much of a threat."

"You didn't seem to care for the way he threw his match on the ground."

"He has a lot of moves. I believe men like him learn a great deal of that as part of their natural talent."

I didn't have anything to add, so I left it at that. A light chill had settled on me while we were sitting still, so I was glad to nudge my horse into motion and pick up a brisk walk in the autumn sun.

At the kitchen table at noon, Dunbar raised his eyebrows in a quizzical expression as he poured chokecherry syrup on his hotcakes. "I had the chance to meet your neighbor Manke this morning."

Grandpa handed him a plate of fried bacon ends. "Katie mentioned it."

"Not all cattlemen are the same. He seems to let his foreman speak for him."

"I believe he lets him run the ranch. It was that way with the foreman he had before this one. Manke has never seemed to me to be much of a cattleman, but he's always made his payment at the bank."

Dunbar nodded, as if he was taking in new information. "How long has he been here?"

"A little under ten years. More like nine. He came here after the big blizzard."

"He seems sure of himself, or that he wants people to think he is. He said something that made me wonder."

"What was that?"

"He said folks around here don't have trouble."

"Everyone has trouble sooner or later."

"I think he meant trouble between people. Not personal trouble like coming down with the grippe or being pummeled by hail. I

27

thought maybe he insisted too much."

"I know what you mean. Like a warehouse I worked in several years ago, before I came out here. This was before labor organizers, but the workers would get together and grumble. The boss would say, 'We don't have a problem. If we did, I'd do somethin' about it.' "

"Something like that."

Grandpa shrugged. "On the other hand, there might be some truth to what Manke said. People don't fight with one another here in the basin. Everyone knows we've got to get along, or things won't work. You can't go cuttin' fences or shootin' someone's livestock. Same in town. Whatever you need, there's one place to buy it. Even if you don't like the bean merchant or he doesn't like you, it's understood that you do business."

"Does anyone ever break the law?"

"Now, that's hard to say. As far as what goes on in the public eye, people don't act up much — like bein' drunk in public, or stealin' from someone else. But I've thought about it, and sometimes I wonder. If someone was good at breaking the law, who would know? Or sometimes things happen, and you never find out the explanation. Like someone disappearing."

"Oh, yes. That sort of thing. I've heard of

it. No one can say for sure that the person left town, but no one finds a body." Dunbar smiled as he tipped his head. "Of course, sometimes they do, even if it's years later."

"Yes, I've heard some of those stories."

Dunbar leveled his gaze. "Did someone disappear around here?"

Grandpa lowered his voice. "I don't know. But there was a fellow about a year ago, before Katie came to stay. He hung around town, and then he wasn't here anymore. Like the way you put it, no one saw him leave town, but no one found him dead in the alley."

"Was he a bum?"

"Not a beggar, from what I understood, but he didn't have his own horse or anything. He came in on the stage."

"And didn't leave."

"Not that anyone knew."

"And what was his name?"

"Zenith. Do you think you know him?"

Dunbar pursed his lips and shook his head. "Doesn't sound familiar to me. Of course, there's no reason it should."

Grandpa scratched his head. "I haven't heard his name mentioned for quite a while myself, or even thought of him, till you mentioned it."

"Just a part of my larger curiosity, which

was stirred up when good neighbor Manke said people didn't have trouble here. I have to admit that I become more interested if there's a morbid possibility. I have a weakness for that."

Grandpa laughed. "I've got more weaknesses than I've got time to tell about, or maybe should even mention. Apple pie, taffy, chocolate drops, ice cream."

"We can make apple pie," I said.

Grandpa regarded me as if he had just remembered I was present. "Yes, and I was thinkin' you two could go to town for some of our regular supplies — bacon and beans and such — and maybe you could buy a pound or two of dried applies."

Dunbar said, "That should be easier to get home than ice cream, even if we could find it."

"I'll draw up a list of things that aren't too perishable. Now that I don't have to send Katie by herself, I might ask you to pick up an item."

"Be glad to."

"A bottle of snakebite medicine. Wards off the grippe as well."

Dunbar said, "I know how to find such a thing."

II

We rode into the town of Perse in the early afternoon. Dunbar had saddled his buckskin for the errand, and I was riding my usual mount, Baldy. The devious Snip trailed behind us on a lead rope, with a pair of saddle panniers for the supplies.

The livery stable sat on our left as we rode in from the north. A crow perched on the gable, shiny black against the blue sky, tipping his head and eyeing us. He croaked as he flapped his wings and flew away.

"Grandpa told me that crows and magpies know how to stay out of range."

"I believe they do," said Dunbar. "Coyotes, too, always lookin' over their shoulder."

We tied up in front of the general store, and Dunbar held the door for me as we walked inside. As the tinkle of the doorbell died away, so did the conversation between two men.

I recognized Mr. Linwood, the owner of the hotel, on our side of the counter. On the business side, Mr. Rhoden, the storekeeper, stood smiling. He raised his voice to greet us as we walked down the aisle.

"Good afternoon. How are things out your way?"

"Well enough, I guess. This is Mr. Dunbar. He's working for us for a while."

Mr. Rhoden nodded. "How do you do." He glanced at Mr. Linwood, who raised his hand in farewell and walked away.

"Fine," said Dunbar.

Still smiling, the storekeeper returned to me. "What can I help you with today?"

"Here's a list of a few things." I unfolded the paper and handed it to him. I knew he liked to tend to things in his preferred order.

Dunbar said to me, "While you're getting these things together, I could go for that other item your grandfather mentioned."

"Oh, yes. Let me give you some money."

Dunbar held up his hand. "It's a small thing. I'll take care of it." He turned away before I could protest. His spurs clinked, and his bootheels sounded on the wooden floor.

I gave my attention to Mr. Rhoden. He was a neat, healthy-looking man in middle age, clean-shaven with well-trimmed hair parted down the middle. He wore a white shirt, black necktie, and gray apron.

"I'll start with the dry stuff," he said. "Beans, rice, flour, coffee. I see you've got dried apples here as well. Would you like some raisins, too?"

"Not if it's not on the list."

"Of course."

As the storekeeper gathered the items, I glanced out the window from time to time to keep an eye on the horses. Dunbar came into view with a cylindrical object wrapped in brown paper. He tucked it into the left-side pannier on Snip and stepped up onto the sidewalk. After taking a casual glance to each side, he came into the store with an easy stride.

Mr. Rhoden said, "I see you've got bags on your horse. I don't have to wrap this up in bundles, then."

"That's right," said Dunbar. "It'll be easier to keep the weight even on both sides."

Mr. Rhoden wiped his hands on his apron. "I wrap the bacon in paper, of course." As he spoke, he seemed to be taking in all of Dunbar's details. "You never know what people want to have wrapped and bagged. Or double-bagged. Time and distance, rough travel, wear and tear."

"Old saying in Spanish," said Dunbar. "Everything comes to an end with use. Even a good cloak wears thin."

Mr. Rhoden gave a light frown as he regarded Dunbar. "You're not from down that way, are you?"

"No, but I've been there. And I've visited with those people up this way as well."

"Good people. Especially the God-fearing ones." Mr. Rhoden ran a string around the wrapped bacon, tied a knot, and broke the string with his hands. "That's got it."

Out on the street, while Dunbar hefted the goods and placed them in the panniers, I took the opportunity to go into the post office. On being told we had no mail, I stepped outside into the sunshine. Dunbar was tying the panniers snug.

"No mail," I said.

"I don't expect any, either, but I might as well check."

"I'll stay with the horses."

Left to myself, I enjoyed the mild sunshine. I recalled how most of the snow had disappeared on the rangeland. Here in town, the only white patches I saw lay in the shadows of buildings.

A voice from the sidewalk behind me caused me to flinch.

"Waitin' for someone?"

I turned to see a tall, slender man looking down at me. I had not seen him before, and from his clothes, I took him to be a newcomer. He wore a narrow-brimmed brown hat, a white shirt with a high collar, a tan jacket, a mustard-colored waistcoat, gray pants, and low, dark shoes.

"Yes, I am," I said.

"That shouldn't keep me from introducing myself." He moved his hand, which held a thin walking stick. "My name is Elton Thomas. I'm an educator by profession." He stepped down from the sidewalk.

"A schoolteacher? Do you work hereabouts?"

"I'm looking for a situation to come my way. In the meanwhile, I do a bit of writing." He waved the stick. "Not so much for the money. I couldn't be a commercial scribbler."

Now that he was closer, I saw that he had a long head, a narrow nose, close-set brown eyes with a blank expression, and a coarse complexion. His shirt collar had not seen a wash for a while, and the rest of him had a filmy quality.

"Don't get me wrong," he said. "I do accept money for my work. But I don't churn it out like these hacks do."

Another voice caused us both to look around.

"And just as well." The voice came from a short man in a black suit and hat. I recognized him as the town doctor.

He tipped his hat, which was of a short stovepipe style. His balding head showed for a second. "Good afternoon, Miss Cooper."

"Moran, actually, but small matter. Good afternoon."

"Is this man posing an inconvenience?"

"Not really. He just introduced himself."

"I see."

The slender man turned his blank expression toward the doctor. "My name is Elton Thomas. I'm an educator. At your service." He gave a short bow of the head.

"I am Dr. Arnold Orme, the physician in this town. You'll forgive the intrusion, but when I saw a stranger imposing his company on this young lady —"

Mr. Thomas's features stiffened. "Think nothing of it. I was doing no harm."

"He wasn't," I said.

"But I'll be on my way nevertheless." With the hand that held the walking stick, Mr. Thomas tipped his hat to me. "A pleasure."

When the schoolteacher was gone, the doctor said, "I hope you don't mind, Miss Moran."

"It's all right." I focused on him, not sure what to think of his intentions. I knew who he was, but not much more. He was a smiling, self-satisfied man, always with an air of sarcasm, I thought. I did not think he was something to be worried about, for he was short and soft, a bit round in the middle. His face had filled out with middle age, and he wore glasses. I knew he was a solid citizen, in that he had a wife and a medical practice. His house and doctor's office were located in the same place, a two-story house with a stone foundation. I was trying to remember if I had read a word for his kind of office, when his voice sounded again.

"I didn't mean to run off your dolichocephalic acquaintance."

I did not know what he meant with such a strange word, but I had the feeling that he was making fun of Mr. Thomas at the same time that he wanted to seem superior in education. I saw that his beady eyes were fixed on me, and I glanced away. To my relief, Dunbar appeared.

He stood about ten feet from the doctor, and silence hung in the air for a moment.

The doctor's eyes searched at Dunbar, then averted. I might say he retreated, for he took half a step backward. He frowned. "I don't believe I know you."

"Name's Dunbar. Cowpuncher by trade. Workin' for Miss Moran and her grandfather."

"I see." The doctor held his hands together at his waist. "I am Dr. Orme, what you cowpunchers call the local sawbones."

Dunbar touched his hat brim. "Pleased to meet you."

"Likewise." The doctor's eyes came back to me. "Well, I should be going. Give my regards to your grandfather, and of course if you need anything, let me know. Has he been in pain?"

"Not that he has mentioned."

"Not that he would. Very well." The doctor took off his hat, made a small flourish in my direction, and settled the hat over his balding head again. "I must be gone."

"Goodbye," I said.

Dunbar said, "Good to meet you."

The doctor spoke over his shoulder. "Of course."

Dunbar stepped down from the sidewalk and began to untie Snip's lead rope. With a wry smile, he said, "I didn't mean to be running off anyone, either."

"Did you hear the word he used? I don't know what he meant."

"Dolichocephalic? It means the head is longer than it is wide." He patted Snip's forehead. "Like our friend here."

"A scientific term."

"Yes, and the phrenologists use it, also."

"Did you see the man he was referring to?"

"The narrow chap? Yes, I did. I also saw the doctor studying you, so I thought I'd watch him for a minute."

"Ah. Then you saw what happened. The thin man is a schoolteacher. I believe he's trying to find work. I'm not sure what the doctor was up to, but he acted as if he was just looking out for me."

"He might be a little deeper than the schoolteacher." Dunbar untied Baldy's reins and handed them to me. "Anything else while we're in town?"

"Not that I can think of."

"Well enough. We won't keep your grandfather waiting."

Hazy clouds were gathering as we headed north out of town. The warmth of the sun, which had not been very strong, was fading. The horses picked their way along at a fast walk, their hooves clip-clopping and their breathing steady.

Half a mile ahead of us, a band of four antelope angled across the trail toward the southeast. Their tan-and-white bodies strung out in single file as they ran.

Dunbar's horse stopped, and so did Baldy and Snip.

"I wonder if they're running from something." Dunbar patted the buckskin's neck.

"Do you think they're spooked?"

"Not too much. If they were really spooked, such as if someone had shot at

39

them, they'd be running in a bunch and kicking up dust. But we'll be on the lookout all the same."

We rode on, and a few minutes later, a rider appeared on the crest ahead of us. He was moving at a lope on a light-colored horse.

Dunbar said, "I wouldn't be surprised if that's the young fellow with the red hair. He was riding a horse like that when we saw him earlier."

"Jeff Hayden," I said. "He was wearing a cap like that, too."

The rider came head-on, and soon enough I saw that it was Jeff. He was bobbing in the saddle as he pulled on the reins and brought the animal to a jolting stop. A low wake of dust caught up with him.

"Afternoon, sir." He pulled off his cap, and his red hair sprang into view. "Katie."

Dunbar said, "You look like you're on your way somewhere. Don't let us hold you up."

"I am, sir." Jeff settled his cap onto his head. "I've got to take some news to town."

"Go ahead. I suppose we'll hear it when we're meant to."

"Oh, I don't think it'll be a secret, sir. But I don't know if it's too much for a girl's ears."

40

I thought his courtesy was overdone, but I did not want to play in and answer him.

"We can wait," said Dunbar.

"I don't know if you should, sir." Jeff glanced at me and returned to Dunbar. "A man's been found dead."

"Indeed? On your boss's land?"

"Right where it meets Mr. Cooper's."

Dunbar remained calm. "Not too far from where we met earlier, then."

"That's right, sir."

"Any idea of the cause of death?"

"Not that I heard. The boss sent me on my way as soon as we found it."

"Then you'd best be going." Dunbar turned to me. "I think we might want to look into this before we go home. Or I can, if you'd prefer not to."

Jeff said, "I think you should go home. It's nothing for a girl to —"

I kept my eyes on Dunbar as I said, "I'll go along with you."

We found Calvin Manke and Hunt Crawford standing by their horses on the side of the trail, not far from the small pile of rocks that marked the northwest corner of Grandpa's land. As we rode up to the scene, the two men moved their horses aside. A hu-

41

man form in drab clothing lay on the ground.

Dunbar and I dismounted. He said, "We met your young rider about a mile back. He said you had found a man dead."

Crawford spoke. "We did."

Dunbar and I walked forward. He held onto his horse and Snip as I led Baldy. We stopped a couple of yards from the body. The deceased man was of average size and build, lying facedown. He had straight, light-colored hair.

"What does it look like?" Dunbar asked.

Crawford said, "I'd say he was dumped here. No hat, no horse, nothin'."

"Any signs of how he might have come to die?"

"Not that we could see. No blood. No bullet or stab wounds." Crawford glanced at me, then spoke to Dunbar. "Isn't this a little strong for a girl?"

"Depends on how you speak."

Crawford wiped his long coat sleeve across the bottom of his nose and said nothing.

Dunbar knelt by the body and studied it. "Do you know who he is?"

"We think he's a fella named Whirledge. Seen him around town."

"I wonder how he would end up out here."

Calvin Manke had been silent all this

time, but now he exploded. "I don't like any of this! I don't like him bein' on my land, and I don't like you two bein' here, either."

"Fine with us." Dunbar stood up and glanced at me. "Shall we go?"

As we turned to lead our horses away, Manke's voice rose up behind us. "And don't come back."

Grandpa's eyes grew wide as he heard the news. "This doesn't sound good at all. Take someone who hangs around town and leave his body out on the range. Just meant to confuse people."

Dunbar said, "That's what some people do when they commit homicide."

"I suppose."

"So much for everyone getting along together."

"I should say. And Manke's offended by it?"

"Seems to be."

Grandpa pursed his lips. "Well, no tellin' who might have a reason."

Dunbar said, "Just a thought, but the last time we talked about anything like this, you mentioned a man named Zenith who disappeared. Do you think the two could be related?"

"No tellin' about that, either."

"Do you know of anyone who might have an idea?"

Grandpa shook his head. "I don't know. It's got me baffled."

We finished putting away the supplies, and Dunbar took the horses to the barn as Grandpa and I went to work on supper.

Dunbar came in, hung his hat on a peg, and stood in front of the stove. He held his hands out, palms forward, to take in the heat.

In that moment I noticed something that I think I had seen before but hadn't registered. In the palm of his right hand, Dunbar had a dark spot, as if he had been branded or burned in the hand at some time in the past. He did not seem to make any attempt to either show it or not let it be seen, so I paid it no more attention. That is, I did not stare at it, but it did make me think about things I had read about transported felons being burned in the hand so they couldn't go back to England, and slaves being branded in a similar way so they could be identified if they ran away. I wondered if Dunbar had been through some kind of an ordeal or if the scar or dark spot was the simple result of some work he had done. I remembered a story I had read about a boy who ran away from a haying crew but was found out by the mark left in his palm by the pitchfork handle.

Grandpa was slicing potatoes on the sideboard. He paused and said, "Going back to what you asked earlier about whether there might be someone who would know of any kind of relationship between Zenith and Whirledge — well, now that I think of it, there may be one fellow who might know something. A man named Sam Stroud who used to hang around town. He worked in the butcher shop until drink got the best of him. Then he worked as a swamper at the saloon. He was known to mooch drinks off of regulars like Tom Whirledge, and he might well have known Zenith."

"And what did Whirledge do for a living?"

"Odd jobs. Load and unload freight wagons. Fix things on people's houses and buildings. If a cat died underneath someone's house, they'd get him to drag it out and bury it. They say he could fix wagon wheels and broken axles, but they wouldn't let him work at the blacksmith shop. By the way, how was Snip running today?"

"All right."

"I think it's time to pull his shoes off."

"I could do that for you. In the morning,

if you'd like."

"That would be good." Grandpa shifted his voice and said, "Katie, was there any mail today?"

"No," I said.

"All the news is out in the country, then."

"Seems to be."

The conversation took a lull until Dunbar spoke. "I met one of your prominent citizens when we were in town. The doctor."

Grandpa said, "Oh, him."

"Not very sociable with me, but he seemed like a busybody."

"He's something like that."

"I would guess from his actions that he's been here for a while."

Grandpa drew his brows together. "More than ten years. Maybe twelve or thirteen. Well before the big blizzard."

"Is he your kind of country doctor who makes the rounds in his buggy?"

"Not much. He stays in town. He goes to people's houses, but anyone from the country has to go into town to see him."

"I suppose he does well enough that way."

"Oh, yes. He's the only doctor around. He set my leg."

"I gathered that, about your leg. He's probably been in every house in town, then."

"Except for the shacks and hovels. But

46

even at that, every man, woman, or child who has come down with something has been seen by him one way or another."

When Dunbar was out doing chores the next morning, Grandpa sat near the stove with his leg propped up as he drank coffee.

"Sometimes I wonder about Dunbar," he said. "Why he's here. He seems to take quite an interest in strange doin's."

I said, "I recall him saying that he had a weakness for morbid things."

"Hah. I don't know whether he might be some kind of a detective. If he is, I don't think he's a bad kind."

"What kind is that — the bad one?"

"There's what they call a stock detective or a range detective. They go around lookin' for men that are accused of bein' rustlers."

"Like a bounty hunter?"

"Sometimes. Some of them are little more than paid killers."

"Do you have a kind of a bad sense about Dunbar, then?" I asked.

"No, I don't."

"Neither do I. I've had a good sense about him since I first met him."

"So have I. But there's such a thing as a confidence man. He earns your confidence, and then he turns it to his own purposes."

"I'll be on the lookout," I said.

"So will I, even if I think he's all right."

Grandpa and I went out to watch and to lend a hand if necessary as Dunbar pulled the shoes off of Snip. He had the horse snubbed to a sturdy corner post and was bent over a raised hoof, prying and pulling with a pair of nippers. When he worked the first shoe free, he dropped the hoof and stood up, taking a long, deep breath.

"He doesn't fight you, does he?" Grandpa asked.

"No, but he likes to lean on me."

"That's an old game."

"Lots of 'em know it." Dunbar moved to a hind leg, lifted it back, and slipped his knee under. Then he let the hoof down and stood aside.

I heard the footfalls of a horse and realized Dunbar had heard them first. I turned to see Jeff Hayden riding into the yard on a small sorrel horse.

"How do you do, Mr. Cooper?"

"Well enough," said Grandpa.

"What are you-all up to?"

"Dunbar's pulling the shoes off of Snip."

"Oh, yeah. I know somethin' about that."

"And yourself?"

"Well, sir, I came to say that I hope you-all don't hold anything against my boss. I understand he got cross yesterday."

"He might have. Dunbar told me about it, but like he said, we can't let that trouble us. We've got to work with your outfit when it comes time to cut our cattle out."

"That's right." Jeff took off his cap and smiled at me, then spoke again to Grandpa. "You see, Mr. Manke's missin' some fifty head of steers, he thinks, and findin' this dead body on his land was the straw that broke the camel's back."

Dunbar had walked to the edge of the corral where we stood. He looked across the top rail at Jeff and said, "Thanks for your kind words. Did you come on your own, or did your boss send you?"

Jeff's face went blank. "Well, I came on my own."

"Thanks again." Dunbar turned. "I need to get back to my work."

When Jeff was long gone and Dunbar had finished with Snip's shoes, Grandpa said, "You wonder what to think about that kid droppin' by."

Dunbar shrugged. "He might be better off not taking the initiative to stick up for someone who keeps his motives to himself."

Grandpa said, "That's how I felt, but I didn't know how much good it would do to tell him."

Dunbar gave a small shake of the head. "Maybe he'll learn it on his own."

Dunbar and I rode out of the ranch yard at midmorning. He told Grandpa that even though he didn't think he would find anything, he thought he should go out and look for signs of any wrongdoing on our property. He suggested that I go along so that we would have the appearance of checking cattle.

As we rode, he hummed a tune. I had heard him sing a couple of lines to the same melody earlier, when he was brushing the roan. The verses were new to me.

And it wasn't women or whiskey
Caused the death of Whistling Jim.

He did not sing the words now when he knew I was around, but I thought he was rather cheerful about a theme that was, to use a word of his, morbid.

Although the sunshine was not strong, it warmed the world around us. After we had ridden for about an hour, we stopped to rest the horses at a low sandstone bluff that caught the sun and reflected a little of the warmth. I stood with my back to the bluff and my face to the sun.

"This is nice," I said. "Sometimes it seems as if the orphanage was in another life, another world. I don't miss it, even though it had some good parts to it."

"I would guess you had something of an education. You speak well."

"Thank you. I don't think everyone who came out of there had good speech habits. But I took well to those subjects, and I liked to read."

"What kinds of things did you read?"

I felt that he was making conversation, but I also felt he might be interested in my answer. "Quite a few of the regular schoolbook poems," I said, "like 'The Ballad of the Oysterman,' 'The Village Blacksmith,' 'Paul Revere's Ride,' and others. Longer poems as well, like *The Song of Hiawatha, The Courtship of Miles Standish,* and *Evangeline.* Then books, like *Uncle Tom's Cabin* and *Silas Marner.* Oh, and stories like 'Rip Van Winkle' and 'The Legend of Sleepy Hollow.' And now that I think of it, I also made my way through *Wuthering Heights.*"

"And how did you like that?"

"I didn't care for all of the characters being in turmoil with one another all the time, but I did like the descriptions of the moors and the bleak countryside."

"Good mournful stuff," said Dunbar. "But I think it would have been better if it ended like a real tragedy." Then, as if to amend himself, he said, "Not that it matters to that many people."

"True. Not everyone had the habit of reading books. Some of them were good for playing checkers and cards and other simple games. There was one game I thought was peculiar. The ones who played it had a couple of different names for it, not very nice, but it was a harmless game in itself."

"What was it called, or would you rather not say?"

"I don't care to talk that way myself, but I can say it. Sometimes they called the game Indian Poker and sometimes they called it Mexican Sweat. It consisted of holding one card on the forehead." I held up my hand as if I had a card in it.

"I know of the game," he said. "It's an interesting way to try to get the best of someone. Rather than bet on what you know you have, you bet against what you know your opponent has."

"That's right."

"And at the same time, you don't know what you have or what the world can see."

"Yes, it was peculiar in that way, and like I said, it seemed harmless. I never knew

52

anyone to win or lose more than a few pennies at it."

Silence fell, and I wondered when we would mount up and move on. Dunbar must have thought it was time as well.

"I think these horses are rested," he said. "Let's move along before we cool down too much."

A few minutes later, out on the main trail, we crossed paths again with Calvin Manke and Hunt Crawford. We all came to a stop. As before, Manke did not take note of our horses or gear. He sat on his stout brown horse with his boots pointing outward and both hands on the saddle horn.

"We're looking for evidence," he said. "I imagine you're doing the same."

"Part of the time," said Dunbar.

Manke did not seem to hear Dunbar's answer, nor did he look straight at us as he spoke. "We need to work together. Share what we know or find out about this business. We need to get to the bottom of it."

"I hope someone can," said Dunbar.

I stole a glance at Hunt Crawford, and I saw a blank stare in his washed-out eyes. I wondered what he was thinking. He came to, blinked his eyes, and said, "We've got to get this stuff out of the way. We've got some hard work comin' up."

He turned his horse and ignored me, even as his stirrup hit mine. Dunbar flinched but held still. Manke's horse turned of its own accord and followed Crawford's. The boss man bounced in the saddle as he gathered his reins and rode away.

III

Dunbar shaved while Grandpa cooked the oatmeal the next morning. The coffee boiled, and Grandpa set it aside to let the grounds settle.

Grandpa sniffed. "I wish I had some raisins to put in this mush. Give it a little more flavor."

I said, "Mr. Rhoden offered to sell me some, but I told him we should stick to what we had on the list."

Grandpa tapped the spoon on the lip of the enamel pot. "It's just as well. If you stick to your list, you have a better chance of living within your means."

Dunbar relaxed his face after stretching it to one side and another in the mirror. "Raisins could be within our reach," he said. "I was thinking of going into town today."

I hadn't wondered before why he was shaving on this day, but now I thought it made sense.

Grandpa said, "Is there any reason in particular, or is that something I shouldn't ask?"

Dunbar had a light tone as he said, "I don't mind the question. I thought I might try to find Sam Stroud. There's also the possibility that someone I know might come in on the stage."

"Oh." Grandpa rested the spoon on the edge of the pot. "If you don't mind, I'll ask another question."

"Go ahead." Dunbar waved his hand, and I noticed the dark spot in his palm.

"Are you a Pinkerton man or some kind of range detective?"

"I work on my own," said Dunbar. He gave Grandpa a knowing look, and with a smile he said, "I'm a cowpuncher with curiosity."

"Well, I won't ask any more questions. There's no good in being too inquisitive."

"I don't mind sharing some information and some things that I know. It helps me learn more." Dunbar smiled again. "I can't very well break bread with you under your roof, or eat your porridge, and think that I can ask questions and not have to answer any. And besides, I was going to invite Katie to go along today."

I felt a catch in my throat. "To look for

Sam Stroud?"

Grandpa said, "If you're going to look for him, I think you'll go into places that Katie ought to stay out of, at least while she's still a juvenile."

I had not heard myself referred to by that word, but I had come across it in a school-book on natural science, where the term referred to a young bird that did not have its full plumage.

Dunbar laughed. "I didn't plan to drag her into dens of iniquity. I thought she might like to meet the person coming in on the stage. A lady named Mrs. Deville."

All the way into town, I wondered what Mrs. Deville looked like. I imagined her as middle-aged and filled out, like a couple of women who worked in the kitchen in the orphanage. I also pictured her as plain and not very shapely, like a woman I had met on the train. She wore a suit like a man's and said she had a boarding house in Broken Bow. In another version, I imagined Mrs. Deville with a dark dress buttoned up to her chin and a hymn book in her hands, like the women who looked right through us when a group of us from the orphanage sat in church.

When I took into account Dunbar's having taken the trouble to shave and to put on a plum-colored neckerchief, I began to think that my images of Mrs. Deville were too drab and strict. I conjured a picture of a woman with lipstick and mascara, wearing a tight-fitting dress, holding a box of knives for the knife thrower in the circus.

My thoughts came back to the present as we rode into town from the north. A crow on the peak of the livery stable flew away, wheezing a croak. A dun horse stood hip-shot in front of the Twin Forks Saloon, and a ranch wagon was pulled up alongside the general store.

Because of the wagon, we were unable to tie up in front of the store, so we rode to the next hitching rail, which was in front of the post office, and dismounted. We tied our horses and made our way to the store.

Once inside, as the tinkle of the doorbell faded and our footsteps sounded on the floor, Mr. Rhoden appeared at the counter. As before, he was wearing a white shirt, black necktie, and gray apron. He put on a smile and waited until we were ten feet away, then beamed at me.

"Good to see you again. What can I help you with today?"

"Grandpa asked us to pick up some raisins while we were in town."

"Oh. Anything else, or just a small order today?"

"Just that," said Dunbar. He laid a silver dollar on the counter.

I frowned at him and said, "Grandpa gave me —"

Dunbar held up his hand. "Allow me."

"But you bought the snakebite medicine last time."

His face had the kind of expression that came to mind when I came across the word *mirthful.* He said, "And I might do it again."

He and Grandpa had taken only one nip out of the new bottle, so I imagined he was going to buy another one in the process of looking for Sam Stroud.

Outside, I stood in the street in the fragile sunlight as Dunbar made his way to the saloon. The door was open, and as Dunbar approached it, he stopped to let a man walk out. At first I thought the man might be a patron, perhaps the owner of the dun horse tied at the hitching rail, but I saw that he was wearing an apron and carrying a bucket. He was a short, slight man with light-colored hair and a scruffy beard. He wore dust-colored work clothes, and his dull white apron hung long and loose. Leaning against the weight he carried, he walked down the sidewalk past the horse a few

58

yards. With a swing and a heave, he pitched the water out into the street.

Dunbar waited for him as he trudged toward the saloon door. He walked leaning forward, and when he stopped to talk to Dunbar, he stood up straight, and his bucket caught up with him. It occurred to me that the man was a swamper, as Grandpa said Sam Stroud had been, but I doubted that Dunbar had found his man. The two of them exchanged a few words in a matter-of-fact tone, and Dunbar waved his arm to usher the man in ahead of him.

I waited for several long minutes. The swamper came out with a broom and began sweeping the sidewalk. Dunbar appeared, holding in his left hand a familiar-shaped object wrapped in brown paper. He stopped, spoke a couple of words, and handed the man what I guessed to be a coin. I heard the man say, "Thank you," and their visit ended.

Dunbar stepped down into the street and joined me where I stood with the horses. In his cheerful tone he said, "I think this will fit in your saddlebag better than in mine, if you don't mind."

"Not at all."

As he stowed the package, he spoke to me over his shoulder. "I'm going to go in here and see if I have a message." He tipped his head, motioning with his hat brim toward the post office. The place also served as the telegraph office and the stagecoach ticket office, so I imagined he was expecting some kind of information about Mrs. Deville, who appeared in my mind now like one of the ladies, all brooches and hatpins, who used to come to the orphanage to donate used clothing.

I stood in the street with my back to the sidewalk, comfortable at being left out of these more adult affairs. A voice from behind me made my shoulders tense.

"How nice that we meet again."

I turned to meet the narrow-faced, thin-chested figure of Mr. Thomas, the school-teacher, dressed as before in his tan jacket, mustard-colored waistcoat, and gray pants. His close-set eyes with their unusual blank expression settled on me.

"Waiting for your boss?" he asked.

"Not quite."

"Oh. I thought you were a working girl."

"I work, but not for someone who pays me or owns me. I live with my grandfather on a ranch, and this man in the dark hat is working for us for the time being."

"Some farms and ranches have working girls."

I sensed that he wanted to place himself in a station above me, but I also thought he might have picked me out with some accuracy. I had come to understand that people who had been in reform schools and orphanages had a recognizable air or quality about them. I said, "I know that. And I have known some of them. I was in an orphanage myself, and I'm not ashamed to say it. Some of the girls there became chore girls and farm helpers and housekeepers. Some of them were indentured. I was lucky that I didn't have to go into that."

"Indentured?"

"Yes. They signed indentures."

"Oh, I know what it means. As a matter of fact, I know something that many people don't. Do you know where the term came from?"

"No, I don't."

He drew himself straight up and said, "You see, back in the old days, when they brought people over from England, some of them couldn't write their own names. So they made an impression with their teeth in wax."

"I hadn't heard that before."

He touched the narrow brim of his brown hat. "Always happy to share a bit of knowledge." With a quick motion, he looked to his left, where Dunbar was coming out of the post office. "Well, here's your hired man, so I'll let you go." He touched his hat brim again and walked away to his right.

Dunbar folded a slip of paper and tucked it into his vest pocket, then stepped down into the street to join me. "It'll be a little while. Forty-five minutes to an hour. Is there anything else you'd like to do while we're in town?"

"Not that I can think of." I peered to my left to make sure Mr. Thomas was out of hearing range. "The educator paid me a short visit."

"I saw that."

"He told me something that I wonder if it's true."

Dunbar's eyes narrowed. "Some kind of news?"

"Oh, no. What he called knowledge. I just don't know how genuine it is."

"Well, what was it?"

I looked again to be sure the man was gone. "He asked me if I was a working girl, and I said no, and then I told him about girls I had known and their terms of service. Some of them were indentured."

"Sure."

"And he went on to tell me that those terms were called indentures because people who couldn't sign their own name made an impression in wax with their teeth."

Dunbar laughed. "That's a quaint story, but I wouldn't give it much credit. People who couldn't sign documents still made a mark. And someone might even write next to it, 'Wilson his mark,' or something similar. That was a common practice, not only in documents, but when people signed things like a manifest, or a passenger list. Or if they signed on for a voyage, like on merchant or whaling ships. Men from places that didn't have alphabets, like South Sea Islanders, still had a sign or a symbol that represented them. Even in the pirate stories, they sign with a mark, and each man has his own."

I laughed. "In a world of skull and cross-bones."

"That's the idea. And they still do it today, on things like mining claims. They make their mark. But I never heard or read of someone signing with his teeth in wax."

"Where does the term come from, then?"

"Oh. That's interesting in itself. In earlier times, when two parties would draw up a contract, such as for an apprentice, they would make out two handwritten copies side by side on the same page, as on a piece of parchment, and then they would cut it down the middle with jagged or zigzag cuts that could be matched later. The cut edges looked like teeth, and that's where the term came from." Dunbar paused. "I don't want to disparage the schoolteacher, and I don't want to begrudge anyone who wants to make a living, but I think that with this explanation, he's being something of a charlatan."

"What does that mean?"

"A charlatan is like a quack — someone who pretends to have knowledge and makes a show of it."

"Like a pedant?"

Dunbar laughed. "A pedant shows off knowledge he does have. I'm afraid I catch myself at that sometimes."

I was tempted to ask him what he knew about transported felons, for I had read that they had come to the colonies along with indentured servants. I restrained myself and said, "So a pedant would go on and on, for example, about whaling ships."

"Yes, right down to the scrimshaw."

"What's that?"

"You see? I just did it. Scrimshaw is the art, or craft, you might say, of carving whalebone. Some of it gets pretty fine and detailed."

"I've seen it. I even saw a whaling ship,

64

with all the masts and sails carved out."

"Here's company," said Dunbar.

I followed his gaze to the sidewalk, where Dr. Orme had stopped and tipped his head, as if to see me better through his glasses. He lifted his short stovepipe hat about half an inch and said, "Miss Moran." Brushing Dunbar with a glance, he said, "And to you."

"Good day," said Dunbar.

Back to me, the doctor said, "And how are things out on the range? Have you found out who's been leaving bodies out there, or are you all sitting around playing bridge and eating cucumber sandwiches?"

Dunbar said, "I didn't know there was more than one."

The doctor's beady eyes held on Dunbar for a few seconds. I thought he was trying to decide whether to say something smart or to retreat. At length he said, "I have to admit I don't know much about it." He returned to me. "My regards to your grandfather. He's doing well, I hope."

"Yes, and thank you."

The doctor pursed his lips and strolled into the post office.

"We can walk the horses," said Dunbar. "Keep them from cooling down too much." He lowered his voice to a confidential tone.

65

"By the way, I'd like you to receive Mrs. Deville, if you would."

The sun had reached its high point in the sky when the tan-and-maroon stagecoach rolled into town from the south. The team of six horses came to a jingling, rustling stop as the driver called, "Whoah!"

The driver set the brake, climbed down, and opened the door of the coach. The body of the vehicle rocked on its springs and creaked, and a large person filled the doorway.

This can't be Mrs. Deville, I thought, and I was right. The large person proved to be a man wearing a brown fur cap and a gray woolen duster. He labored as he eased himself to the ground and took a long breath, then moved aside.

A woman appeared. *This is her,* I thought. She stepped down with no trouble, took a few steps away from the coach, and stood up straight with her hands together at her waist.

She matched my idea of a handsome woman. She had dark hair pinned up beneath a cap of clean gray wool. Her eyes were dark and shiny, and she had well-shaped lips. She wore a traveling coat that matched her cap in color and texture. Below

66

the coat, the bottom of a charcoal-colored dress reached to the middle of a pair of black, buttoned shoes. Glancing at her face again, I guessed that she was about Dunbar's age or a little younger — perhaps in her early thirties.

Her eyes met mine, and I felt a warmth go through me. I had never been a pretty girl, and I was used to well-to-do women looking at me as if I was a servant, but this lady was not of that sort. She stepped toward me and held out her hand, which was neither dainty nor rough.

"My name is Medora Deville," she said. "Are you waiting for me?"

"Yes," I said. I gave her my hand, and we released. "This is Mr. Dunbar. I don't know if you've met him."

He took off his hat without speaking, and she nodded to him.

I said, "I suppose you would like to go to the hotel."

"As soon as they take down my bag."

"Of course." I met her eyes again, and I was quite sure we would get along.

The driver waited for two more passengers to step down, a couple of men who looked like brothers. They were wearing range rider hats and drover coats, and they each took out the makings for a cigarette. As the driver crawled up to untie a traveling bag, I saw two saddles tied to the top of the stage as well.

Dunbar stood near and reached up as the driver handed down a dark Gladstone bag.

"That's it," said Mrs. Deville. "Nothing else."

The large man in the fur cap began coughing and moved away from the two men who were sharing a match to light their cigarettes. The driver crossed in front of them on his way into the post office.

Dunbar held the bag at his side. "Ready?"

"Yes," said Mrs. Deville.

The three of us turned around to head in the direction of the hotel, and we stopped short at the presence of a man in a floppy-brimmed, tall-crowned hat and a dull black overcoat. I recognized the needle nose and washed-out, close-set eyes of Hunt Crawford.

"How do you do," he said. Directing his attention to Mrs. Deville, he swept off his hat and bowed his head. His straw-colored hair had an unwashed appearance, and I detected the stale odor of a man who needed a bath.

Mrs. Deville did not answer.

"Welcome to our town." Crawford settled

his hat on his head. "I'll take your bag for you."

"There's no need," she said. "This man has offered to help."

Crawford leveled his eyes on Dunbar. "Why don't you get out of the way? We like to welcome visitors, and it's best done by someone who's from here."

"The lady said she doesn't need you."

Crawford's face tightened. "Look here, mister. Maybe you don't understand me, so I'll have to talk plainer. We don't need strangers and drifters hornin' in."

"You should take the lady's word."

Crawford turned his head and softened his features as he smiled at Mrs. Deville.

With her dark eyes steady, she said, "I don't need your help." She made a quarter turn to her left and said to me, "Let's go this way."

I moved aside half a step, but I kept an eye on Hunt Crawford. I saw his yellow teeth as he spoke in a strained voice to Dunbar.

"I'll take care of you later."

"You can try."

I felt as if I had forgotten to breathe for a moment, but the tension faded away as the three of us walked toward the Continental Hotel.

Inside, the lobby was well lit, and the air was warm. Mr. Linwood stood behind the reception desk. His wavy blond hair was in perfect place, and his broad face was shining.

"Good afternoon," he said. "Or is it quite noon yet? I believe it is. Yes."

"And good afternoon to you," said Mrs. Deville. "I would like a room."

Mr. Linwood glanced to each side at me and at Dunbar. "By yourself? One night, or more?"

"One night to begin with, but I'm likely to stay more. And, yes, by myself."

Mr. Linwood smiled as he turned the register around for her to sign. "And what brings you to town, if you don't mind my asking?"

Mrs. Deville raised her eyebrows as she took up the pen. "I'm on personal business."

"Oh, looking out for business prospects."

Mrs. Deville left it at that. She stood back, untied the belt from around her coat, and reached inside. She drew out a small purse.

"You can pay later," said Mr. Linwood. His eyes went over her. "We have full service. Dining room. Hot baths. Direct heat." He waved his arm in the direction of a large cast-iron stove, shiny black with a

70

brass rail around the base. A full scuttle of coal stood next to it.

"Thank you," she said. "I think I might warm my hands." She turned to me. "Thank you very much. I don't believe I caught your name."

"Katie Moran."

She gave me her hand, and it was not cold at all. She turned to Dunbar and gave him her hand as well. "And thank you, sir."

He smiled. "Don't mention it."

I had no doubt that they knew each other, but they gave no further sign. Mrs. Deville moved to the stove and held out her hands as Dunbar and I turned to leave.

"Thank you both," said Mr. Linwood.

"And thanks to you," said Dunbar.

Outside on the sidewalk, Dunbar looked both ways before stepping down into the street. He turned to offer me a hand, but I waved him away and took a long step myself. As we turned right and headed toward our horses, which we had tied in front of the post office again, a familiar voice sounded from behind.

"Just a minute."

We turned to face Hunt Crawford, who had stepped into the street behind us and was striding forward with his dark wool overcoat open. I caught a glimpse of a holster and six-gun riding on his hip, and I returned to his hard stare. I was sure he had been waiting beyond the far corner of the hotel.

As he came to a stop within arm's length, he trained his close-set eyes on Dunbar. I guessed he had had success bearing down on men that way in the past, but it did not seem to have much effect now. Dunbar gave him a matter-of-fact look.

Crawford took a breath with his mouth open, then made a coarse sound in his throat, turned, and spit. He wiped the bottom of his nose with his long sleeve. "Do you think you still want to tell me wot's wot?"

Dunbar kept his eyes on the man as he said, "You would have done just as well to leave the lady alone earlier, and you'd do well if you did the same now — that is, leave well enough alone."

Crawford poked out his cheek. He rocked back and came forward. "Wal, maybe things aren't well enough."

Dunbar kept a calm expression as he waited for more.

"It's in our interests to know what kind of people come to this place." Crawford wiped the heel of his hand on his mouth and said, "For all I know, she could be some kind of a madam."

Dunbar's fist came out of nowhere, landed on Crawford's jaw below his cheekbone, and dropped him to the ground.

Crawford rolled to one side and pushed himself to his feet. He rubbed his jaw as he said, "You'll be sorry for this."

Beyond him, visible from the light in the hotel lobby, Mrs. Deville stood at the window, watching. A couple of minutes earlier, she had given me her hand, which I thought was not the hand of a working-class woman or of a fine lady, but something in between. Now I sensed a vast difference between her and this uncouth man who had just made a slur. From the casual language of the orphanage, I had derived some idea of what a madam was, and I was appalled that this man could say such a thing.

Up until the instant Dunbar hit him, Crawford had given me a sick feeling in my stomach. Now I felt better, as if justice had triumphed.

But Crawford was not one to walk away without speaking one more time. His washed-out eyes were full of resentment as he glared at Dunbar, and his voice was tight. "This isn't over."

Dunbar said, "It would be if you were wiser."

Crawford raised his head as he snorted inward, hacked to clear his throat, and spit a gob of phlegm to the side. I was sure he made an effort to ignore me as he turned away.

Dunbar stood silent, watching. His chest rose and fell with his breathing. I thought he knew his man very well. Even more, I was impressed by what seemed like a natural sense, an instinctive knowledge of what to do and when.

I also believed what Crawford had said, that this was not over.

IV

Dunbar finished his deer stew and pushed away the empty bowl. "That was good."

"Thanks," said Grandpa. "That's some of the same deer that Katie hunted. And I grew the spuds."

"That's the best kind of food," said Dunbar, "when you can raise it or gather it yourself." He smiled at me. After a moment of silence, he drummed his fingers on the table and stopped.

Grandpa said, "Somethin' on your mind?"

"I don't know if there's any work pressing for this afternoon. What's left of it."

Grandpa shrugged. "Nothing urgent."

Dunbar rubbed the back of his neck. "I think I might go for a ride. I'll be back sometime after dark." He added, "I'll take both my horses, but think nothing of it."

"I won't. Whenever you get back, there'll be supper. You can see how much stew I cooked, so you know what's on the menu."

"I'll look forward to it. It'll be an encouragement for me not to stay out too late."

A wind began to blow from the northwest in late afternoon. Grandpa said it smelled like rain, not snow. I wondered if Dunbar took two horses because he planned to ride hard and wanted to change mounts or if he expected to have someone else ride the buckskin. I did not envy anyone who had to ride in such weather. The wind kept blowing, and a thin, cold rain began to fall. The sun went down. More than enough time elapsed for Dunbar to ride to town and back. I imagined him out roaming somewhere in Temple Basin.

I finished the kitchen work and took a chair by the stove. I thought of reading a book, but I was tired. My eyes began to grow heavy. Eight o'clock passed. I drowsed off, and I awoke to see the clock at half past eight. I shook my head and sat up. Before long, my head was dipping again.

The sound of horse hooves carried from outside, and I sat up. I rubbed my eyes. A minute later, the door opened, and Dunbar ushered in a slight man wrapped in a wet denim coat and topped off by a dripping short-billed wool cap. Dunbar's canvas coat was also sodden, and water ran off the brim of his black hat.

I stared as the stranger took off the cap and denim coat. He was below average height, with a slender build. He hunched at the shoulders, and his head hung forward. Thick, dark hair covered his head, and he had bushy eyebrows as well as a reddish face with dark stubble.

Dunbar shook water off his hat as he said, "This is Mr. Sam Stroud."

Grandpa said, "Good evenin', Sam."

The man raised his head. "Hullo, Will." He blinked his eyes. "Who's this?"

"Katie. My granddaughter."

"Pleased to meet yuh." He squinted in the lamplight as he stared at me.

"Likewise," I said.

His face relaxed, but the color did not fade. He had flushed cheeks with a purple nose and a mask of broken veins across his cheekbones. The whites of his eyes were yellow. I saw that he was a wreck of a man, the kind I would avoid if I met him on the street. But here he was, standing in the lamplight inside our house.

Dunbar took off his coat. "Do you mind if we sit near the stove?"

"Not at all," said Grandpa. "We can get you something to eat as well." His eyes went from Dunbar to Stroud and back to Dunbar. "And maybe some spirits?"

"Good idea. Drive off the chill." Dunbar and Stroud took seats near the stove.

Grandpa set three glasses on the table and brought out the bottle of whiskey that he and Dunbar had opened the night before. Stroud's eyebrows went up. Grandpa poured about an inch and a half of the amber liquid into each glass. "Is that three fingers?" he asked.

Stroud said, "Not quite, but it's good enough to start with." He kept his eye on the bottle as Grandpa set it in the middle of the table. He waited for Grandpa to set a glass in front of him, but he did not wait for the others to take hold of theirs. With his eyes narrowed, he took a sip, licked his lips, and drank more. He winced as the whiskey went down, then let out a long "aahh."

Dunbar held his glass at the base but did not lift it. He sat up straight and said, "I brought Sam here so I could ask him a couple of questions. I thought having someone else hear the answers might be a good safeguard, though I don't expect anything to happen to either of us."

I had stood back from the table to make myself scarce and to keep an eye on the pot of stew that I had set on the stove to heat. Sam Stroud paid me no attention as he took another drink, grimaced, and licked his lips.

Dunbar raised his glass and took a sip. "Well, Sam, as I mentioned, I'm interested in knowing about a man named Zenith who came through these parts a while back."

"Yep."

"And a man named Whirledge, who was found dead a couple of days ago."

"Him, too, uh-huh."

"I don't want to put words in your mouth, so I'll let you speak first." Dunbar glanced around and came back to Sam. "Just for the record, I haven't heard any of this from you already."

"That's right."

"So go ahead."

The man's face clouded as he strained his eyes, staring at his glass. "I'd put it at a little over a year ago. I was hangin' around the saloon, doin' odd jobs, and this stranger come to town. Said his name was Zenith. He was one of those fellows that liked to talk and not say much, like he wanted to

78

hear what others might say but he had things himself to keep under his hat. He got me off to the side and bought me a couple of drinks. Started askin' me questions." Stroud tipped his head to the side and took in a long, sniffing breath.

Dunbar took a sip of whiskey in an unhurried way, and so did Grandpa.

Stroud gave a short cough and resumed talking. "So he got around to askin' me if I knew a man with thus-and-such a description — kind of short, soft, about middle-aged by now, wore glasses earlier and would still be wearin' 'em, prob'ly took up some polite kind of work." Stroud took a breath with his mouth open. "I said it sounded like the doctor. Zenith says, 'A doctor, eh?' I said 'yes,' and I gave him the doctor's name." Stroud took another breath. "And now he got real interested, and he wanted to know if I knew anyone who could get him some inside information. I asked him what kind, and he said, like old papers, anything that might have a man's earlier name on it. He didn't tell me the name, and I didn't ask."

Dunbar nodded for him to go on.

"He wanted to know if there was someone who could get inside the doctor's house. He didn't want to try it himself. I told him I didn't do that kind of work and wouldn't be any good at it. But I thought of someone who might." Stroud lifted his glass and set it down. "A man named Tom Whirledge."

"Oh," said Grandpa.

"Not that Tom was anyone to break into someone's house. But he did work that took him into people's offices and store buildings and houses, and I knew he had done some work on the doctor's house. He had told me the doctor was kind of prissy and had a water closet in the back of the house, inside. It emptied into a cesspool, but it didn't always work right, so Tom would go tinker with it to unclog it."

Grandpa said, "I've known people who didn't want those things inside their house, and I can understand why."

Stroud drank from his glass. "It doesn't matter to me. I've never cared for the doctor. I didn't know how I felt about someone snoopin' in his house. But this fellow made it worth a little to me to arrange a meeting with Tom Whirledge. So we met in Zenith's hotel room, quiet and secret, and Zenith told Tom what he wanted. Anything with the doctor's earlier name on it." Stroud paused.

Dunbar said, "And did he give the earlier name?"

"Yes, he did. I didn't ask, but of course Tom did. Zenith said the man's earlier name — that is, the man he was looking for — was Fell Perkins."

Grandpa shook his head. "Never heard of him before."

"Neither had I, and maybe it didn't belong to the doctor, because I never heard it again." Stroud raised his eyelids as he stared at his glass. "That was the last time I saw Zenith. He just disappeared. I saw Tom Whirledge a few times after that, but we never talked about very much, and we never came close to mentioning Zenith or the name he gave Tom."

Dunbar said, "And you've not told anyone else about this?"

Stroud shook his head. "Not at all. You're the first, and, I hope, the last. The best thing you can do for me, in addition to what you've done so far, is take me back to where you found me."

"Not tonight," said Grandpa. "You need to dry out your clothes and get some hot grub into you."

"Well, I don't want to travel in the day-time. I just want to get back to Ashton and mind my own business."

"Make use of the warmth while we've got it here," said Dunbar, waving his hand at

81

the stove. "We've got a good dry barn to sleep in as well. We'll let this rain pass over, and I can take you back tomorrow evening." He pointed at the bottle. "And fear not. There's another full one of those."

Bacon was crackling in the pan when Dunbar showed up in the kitchen the next morning. He was wearing a gray wool cap, as he had left his hat to dry by the stove the night before.

"I fed the horses," he said. "The sky is clearing out." He took a seat at the table.

Grandpa poked at the bacon. "How's our guest?"

"Sleeping well."

"That was an interesting story he told us."

"Indeed it was."

"It strengthened my suspicion that Zenith is no longer in the land of the living."

"Mine, too," said Dunbar.

"Do you think there's anything to be gained by being able to prove it?"

"Oh, yes. But we'd have to find the body, and it's a big world out there." Dunbar waved his hand.

"You think the body is stashed somewhere in the country?"

"It's a hunch."

"Temple Basin's a big place for that."

Grandpa began to turn the bacon.

Dunbar took off his cap and set it on the chair where Sam Stroud had sat. "People have different ways to hide bodies. Some folks want to get the body as far away as possible. Others want to bury it right beneath 'em, like in their cellar." He pointed downward. "So they've always got it near, and they know right where it is."

"And what's your hunch on this one?"

"Kind of in between the two."

"So you don't think it's underneath the doctor's house, or out by his cesspool."

Dunbar laughed. "Oh, no. I don't think the doctor's got it in him to kill another man, much less dig a hole to bury one."

Grandpa's eyes narrowed. "You think it's someone who's not much of a cattleman?"

"Could be. I had never heard of him or Zenith either one before I came here, but it looks as if things are more complicated than I thought. If I can smoke him out, things will begin to seem more certain to me."

"How do you plan to do that?"

"I think I need to go to town again, and I could use Katie's help."

Grandpa's features went still. "What for?"

"To have a private meeting with Mrs. Deville."

"Oh. In her room."

"To avoid eavesdroppers."

Grandpa's chest rose and fell. "I suppose it would be all right."

"Do you think I could borrow Snip? I'd like to let my two horses rest."

"Sure. He could use the exercise."

Mr. Linwood did not question me when I told him I would like to visit with Mrs. Deville on a business matter. He went down the hallway to her room and returned in a few minutes.

"Mrs. Deville says she will see you." His eyes moved to Dunbar. "I didn't say anything to her about you."

"He's my chaperone," I said. I felt brilliant for the moment as Mr. Linwood's eyes widened and he turned to stare at me.

"Very well," he said. "This way." He led us down the hallway, stopped at a door, and knocked. "Your visit," he said.

Mrs. Deville opened the door and stood aside to let us into the room. Her dark, wavy hair hung loose to her shoulders, and her dark eyes had the same friendly shine as before. She wore a dark blue wool dress that did not hide her shapely figure, and her feet looked snug in a pair of brown, fur-lined slippers.

Dunbar stood by with his hat in hand as

she closed the door.

"We can sit down," she said.

I saw that there were only two chairs.

Mrs. Deville smiled at me and said, "Would you like to sit on the bed?"

My thoughts went back to something Grandpa had said when we were traveling on the train. He told me never to go into a room by myself with a man or a woman, and if I did end up in such a situation and the other person invited me to sit on the bed, I should not do it. Now in the presence of two people I thought were trustworthy, I still did not go against my grandfather's advice.

"I'd rather sit on a chair," I said.

"Quite all right. I'll sit there. Please sit down, both of you."

When we were all settled, she folded her hands and said, "What a pleasant visit. The only other person I've talked to, other than the hotel owner, has been a man named Mr. Thomas. Perhaps you know him."

I nodded.

"I went to the store to buy some lozenges, and he met me on the sidewalk. Not a harmful sort, I don't think, but I had to work to get loose from him. Enough of that, though. What shall we talk about today?"

I turned to Dunbar.

"I'll make it as brief as I can," he said. "Not long after I arrived, and shortly before you did, a man was found dead out on the range. Maybe you heard of it. A man named Whirledge. Katie's grandfather told me of a man who might know something about the dead man and about another man who disappeared about a year ago."

Mrs. Deville nodded.

"I was able to find the man and get him to tell his story, in the presence of Katie and her grandfather, just for good measure."

Mrs. Deville smiled at me.

"According to this man, Sam Stroud, the man who disappeared had come to town to ask questions about the doctor."

"I see."

"And he had kept company with Whirledge, the man who was found dead." Dunbar took a breath. "As I told Katie and her grandfather, I think someone else has been silencing these men. I've got a suspect, but I need a way of flushing him out. I think he's got the body buried somewhere, and I need a way to make him go check on it."

"Very well."

I thought Mrs. Deville had great repose, and I had the impression that this was not the first time she had worked with Dunbar.

"Here's an idea," he said. "You could put

86

out the word that you are representing someone's estate. The first beneficiary has disappeared and may be deceased. The estate wishes to find the beneficiary and is willing to pay a reward for confirmation of his whereabouts if he is deceased."

"How much is the reward?"

"Let us say a cool thousand."

Mrs. Deville made a small whistling sound.

"Maybe that's too much. Make it five hundred if you think that's better. Anyway, for confirmation, we'll have to have some identifying mark or feature. Something that will last a year and more as a body decomposes."

I felt an unpleasant expression creeping onto my face, but I sat up and took a deep breath as I saw these two clear-minded people making a plan.

Dunbar continued. "The feature could be something that was not obvious before. People would remember a silver tooth, or more to the point, that he didn't have one. But we want something durable in that way, like a denture."

"A denture?"

"An artificial tooth, or maybe a set of two teeth, in a plate — say, on the left jaw. Again, something that would not have been

87

noticeable right away."

"And you think that will make your suspect want to dig up the body?"

"If not that, at least to check on it, to make sure no one else has dug it up."

Mrs. Deville let out a breath. "We can try it. We need a name for the missing man."

Dunbar glanced at the door as he spoke in a lowered tone. "All I have is a last name, Zenith. We could give him a first name like John."

"That might be bad luck," said Mrs. Deville. "I knew a boy in school named Johnny Zenith."

"How about Richard?"

"It sounds reasonable." She drew her brows together. "When should I put out my notice?"

Dunbar brushed his hand over his mustache. "I think late this afternoon would be good. News could reach my suspect by tonight, and if the ruse works, he'll be fidgeting to go out first thing in the morning."

"And his name?"

Dunbar spoke again in a low voice. "I'd rather not say it. But he's a cattleman *manqué.*"

A knock sounded at the door, and I flinched. The room went silent. Mrs. Deville stood up, crossed in front of us, and paused at the door.

"What is it?"

Mr. Linwood's voice came through the door panel. "A man named Mr. Thomas sends his regards and would like to wait for you in the lobby until you are available."

"Please tell Mr. Thomas I am busy for the rest of the day."

"Very well. I'll do that."

When the footsteps retreated, Dunbar said, "I think we're done for the time being, don't you?"

"I think so." Mrs. Deville turned to me and smiled. "Thank you for coming. It was a pleasure to see you again."

I stood up, took her hand, and met her friendly eyes. "Thank you. It was nice to see you, as well."

Dunbar and I walked down the hallway toward the lobby. As we paused to take leave, my glance traveled beyond the reception desk and took in Mr. Thomas standing by the cast-iron stove. He had his walking stick tucked under his arm as he held the palms of this hands toward the heat, and he had a sad expression on his face. He made a slow turn to regard us as we thanked Mr. Linwood, and he gave a cold stare at Dunbar.

Outside, I said, "He looks as if he's miffed."

"Can't help that," said Dunbar. "It's not as if we're making fun of him, like the schoolteacher of Sleepy Hollow. And he's not all that bad. I admit I owe him for the idea of the denture."

Dark clouds were gathering in the west as we rode to the ranch.

"What kind of weather does it look like?" I asked.

"I wouldn't be surprised if it snowed again. I don't mind. It's better than cold rain. And I have to take Sam Stroud home tonight."

A couple of inches of snow covered the ground when I looked out the next morning. Daylight straggled beneath an overcast sky.

Dunbar showed up at the regular time for breakfast. The kitchen was warm as Grandpa set down the enamel pot of oatmeal mush with raisins.

"I'll get some tin cow," he said. He rummaged in the cupboard, brought out an airtight can of milk, and punched two holes in it. "No trouble last night?"

"None at all. It started to snow when I was on my way back, but it was not a bad

90

night. Quiet."

"And what's your plan for today?"

"I thought it would be a good day to check cattle. I'm happy to have this snow. Easier to see tracks."

Dunbar handed me his small pair of binoculars. At a distance of more than a mile, the two riders had been specks against the snow. Now as I found them in the field glasses, I recognized the two men. Calvin Manke was wearing his sheepskin coat and flat-topped hat, and he sat on his brown horse with his boots sticking out. Hunt Crawford, in his dull black overcoat and floppy, light-colored hat, slouched in the saddle on a sorrel horse. The two men were headed south, in the general direction of the Lazy M Bar headquarters.

"It looks like they're going home," I said. "It's too bad we didn't find them sooner."

Dunbar said, "It's just as well, if not better, this way. We'll let them put another mile or so behind 'em, and then we can go down and follow their backtrail."

I lowered the binoculars. "That's so simple, I wonder why I didn't think of it."

"You would have."

"If I hadn't spoken first."

"It would have occurred to you when you went down to cut their trail."

The afternoon was fading when we reached the far end of the two men's trail. We saw where they had come in on a more round-about route from the west and had ridden around a patch of ground at the base of a low bluff that looked like dried mud. In the middle of the undisturbed ground, the blanket of snow brought out the form of a slight mound about three feet wide and six feet long.

"They showed good restraint," said Dunbar. "They just wanted to make sure it was still here."

"You don't think they're interested in the reward?"

"I'm sure they'd like to have it, but it would be hard to explain how they came by the evidence. And if they have any sense at all, which I think we ought to grant them, they'd be skeptical of the story anyway."

I met Dunbar's eyes. "You don't think we should take a look, do you?"

"Oh, no. this is good enough for me. I'm convinced there's a man buried here, and I know better than our friends do that the dental work is just a fiction."

"So this is it?"

"For right now. I'd say we've seen the card on Mr. Manke's forehead."

Neither of us had dismounted. Dunbar was riding Snip again, and the horse had given no trouble. But with no warning, Snip jerked his head up and let out a whinny that carried loud and sharp on the cold air.

Dunbar pulled on the reins and turned the horse. Baldy moved his hind end around and settled under me. I found myself looking in the direction we had just come from.

A rider was headed our way on a horse that looked yellow against the white background. The man was wearing a gray overcoat of coarse wool and a brown corduroy cap trimmed with rabbit fur. Everything seemed out of place until the man drew closer and I recognized the dolichocephalic head, narrow nose, and close-set eyes of Mr. Thomas the educator.

He stopped about fifteen feet away, holding the reins tight and choking the saddle horn. His breath showed as he said, "I know what you're up to."

"You may not know as much as you think," said Dunbar. "You'd be better off if you stayed out of the way."

Mr. Thomas gave a somber expression. "You think you're going to scare me off?"

"Suit yourself," said Dunbar. "But men

93

have been killed."

"Since you came to town, from what I hear."

"Oh, go on. You'd be better not to take cards in this game, friend."

"It's a game, is it?"

"Only in a manner of speaking. There're men that have things to hide, and they'll kill to do it. I wouldn't want to see you get caught in the middle."

"I bet I could find someone who'd like to know you made that kind of accusation."

Dunbar spoke in a patient tone. "You know enough to get hurt, and not by me. I'll give you one more piece of advice. Keep your mouth shut and your eyes and ears open. At about noontime tomorrow, we'll have a public meeting in town, and you'll see what else there is to know."

Mr. Thomas made a slow turn of the head as he kept his sullen stare on Dunbar. "You think you're smart," he said. "We'll find out."

V

A crowd of at least thirty people had gathered in the dining area of the Continental Hotel. Mrs. Deville had set the meeting for one o'clock so that Mr. Linwood could accommodate his noon guests and then serve coffee and pastries to anyone who wished. All of the tables were full, while several men and a few women gathered in back by the double doors that led to the lobby.

Those who had finished lunch included Mr. Rhoden and Mr. Linwood at their table with a couple of other businessmen; Dr. Orme with the postman, the barber, and the red-nosed Methodist preacher; Calvin Manke, Hunt Crawford, the blacksmith, and the livery stable owner; Mr. Thomas, seated with three men who did not pay him any attention; and a group of four ladies who had an air of civic correctness. I recognized some of the people at the other tables but only from having seen them on the street. For my part, I sat with Dunbar, Mrs. Deville, and an empty chair.

At a little after one, Mr. Linwood stood up, tapped a spoon on a glass, and quieted the hubbub. "Good afternoon," he began. "I imagine most of you have gathered to hear about a missing beneficiary, a reward, and anything related. To that purpose, and without further ado, I will introduce Mrs. Medora Deville, who represents the estate."

An uncertain applause rippled through the room as Mrs. Deville stood up and faced the room. She was wearing her dark blue wool dress and had her hair pinned up, and I thought she looked quite businesslike. She spoke in a calm, clear voice.

"Thank you, Mr. Linwood, and thank all of you who have come to show your interest. As many of you know, this is a case entailing one or more deceased persons, so before we talk about money, we need to clarify some information about the people. To that purpose," and here she paused with a half smile, "I introduce Mr. Dunbar."

A clearing of throats and a scuffing of chairs followed as Dunbar took his place before the group. His hair was combed, and he had a clean shave. He wore a pearl gray shirt beneath his charcoal-colored vest, and his dark-handled revolver hung within view. His eyes scanned the crowd as he began.

"I join Mrs. Deville in thanking you for your interest. Although this seems to be a case of someone else's money, the circumstances should matter to all of us. So I will begin by discussing the disappearance of a man named Zenith." He paused to let a wave of muttering pass. "I will submit to you that Mr. Zenith disappeared because he knew something about a prominent member of this community."

I caught a glance of Dr. Orme, who raised his eyebrows and shrugged at the Methodist minister.

"This man is not what he seems," Dunbar went on. "He came to this town and presented himself as a doctor, but he has no training and no credentials in that area."

A mixture of gasps and exclamations broke out as all eyes turned upon the doctor's table. He sat up, put on a severe expression, and brushed his chest. He cleared his throat and said, "Excuse me, but I can't let you besmirch my reputation like that. There's nothing —"

"There is, and you know it. And you also know, as Zenith did, that your original name is not Arnold Orme." Dunbar's eyes swept the crowd. "To the contrary, this man's name is Fell Perkins."

The doctor's face went white, and his features looked stricken. "You have no right —" he began.

Mr. Rhoden thumped the table and stood up. "See here! You can't just come in here and ruin a man's reputation, as he says. And besides, what does that have to do with the missing man?"

Dunbar spoke in a calm voice. "I'll put the story together for you, if I may."

Mr. Rhoden sat down.

"This man here," Dunbar resumed, "has a prior life. Zenith knew about it and

97

tracked him here, I imagine with the motive of blackmailing him. When he found out the man was posing as a doctor, he had even more to hold against him."

"No, wait," said Mr. Rhoden. "First things first. That is, before we go any further, I want to know whether there is any truth to your accusation that the doctor is a —"

"Fraud? Ask him to produce a license or a diploma or a certificate. He can't."

All eyes turned again to the doctor, or at least to the man who was still dressed in the clothes of the practitioner. The man himself had sunk in his chair.

Mr. Rhoden directed his glare across two tables. "Well, can you?"

The doctor kept his eyes down as he shook his head and said, "No, I can't."

Murmurs and whispers went around the room. Mr. Rhoden seemed lost in thought as he stared at the doctor.

Calvin Manke stood up and spoke. "Well, let's wait another minute. Just because a man doesn't have a piece of paper doesn't mean he's no good at what he did. I've known doctors that never went near a college but could save the life of a horse or a cow. And out here on the frontier, I'd say anyone who can save a life is welcome."

A louder rumble began as Manke sat

down, but Mr. Rhoden cut it short by slapping the table again. "Be that as it may, there's something to this." He looked around, and he now had a troubled expression on his face. He swallowed and said, "We've trusted this man. We've let him into our houses. He has examined us, and our wives, and our sons and daughters. That's not the same as a horse or a cow."

I could feel a change, a wave of dread, make its way through the room. The four ladies sitting together were all staring at the table, their eyes vacant as Mr. Rhoden's had been. One of them began to shake her head, and with her mouth trembling, she said, "I can't, I can't . . ." and she stood up. The other three rose from their seats as well, and the four of them marched out of the room.

"Very well," said Mr. Rhoden, directing his gaze at Dunbar again. "For what purpose are you exposing all of this? I have to say I'm feeling revulsion for this man with his prying fingers, but I want to know why you're doing this. Did you come here just to shame him? Or do you have some other idea?"

"I can answer that," said Dunbar. "As I said earlier, this man had a prior life. When he went by his real name of Fell Perkins, he lived in El Paso, Texas, and he was a priest. This was almost thirty years ago." Dunbar paused, and silence held the room. "One night, just before Easter weekend, he heard the confession of an attractive young woman named Rachel Tilma. He enticed her to the rectory, where he strangled her as he violated her, and then he left the body in a ditch."

The accused man barked out, "It's a lie. All a lie."

"No, it isn't," said Dunbar. "But there was a reluctance within the church and without to pursue the case, and this man was sent to a retreat for disturbed priests. There he confessed to another priest, but because it was a confession, it remained private. From there he changed his name, made a new identity for himself, and ended up here."

"All lies."

"And here he would have lived in peace, except someone knew his secret. And leeched him for money. Then when another man came to town with the same purpose of blackmailing, not knowing he was trespassing on someone's else's claim, he disappeared. Zenith knew the name Fell Perkins, and that was his undoing. Wasn't it?"

The accused man blubbered something that I could not hear.

"What did you say?" said Mr. Rhoden.

"It wasn't me."

Mr. Rhoden turned to Dunbar. "Was it?"

Dunbar shook his head. "No, he didn't do away with Zenith, but he knows who did, for it cost him all the more. And after that, they had to silence Tom Whirledge."

Mr. Rhoden pushed with both hands on the table as his eyes burned at the slumped man. "Who?"

The chubby face and beady eyes turned toward Calvin Manke. "Him."

Manke exploded. "Oh, come on! Here I try to say something to make you look better, and —"

Mr. Rhoden interrupted. "Did you know this man was a priest?"

Manke made a spitting sound. "This rotten old punk? He's nothing of a priest. He's just a cowardly, hypocritical old sack of —"

"Mind your language," said Dunbar.

"I'll speak the way I want."

Mr. Rhoden said, "Did you know of anything he did in El Paso, Texas?"

Manke sneered. "El Paso is a place where old whores go to die."

A gasp went through the crowd. I had heard people use that word at the orphanage, and I had heard the word "punk" to mean something similar, but I was jolted to

101

hear someone say the stronger word now, especially with a respectable-looking woman like Mrs. Deville present.

The ruined man sat up in his chair. "Yes, he knew. And he bled me for years. And anyone else who tried —"

The blast of a gunshot ripped through the room. While everyone had been keeping an eye on Manke and the man now known as Fell Perkins, Hunt Crawford had pushed back from the table, stood up, and fired a pistol from twelve feet away.

A red spot appeared on Perkins's white shirt, and the man toppled out of his chair. Shouts, curses, a woman's scream, and the scraping of chair legs all rose in confusion. Two or three people ran out through the door. Hunt Crawford bolted, and the people standing at the edge of the room made way for him as well.

Calvin Manke stood up with his gun drawn. "If you people know what's good for you, you won't get in my way."

More chairs scraped, and men scrambled.

"Hold it," came Dunbar's voice.

Everything stopped, and all eyes went to Dunbar, who stood with his pistol aimed.

Manke lowered his gun and turned aside.

"Drop it," said Dunbar.

Manke whirled, took a quick step to his

right, and brought the six-shooter up and around. He fired, but the shot went wide, shattering a lamp that sat on a sideboard.

Dunbar returned fire, and the round, shiny face of Calvin Manke dropped out of sight.

"Take care of him," said Dunbar. "I've got to go after the other one."

As I rushed to follow Dunbar, I heard a kneeling man say, "He's done for." I realized he was referring to Manke.

I ran outside, thinking I would see Dunbar chasing Hunt Crawford, but my blood sank to my feet as I stopped short.

In the middle of the street, Hunt Crawford had his arm around the neck of skinny Mr. Thomas and was holding his pistol in the schoolteacher's ribs. Jeff Hayden was walking toward Crawford and leading two horses. Dunbar stood still on the sidewalk with his pistol in his holster. He waved at me with his left hand and said, "Get out of the way."

"All slow now," said Crawford, "or this bird gets it in the gizzard. Jeff, you cross behind me and bring the girl over here."

My eyes grew wide.

"Leave the girl out of it," said Jeff.

"Do as I say, or I'll plug you, too."

"I don't want to."

103

"Don't make me mad. Bring the girl over."

Mr. Thomas twisted his head to look at me, and the thick arm of Crawford's wool overcoat tightened. The schoolteacher's eyes rolled upward.

As Jeff passed behind Crawford, he stopped the horses. He dropped the reins to one horse, set the reins of the other, and sprang into the saddle. Crawford turned toward the movement, and Mr. Thomas sagged to the ground. As the horse galloped away, Crawford fired in its direction. The horse dodged to the right, throwing Jeff Hayden, and kept on running.

Crawford turned around to face Dunbar, who had his pistol drawn. Crawford raised his gun and snapped off a shot that went past Dunbar and crashed through the window of the hotel. Dunbar took steady aim and fired.

Crawford's upraised arm fell, and his six-gun tumbled to the ground. The man followed, and the only sound on the main street of Perse was a man hollering at the runaway horse.

When the meeting resumed in the dining area of the hotel, the two bodies had been carried out, and the floor had been scrubbed.

Mr. Rhoden looked as if he had a case of indigestion as he called the meeting to order. He said, "I'd like Mr. Dunbar to stand up and answer a couple of more questions."

Dunbar took his place as before in front of the audience.

Mr. Rhoden said, "I didn't get a full answer to my question earlier. What I'd like to know, for the benefit of everyone present, is what you came here for. What has come of it, we can see."

Dunbar took a calm breath. "I came to locate Fell Perkins so he could be brought back to El Paso to face trial. As I said earlier, some people had let the case go. I don't want to say that the church covered it up, but certain members of the church, plus certain people in charge of the law, let it fade away. Some people in the community said that if the victim had been from a prominent white family, the outcome might have been different. But with the passing of time, and the passing of some of the people who suppressed the case, more of the original evidence has come to light. And so I took the assignment to find this man."

"And that was all?"

"It was enough, and it turned into more when I got here."

Mr. Linwood spoke up. "I don't think it was enough to shoot him for it."

"I didn't do that," said Dunbar. "One of his blackmailers did."

"I just don't know how much he deserved it. Even if he wasn't a bona fide doctor — well, let me put it this way. If he was a priest, he couldn't have been all bad. And they never proved that he did those things. It was a long time ago. And besides, from the sounds of it, the girl was Mexican. She could have brought it on herself."

Dunbar's eyes glinted. "I'm not here to pronounce guilt or innocence. And as I said in a separate conversation with someone else, I don't think he had it in him to kill another man. But I know they had enough evidence in the death of Rachel Tilma to issue a warrant and want to find the man. And as for the victim, she came from a decent family. She taught Sunday school and went to confession."

Mr. Linwood said, "But I don't think he deserved to be shot."

Dunbar took a breath. "I'll admit I didn't handle things as well as I should have. I had hoped to see the man face trial. But when I got on the trail of these other killings, I felt I had to bring all of that to light."

"You take a lot upon yourself," said Mr.

Linwood.

"Maybe I do. But if the man had been innocent, he wouldn't have been paying a blackmailer. And if the blackmailer and his henchman hadn't silenced a couple of men, they wouldn't have done anything they did today."

"We'll leave it at that," said Mr. Rhoden. "Is there anything more to be said about the beneficiary and the reward?"

"Not really," said Dunbar.

Mr. Rhoden nodded. "And Zenith?"

"I think we found out where he is buried. If you want to go digging for some reason, Mr. Thomas can help you find the location."

"Mr. Thomas?"

"The man who fainted in the street. I believe they took him to the saloon and administered some spirits."

"I don't find it very compelling to dig up a would-be blackmailer," said Mr. Rhoden. "For my part, I can't quite forgive the doctor. That's still got me chewing it over. We trusted him."

"So did Rachel Tilma."

Mrs. Deville left on the stagecoach later that same day. She was dressed in her gray wool cap and overcoat, and Dunbar carried her Gladstone bag. He acted as if he was a butler or a bellboy, but I was sure they would meet again in some other place.

Mrs. Deville gave me her hand. "Thank you for all of your help, Katie. It has been a pleasure to know you."

"I didn't do much."

"You did more than you had to. And I'm sorry you had to hear some of the things you did."

"Thank you. When I first came out west, I thought this was an innocent place because it seemed so simple, but I realize I would have had to face some of these grown-up truths wherever I would have gone."

"Well, you're still young. Enjoy it while you can."

"Thank you. I wish the same to you."

She smiled as she arched her eyebrows. "Enjoy my youth? I suppose it's all relative."

Dunbar left the next morning after breakfast. He tied his belongings onto the buckskin and saddled the blue roan. A light snow had fallen overnight to add to the snow from two days before, and the air was cold enough to show the horses' breaths.

Dunbar did not waste time taking leave. He shook Grandpa's hand and then mine. "So long," he said. "Many thanks for your help."

"And for yours," said Grandpa. "Here and in town."

"I wish I could have done better."

"Thanks for everything," I said.

He touched his hat. "Stay on the good trail you're on, Katie."

With that, he held the lead rope in place and mounted up. He lifted his black hat in farewell and rode away into the snowy rangeland where I had first seen him. The horse hooves pushed up little clouds of snow. I watched as the figures became smaller and disappeared.

I had wanted to tell Dunbar that I thought he had done well, but I did not think I was anyone to express my opinion about him. He seemed very capable and yet so modest as to admit he could have done better. I had no misgivings about how the doctor had come to an end, yet I think it would have been fitting if Dunbar could have taken him or had him taken to El Paso, where he would have faced trial and where, one would hope, he would have been punished for his crime.

ABOUT THE AUTHOR

John D. Nesbitt lives in the plains country of Wyoming, where he teaches English and Spanish at Eastern Wyoming College. He writes western, contemporary, mystery, and retro/noir fiction as well as nonfiction and poetry. John has won many awards for his work, including three awards from the Wyoming State Historical Society (for fiction), two awards from Wyoming Writers for encouragement of other writers and service to the organization, two Wyoming Arts Council literary fellowships (one for fiction, one for nonfiction), five Will Rogers Medallion awards, one Western Fictioneers Peacemaker award, four Peacemaker Finalist awards, four Western Writers of America Spur awards, and two Spur Finalist awards. His recent books include *Castle Butte* and *Great Lonesome,* frontier novels with Five Star.

■ ■ ■ ■

A TOMMY STALLINGS
WESTERN MYSTERY

SCARECROWS

JIM JONES

■ ■ ■ ■

I

"It might be nice if you'd fill me in on the details of this problem I'm supposed to be helpin' you fix."

Tommy Stallings was headed east to Texas on his horse, Rusty. Riding beside him was his cousin, also named Rusty. Tommy had, indeed, named his horse for his cousin, who was under the impression it was because they both had red hair. That was a fact as far as it went . . . Rusty the horse was a red roan . . . but truth be told, it was mainly because they were both stubborn trouble-makers. Both had good hearts though and that made up for a multitude of sins.

"Well, I ain't really had time to do that now, have I?" Rusty, the cousin, responded in that quarrelsome manner that had always irked Tommy. "We been sorta busy, in case you hadn't noticed."

The terrain was changing as they rode east. It happened in a gradual manner so that if you weren't paying attention, you didn't notice right away. All of a sudden, you looked up and the mountains had disappeared, replaced by a flat and endless sea of grass. It was so wide and open it could make a person feel nervous. There was no place to hide.

Until two days before, Tommy Stallings had been the sheriff . . . well, to be precise, the acting sheriff . . . of Colfax County in the New Mexico Territory. Rusty, his cousin, had come from Texas to seek Tommy's help but instead had wound up staying in Cimarron to assist Tommy in breaking up a murderous ring of rustlers who were terrorizing folks in Colfax County. In return, Tommy had agreed to accompany Rusty back to Texas.

"Course I noticed," Tommy responded with a little bit of heat. "In case you forgot, I'm the innocent one who got accused of takin' a bribe and got locked up for it."

"Well, yeah, but you weren't in jail for all that long and besides, the cell didn't even have a lock on it. Strictly speakin', you weren't 'locked up,' you were a guest of Mayor Salazar and the town of Springer. And in the meantime, I was gettin' shot at right and left."

"Hell, they didn't hit you, did they?"

Tommy figured he could banter with Rusty like this all the way to Texas if he was willing to keep it up. "And as you recall, they shot at me, too."

Rusty stared off in the distance for a moment, deep in thought. The thought he was pondering made him sag in the saddle. "No, they didn't hit either one of us, lucky enough. I still can't get over them shootin' Sheriff Averill though. He was one of the finest men I've ever had the honor of knowin'. I can't believe he's gone."

The bitter taste of that reality made Tommy lose his appetite for jawing with his cousin. "You're right, he was one of the best. Whatever I might know about bein' a lawman, I learned from him."

"He was as tough a man as I ever met," Rusty said. "As affable as could be but you sure knew you didn't want to cross him."

"He was tough all right," Tommy agreed. "It was more than that though. I remember he told me that to be a good lawman, you had to be tough, you had to be good with a gun, but more than anything, you had to be smart. I reckon he put away quite a few bad men without ever drawin' his pistol." He chuckled. "He just out-thought 'em."

Rusty nodded, reflecting on what his cousin had said. "Speakin' of bein' smart, I think you're gonna need to use all of your horse sense to figure out this situation Ma and Pa are facin'."

Tommy hadn't seen his aunt and uncle for five years. The last time they were together, he had stormed off in a fit of anger at some perceived slight that he now realized was a total product of his imagination. After his parents and sister were killed by Comanche, his Uncle Joe and Aunt Martha had taken him in. They'd treated him decent and only now with the benefit of hindsight did he realize that his anger had not been at them, it had been at losing his family in such a horrific manner. He'd been away helping Uncle Joe at the ranch when his family was murdered and that had saved him from being slaughtered along with his parents and sister. It was also the source of his overwhelming guilt at surviving while they died. Apart from any help he might give his aunt and uncle with the troubles they were facing in the present time, he knew he owed them a sincere apology for the way he'd treated them and, in particular, for the way he'd left.

"That takes us back around to the part where I need you to fill me in on what we'll be dealin' with when we get to the ranch."

Rusty spent the next hour on the trail

describing the disturbing events that had been plaguing his parents for months. Along the way, Tommy asked multiple questions for which Rusty had no good answers. Tommy was baffled.

"Reckon Nathan Averill was right. We're gonna have to be pretty smart to figure this mess out." He got a wistful look on his face. "I can't believe old Nathan is gone. It's not surprisin' that he's still teachin' us lessons from beyond the grave though. He was as sharp a lawman as I ever heard of."

Rusty nodded. "That's the gospel truth. And you're right, we're gonna have to really push to crack this mystery."

Tommy chuckled. "I do believe I'm up to the chore but I am a little worried about you."

Rusty snorted with disgust and loped ahead of his cousin. Tommy spurred his horse to catch up, laughing.

II

"Come in, come in, it's so good to see you after all these years." His Aunt Martha enfolded Tommy in a smothering hug. His hug in return was a bit tentative. He hadn't been sure how she would receive him. After a moment, she released him and stepped back to look at him. "How many has it been?"

"Seems like it's been a good five years since I left," Tommy said. "A lot's happened since then."

"That's a fact," Aunt Martha replied. A smile spread all the way across her face. "Look at you, you're all grown up."

It was true. When Tommy left the ranch five years before, he'd been a lanky boy of sixteen who shaved every other day even though he didn't need to. Now he was a young man of twenty-one. His frame, while still on the slender side, had filled out and his muscles were hard like fence wire. He was around six feet tall now and his hair was black as an Apache. He had a youthful appearance but that was offset by a look in his eyes that might be sadness.

"Reckon it had to happen sometime," Tommy said. He paused and cleared his throat. "Aunt Martha, I want to tell you how sorry I am about the way I left y'all back then. I said some things that were stupid and just plain not true. I've thought about it almost every day and I know I was a fool." He took a deep breath. "I'm as sorry as I can be."

His aunt looked at him for a moment and then smiled. "Aw, it's nothin'." She waved her hand to suggest that it had all been forgotten. Her eyes indicated otherwise. They reflected gratitude that he'd been man enough to acknowledge his mistakes and apologize. "Growin' up ain't easy, even if a person hadn't had the tough time you did. I never stopped lovin' you."

Now Tommy's eyes reflected a deep gratefulness at the generosity and loving nature of his aunt. He reached out and pulled her into a hug, this time putting his considerable strength into it. She returned the fierce embrace for a moment before pulling away.

"Lawd, Tommy, you come close to crushin' me. You certainly have grown up."

They smiled at each other, a sense of peace hanging in the air. Then she turned and looked at her son, a puzzled expression on her face.

"Who is this ragged rascal you drug along with you?" She stepped back and studied him from head to toe. "He looks like a mountain man or some such. You reckon he's got critters livin' in that tangled beard on his face?"

"Aw, Ma, you know it's me," Rusty said. "And there ain't no critters livin' in my beard." He stepped forward. "Come on, give me a hug."

She stepped backwards with a look of

mock horror on her face. "I swear, I believe you got fleas in that clump a hair hangin' down. You sure it's safe?"

"Ma, you know you're glad to see me," Rusty said with a big grin. "I want my hug."

"All right," she said, "I guess I could spare a hug for you." They embraced for a couple of moments. When she pulled back, she stared at her son and said, "I sure look forward to the day you take a razor to that mess though."

Tommy laughed at his cousin's discomfort. "Aunt Martha, you know he only keeps it because it puts a burr under your saddle. He don't even like it all that much himself."

"I hope he gets tired of it pretty soon," she said. "I seem to recall there's a handsome lad under all that fur but a young lady wouldn't know it to look at him. If he don't shave that thing, he may never get married and I may be stuck with him forever." She shook her head. "Enough of this talk, you boys must be starvin'. Let me fix you some food."

They had broken camp at daybreak and hadn't had a chance to do anything except chew on a little jerky as they rode the final leg of their journey. It was past noon now and they were famished. Aunt Martha had a pot of beans warming on the stove. She dished out a sizable portion onto a tortilla for each of the young men and they dug in. They were shoveling down the food and joking with each other when the door opened and Uncle Joe came in. He stared over at Tommy. Everyone stopped talking. Although Tommy was unsure what to do, he'd learned over the past few years that ignoring problems didn't help. They don't go away on their own. He stood up and cleared his throat.

"Howdy, Uncle Joe," he said. His voice sounded tight, as if his throat was a bit constricted. "I came back to Texas with Rusty. He said y'all had some troubles brewin'. I'm here to help if you'll have me."

His uncle stared at him for an uncomfortable moment, then he nodded. "Got a few problems, that's a fact." He walked over and sat down. His wife served him up a tortilla loaded with beans. "I reckon we could use some help, sure 'nuff. Good to have you back."

That seemed to be all his uncle had to say on the matter. Tommy sat down and resumed eating. Tommy was curious about the cattle rustling epidemic but he remembered how his uncle was. When he was ready to talk on a topic, he'd get to it. When he wasn't, you couldn't pry information out of him if you stuck his bare feet in a camp-fire. Since he was still hungry, Tommy figured his best option would be to follow his uncle's lead and continue eating.

Unlike Uncle Joe, Aunt Martha didn't have to be tortured to carry on an animated conversation. She looked over at her taciturn husband and shook her head.

"Well, if he ain't gonna tell you, I will," she said. "It's got folks plum spooked around here, I promise you."

She glanced at her husband to check his reaction. He didn't say a word, just continued eating. Tommy didn't want to step on anyone's toes or come between his aunt and uncle but he really wanted to know more details.

"Whenever y'all are ready to talk about it, I'd be happy to listen. Rusty filled me in a bit on the ride over from New Mexico."

"Like to scared the poor widow Barclay out of her mind, I'm here to tell you," Aunt Martha remarked.

"What did?" Tommy was confused. "Wait . . . is that Emma Barclay you're talkin' about?"

"Do you know some other Barclay?" Aunt Martha raised an eyebrow as she looked at him.

"No, ma'am," he said, feeling a little foolish. "When I left she wasn't a widow though. She had a husband named Ed if I remember right. I didn't know he'd passed."

"Had a bad horse wreck a couple of years ago," Aunt Martha replied. "Horse stepped in a gopher hole and the danged thing rolled over on him. Broke his neck."

"Sure sorry to hear that." He shook his head. "I reckon that clears up the mystery of who the widow Barclay is but it doesn't tell me what scared her."

"Scarecrows," Aunt Emma said. She took a bite of beans and didn't say anything else.

"Scarecrows?" Now he was even more confused. Aunt Martha took another bite of beans. "What do scarecrows have to do with cattle rustlin'?"

Aunt Martha looked at him like he was a bit slow. "Well, the rustlers was dressed up like scarecrows. I thought that was obvious."

Tommy tried not to lose patience with his aunt. He'd begun working his way back into her good graces and he didn't want to upset her. He also remembered that much like her husband, she had her own way of telling a story and couldn't be rushed.

"I suppose you're right, I guess I missed that part. You're sayin' the cattle rustlers were dressed up like scarecrows."

"Yep."

He waited for more information but none was forthcoming straight away. He took a deep breath and asked, "So what did they do to scare Mrs. Barclay . . . besides dressin' up like scarecrows, of course?"

Aunt Martha rolled her eyes and put her fork down. "I guess you want the whole story. She heard a noise one night and got up to look into it. Took her Winchester with her. She had some cattle in a pen a short ways from the house. She heard the cattle bawlin' and then it sounded like someone was cuttin' the fence." She picked up her fork and took another bite of beans. Tommy waited, calling on his rather short supply of patience.

Uncle Joe spoke up for the first time. "Martha, are you gonna to tell the story to the boy or are you gonna eat your beans?"

Rusty tried not to laugh but couldn't contain himself and almost spit out his food. He looked at his cousin with a grin. "Some things never change."

"Don't you get sassy. You get me riled up, I'll get the shears and shave that mess of a beard right off your face."

"Sorry, Ma," Rusty said. When she looked down at her food, he snuck another grin in for Tommy's benefit.

"So what did she see when she went out

to the pen?" He tried to find some middle ground between waiting for the story to unfold in a logical manner and encouraging his aunt to provide more details.

"She saw a couple of yahoos dressed up like scarecrows. One of 'em was on the ground cuttin' the wire and pullin' the fence back to make an opening. She was so thunderstruck she didn't even think of shootin' at 'em right away."

"What do you mean they were dressed up like scarecrows?"

"They had some kind of sacks on their heads with holes cut over the eyes. She said they looked like scarecrows. She also said they had their hats stuck on top of the sacks." She chuckled. "Not sure why they'd do that. Maybe they're dudes and it was some kind of fashion statement."

Tommy thought it was a little odd, too, but he didn't want to follow his aunt down that rabbit hole. What size hat would you need to fit over a canvas sack? Did John B. Stetson even make one that big? Better to stick with specific details of the rustling. "Did they shoot at her or threaten her?"

"Don't you reckon just dressin' up like scarecrows is pretty threatenin'?" Again, his Aunt Martha looked at him like he was a bit slow. "But no, they didn't shoot at her.

They did hustle up to finish their business. Ran off maybe fifteen head but they left another twenty. It appeared that she spooked 'em." Martha grinned. "Not as much as they spooked her though, I guarantee. She collected her wits and got off a couple of shots as they rode off but she didn't hit nothin'."

"So two outlaws dressed in some sort of disguises . . ."

Aunt Martha interrupted. "They wasn't dressed in 'some sort of disguises,' Tommy Stallings, they was dressed up like scarecrows."

Tommy had a limited amount of patience and he feared it was running in short supply. He nodded and took a deep breath. "You're right, they were dressed like scarecrows. They didn't threaten her but they pulled down part of the fence of her pen and ran off some cattle."

His Aunt Martha nodded and smiled at him. "I think you got it. I'm not sure what was so confusin' to you."

Uncle Joe cleared his throat. "Reckon what was confusin' to him was the way you told the story, Martha."

Aunt Martha glowered at her husband. "Don't you be criticizin' how I tell a story, Joe Stallings. At least I talk instead of sittin' there like a dang fence post in the middle of the prairie."

Uncle Joe ignored his wife and turned to his nephew. "They raided us a couple of times in the past few months. It was right after that when Rusty took it in his head to go lookin' for you in the New Mexico Territory."

"How many head did they get?" Tommy was interested to hear how ambitious these two desperados were.

"Took ten head the first time, fifteen the second. That don't sound like a lot and maybe to some of them big outfits, it'd be just a drop in the bucket. We're small-time though and that hit us pretty hard."

"Have they hit any of the larger ranches?"

"They didn't at first. I think they were bein' cautious and figured they'd avoid pokin' the bear. After a while though, they appeared to get cocky and they started stealin' from the large spreads too." Uncle Joe shook his head. "It took a little time to get their attention. Fifteen head ain't much to those ranches. It took a couple or three of those midnight raids to make 'em sit up and take notice."

"What'd they do?"

"They got in touch with the Stock-Raisers' Association, asked them for help. I hope you can make more progress with this mess than that Slaughter fella."

His aunt's meandering story about the "scarecrows" had already tested his patience. Now he was baffled by what his uncle was saying. Still, he could never have enough lessons on the value of patience. Here another opportunity appeared almost at once.

"I don't know who the 'Slaughter fella' is, Uncle Joe."

"He's that agent for the Stock-Raisers' Association. Nice enough young fella but he hasn't made a lick of progress on solvin' this mess."

Tommy knew a little about the Stock-Raisers' Association of Northwest Texas. It had been formed almost ten years ago in Graham, Texas. A group of cattlemen who were fed up with the rampant rustling got together and established an agency whose job it was to investigate cattle theft and put an end to it. Their agents carried badges and were authorized to make arrests. By all the account he'd heard, they'd made a pretty decent dent in the thievery but they still had a ways to go before they stamped it out.

He considered the situation. "Reckon it'd be smart for me to check in with Agent

Slaughter before I get too busy lookin' into this mess myself. Some lawmen are a might touchy about other folks intrudin' on their business."

"I expect you're right." Uncle Joe resumed eating. After a couple of bites, he looked up again. "I appreciate your helpin' out. It's good to have you back."

III

"Rusty Stallings, how you doin'?" Tommy and Rusty were headed into Oneida to look for the Stock-Raisers' Association agent. They were surprised when he topped the rise and appeared right in front of them. "I'm fine, Bill. You're out and about kinda early. You trackin' down cattle rustlers?"

Bill Slaughter was short and stocky. He looked to be about fifteen but Tommy knew that couldn't be true. Like Rusty, he had red hair and freckles. Tommy wondered if he'd taken a wrong turn into a vegetable garden what with all these red-haired carrot tops around. Considering he was outnumbered two to one, he chose not to remark on that.

"That's exactly what I'm doin', Rusty. Who's your friend?"

"Let me introduce you to my cousin,

131

Tommy Stallings. I've been out in the New Mexico Territory savin' his bacon. He came back with me to help Ma and Pa out with protectin' the ranch against these cattle thieves."

"Pleased to meet you," Slaughter said, extending his hand.

Tommy shook it and noticed the man had a firm grip but that he didn't make a show about trying to crush your hand as he shook it. He appreciated that. "My pleasure, Agent Slaughter."

"No need to be so proper," Slaughter said. "You can call me Bill." He cocked his head. "So how was Rusty savin' your bacon out there in New Mexico?"

"How well do you know Rusty?"

Slaughter said, "I've gotten pretty familiar with him since I been lookin' into this latest cattle rustlin' deal."

"Well," Tommy said, "then you're aware he's been known to shade the truth from time to time."

Slaughter laughed. "He does like to tell a good story and he's not inclined to let the facts get in the way."

"That's correct," he said with a chuckle. Then his expression turned serious. "Truth be told though, he did help me out a whole lot. We couldn't have got done what we did without him."

"And what was it you were doin'?"

"I was the sheriff in Colfax County up in the northern part of the territory. We have our own problems with cattle rustlers out there and we had us a vicious bunch roamin' around. They not only were stealin' stock, they were killin' folks." Tommy glanced at his cousin. "It was tough. He done good."

"I can't say that surprises me," Slaughter responded. "He ain't nearly as goofy as he looks. Ain't smart enough to be scared neither."

"Y'all do know I'm right here, don't you?" Rusty wore a wounded expression on his face.

Slaughter chuckled and Tommy poked Rusty in the shoulder. "Don't get all hurt on me, cousin. You know I'm just hoorahin' you."

"So you're a sheriff, you say?" Slaughter said.

"I was," he replied. "I quit to come back here. I don't know how long I'll be in these parts. I couldn't leave the folks in Colfax County hangin' so I give 'em my notice."

"You plannin' on investigatin' this 'scarecrow' mess?" Slaughter spoke in a casual tone but seemed quite intent on hearing his answer.

"I ain't plannin' on doin' nothin' without it bein' all right with you," Tommy replied. "This is your neck of the woods. I wouldn't jump in without your say-so. I don't want to step on anybody's toes."

The agent nodded. "I appreciate that. Fact is, though, it's just me investigatin' and I could use some help. I'll put you to work if you're willin'." He laughed. "Rusty's already been helpin' me out. I'll pay you twice what I been payin' him."

"You ain't been payin' me nothin'," Rusty exclaimed.

"That's right," Slaughter responded with a straight face. "And I'll be happy to double that for your cousin."

Tommy thought he might come to like Bill Slaughter.

My dearest Mollie,
Oct. 10, 1886
I wanted to write and tell you how much I miss you. Rusty is not bad compeny and my cousin is not that bad either. Ha ha, I made a joke. In my mind, I can see you roll your eyes. Anyhow I do not like them nearly as much as I like you. I hope things are going well for you at school and those little devels you call students are treating you right. I pity the ones that do not.

Things are good hear. My aunt and uncle forgave me I guess. They are bein pretty nice. I met a fella who is an agent for the cattle growers, he's nice tho he has red hair like both Rustys. Ha ha. He wants me to work with him to catch these cattle theves. Did I menshun they dress up like scarecrows? I do not have any ideas about whose done these things. I want to help my aunt and uncle but I do not know if I am smart enough to figure it out. I got to go now. I love you. ps Please do not fix my spellin, I know you are a teacher but it makes me feel dum when you do it.

Youre lovin husband,
Tom Stallings

IV

Between bites, Uncle Joe asked, "What did that boy, Slaughter, have to say?"

They were seated around the table eating the evening meal of beefsteak and potatoes. Aunt Martha had whipped up some biscuits and she had a jug of molasses ready to sweeten them. It made Tommy think of times when he was younger and lived with his aunt and uncle. Sometimes, when he remembered those days, it felt like he had been angry all the time. Sitting there with what was left of his family though, he realized that there had been good times too, many of them right here at this table.

"For the most part, he said the same things y'all said about the scarecrows," he replied. "He did ask me if I'd help out with the investigation."

"What'd you tell him?" Aunt Martha passed another round of potatoes his way as she inquired. Before he could answer, she said, "Oh and I'll take that letter you wrote to your wife in to town when I go in for supplies tomorrow or the next day. It might get there in a week or two if you're lucky."

Town was Oneida, about ten miles south from the ranch. As the crow flies, it wasn't all that far west to Cimarron, maybe two hundred and fifty miles. He didn't know why it might take as much as two weeks for a letter to get there since he and his cousin had ridden the distance in a little over seven days. Maybe the folks who carried the mail weren't in any kind of a rush. He also wished his spelling was better. He hadn't known how to read or write when he came to live with his aunt and uncle after his family was killed. Aunt Martha had taught him, something he was grateful for even though he'd never told her that. It did bother him that Rusty was a better speller than he was but he'd had a head start in learning.

"Thanks, Aunt Martha, I sure appreciate it. I want to let Mollie know what's goin' on so she's not worried." He helped himself to more potatoes. "And I told Agent Slaughter that I would very much like to help track down these rustlers if he didn't feel like I would be buttin' in."

"What'd he say to that?" Uncle Joe said without looking up from his plate.

"He didn't seem to mind, said he'd welcome the help. Seems like a decent fella to me though I didn't get the impression he had any notion who was doin' the rustlin'."

"That's a fact," Uncle Joe responded. He looked up from his plate and stared at his nephew for a moment before asking, "What's your take on this?"

Tommy was caught off guard. He hemmed and hawed for a minute before shrugging. "Don't reckon I have much of a notion so far. 'Course, I just got here. I ain't had much chance to investigate yet."

His uncle stared at him for a moment longer, then he grunted and returned to his meal.

The moon was half full and it provided enough light for the two individuals to see. Both had canvas bags with eyeholes cut in them pulled over their heads. As they began pushing the cattle, some of them bawled a bit but they were far enough away from the ranch house that the ruckus shouldn't wake the occupants. They'd learned their lesson at the Barclay spread . . . if the cows were too close to the house, leave them alone. It helped that this bunch was out in the open so they didn't need to cut any barbwire.

They cut out about twenty head and started moving them northwest where they would join the herd they'd been gathering. Tomorrow, they would use their running irons to alter the brands. After a few more midnight raids on local ranches, they'd drive them north to Oklahoma where buyers waited. They'd been up this trail before and knew people who didn't ask questions.

No one woke up and their actions went unobserved except by a whitetail buck and two does who were watching from a stand of trees. Whatever they thought, they kept it to themselves. If anyone else had seen them, they wouldn't have been able to identify them. And, in fact, they did resemble scarecrows.

V

"So they did it again?" Rusty shook his head in disbelief.

"Yep," Agent Slaughter replied. "This time, no one saw them. John Steele reported it to me, said they made off with twenty head. Ran 'em right out, easy as you please."

Tommy frowned. "How do you know it was the same fellas?"

"Well, I don't know for sure," Slaughter said. "They got a pattern they seem to follow though and it doesn't change much from one time to the next. I'm assumin' it's the same ones."

"I expect you're right but it's a good idea to keep an open mind in these things." Rusty laughed and Tommy shot a ferocious look at him.

"What?" His cousin stood with an innocent expression on his face. "I was just impressed with how smart you sound." A wicked grin crossed his lips. "How long were you sheriff?"

"Long enough to learn a thing or two," he said. "Don't forget I had the benefit of workin' with one of the best lawmen who ever pinned on a badge."

"That's a fact. Nathan Averill was one of the best ever, no doubt about it."

"Tomás Marés was a pretty sharp fella himself when it comes to it," Tommy added.

"You're right," Rusty said, his wicked grin returning. "Some of their smarts was bound to rub off, even on a hard-head like you."

Slaughter chuckled. "You boys are pretty good at givin' each other a hard time. Reckon you been at it for quite a while."

"We do have some experience, that's for sure," Tommy said. "But back to the important thing, I wasn't sayin' you were wrong, Bill, I was just sayin' we don't really know anything for sure at this point."

"You're right." He frowned and was quiet for a moment. "You know, if I didn't know better, I'd say there was a good chance this was the work of an old cattle thief that was around here a while back, old Jim Sully."

"Why's that?"

"The way these boys are operating only at night, cutting the wire, not taking more than twenty head at a time."

Tommy took off his hat and scratched his head. "Well then, how can you be so sure it ain't this Sully fella?"

Slaughter laughed. "I know it for a fact. They hung him five years ago."

Rusty grinned. "Reckon he's got a pretty good alibi, don't he?" He elbowed his cousin. "What you think, Mr. Investigator?"

140

Tommy shot him a dirty look. "Yeah, that's a pretty solid alibi." He thought for a moment. "Did he work alone or did he have a gang? Seems like you'd need at least a couple of cowboys workin' together to do it right. Maybe somebody who learned the trade from him has started back up causin' trouble."

Slaughter shook his head. "He had two fellas we know of who ran with him. They didn't do this neither."

"Let me guess," Rusty said. "They hung them boys, too."

"That's right, they did. Caught Sully and the two of 'em in the act. Had a quick trial and then hung 'em. They ain't around to cause anybody problems anymore."

This all sounded like a dead end and yet he had a nagging feeling that maybe there was something there that he hadn't figured out yet. If he kept asking questions, Rusty would needle him but he couldn't let it go.

"You know for certain there wasn't anyone else mixed up in their dirty work? Maybe someone else had run with 'em but wasn't there the time they caught these fellas."

The agent pondered the question. "Not that I know of but that doesn't mean it's impossible."

"You reckon there's anyone around who

remembers this Sully fella? Maybe they know who he ran with."

"I can't think of anybody," Slaughter said. "Only folks left that had any kind of connection with Jim Sully are his two daughters."

"What do we know about them?"

Rusty guffawed.

Tommy ignored his cousin's laughter. "Do they live around here?"

Rusty would not be ignored. "Yeah, those Sully girls are dangerous desperados. Prob'ly got 'em a gang of old maids and they been terrorizin' the countryside."

He tried to think of a clever response to the jibe. He couldn't think of anything. On reflection, he figured there was a good chance Rusty was right. He hated it when his cousin was right, especially when it came at his expense.

Agent Slaughter jumped back in the conversation. "I kind of doubt that, Rusty," he said with a chuckle. He gave the whole notion some thought. "You know, they might remember somebody who ran with their daddy though. I wasn't around when all this happened but I think they were about seventeen and fifteen at the time. It's been pert near five years but it's worth a try."

Shooting his cousin a look of triumph, he said, "You're right, it couldn't hurt. It's not like we're overburdened with leads as it is. Might as well follow this thread and see what comes untangled."

Rusty sniffed and looked at Slaughter. "I sorta remember them girls but I didn't know 'em well. Are they still around these parts?"

He nodded. "Their daddy had a small spread a little bit east of here. Far as I know, they still run it."

"There you go," Tommy said. "Why don't we head that way and ask these ladies some questions."

"Let's do it," Slaughter said. "It ain't but an hour's ride."

Rusty muttered something under his breath. "I didn't catch that," Tommy said.

His cousin looked at him and shook his head in disgust. "I said looks like we're fixin' to waste a couple of hours."

"So how'd you get into this stock-grower's outfit, Bill?" They rode along with the Stock-Raisers' agent in the middle and the Stallings boys on either side. The panhandle wind was blustery and it cut right through Tommy's coat. It got chilly in the New Mexico Territory but now he remembered how cold a fella could get out there on the Texas plains where there was nothing to block the wind.

"My daddy was a sheriff down in Georgetown, a tad north of Austin," Slaughter replied. "When I was a kid, he used to let me ride with him when he'd go out lookin' around. Never let me get caught up in any gunfights or nothin' but I sure heard a lot of stories about cattle rustlers."

"Bet he had some tales to tell," Rusty chuckled. "Plenty of rustlin' down that part of Texas. Is he still in the law enforcement business?"

The man was quiet for a moment. "Nope, he got shot. It was cattle rustlers which I reckon tells you why I do this."

They rode along without a word for a while and then Rusty broke the silence. "I sure am sorry, Bill. I didn't know."

Slaughter nodded. "I know that Rusty, no hard feelin's. That is the reason I hunt these scofflaws down though. They're a bane to the cattlemen and we need to wipe 'em out."

"You'll get no argument from me on that," Tommy said. "Like we were tellin' you, we just tracked down some vicious outlaws ourselves. Seems like you take one down and two more pop up and take their place."

"That's the way it is around these parts

for sure," he replied. "Our bunch has arrested and hung a whole passel of rustlers over the past nine years but every time we turn around, seems like there's another one preyin' on smaller ranch outfits."

"Doesn't seem like this gang is inclined to violence though from what you know so far."

"Not yet maybe, but I don't reckon it would take much to get 'em started murderin' folks. That's the way these devils operate." The muscles in Bill Slaughter's jaw tensed up and for a moment he was quiet. "I know this much, if I catch 'em in the act, I won't waste any time askin' questions."

Tommy wasn't sure how to respond to this statement. In his rather short career as a lawman, he'd shot several outlaws but he was clear in his conscience that it had always come down to them or him, and in all cases, they had fired first. His mentors, Nathan Averill and Tomás Marés, had drummed it into his young, and at times thick, skull that he was a lawman, not a vigilante. It sounded to him like Agent Bill Slaughter might not share that point of view. They rode on without speaking. In twenty minutes or so, they could see the outline of a ranch house on the horizon. Slaughter stopped and the other two followed suit.

"I'll let 'em know who I am," he said, "that way they'll understand this is official business. Reckon you boys might do the talkin' after that." When Rusty looked at him with a puzzled expression, he said, "My people hung their daddy. I doubt they'll be inclined to be friendly towards me even though that was before my time."

Tommy nodded. "I expect you're right. I been out in the New Mexico Territory the last five years. I got no dog in the fight as far as they know."

Slaughter took his hat off and scratched his head. "Five years you say. You must've left right around the time the agency hung their daddy."

"I don't recall hearin' anything about it before I left," he said. "I was young and dumb though, maybe I wasn't payin' close enough attention."

"At least you ain't so young anymore," Rusty said without missing a lick.

Tommy shook his head. "I got to hand it to you, cousin. You never miss a chance to get a good shot in."

Rusty beamed.

They rode on until they could see the ranch house. It was sagging and in need of a coat of whitewash. About twenty feet to the west of the house stood stables and a small corral. "Stood" wasn't an accurate description. The structures were on the verge of falling down.

"Don't look like these ladies have been all that successful in their careers as ranchers," Rusty said. "Place looks like it could use a man's touch."

When they got a little closer, they saw a woman of indeterminate age walk out into the yard. She was carrying an old Winchester that looked like it had seen better days. The boys proceeded with caution. As they got to within twenty feet of her, she held up her left hand, indicating that they should stop. They did. The woman was wearing a battered Stetson, a denim shirt, and dusty denim pants. She was weathered looking but attractive. Her age could have been anywhere between twenty and forty. She looked them up and down.

"You're Rusty Stallings, ain't you?"

The redhead doffed his hat and bowed in the saddle. "Yes, ma'am, I am, at your service. So you heard of me, have you?" He turned his head towards his cousin and whispered, "Reckon I got me a reputation."

The woman snorted. "I heard you used to be almost handsome till you grew that red, tangled bird's nest on your face. Now nobody knows what you look like."

Rusty turned red. Slaughter turned his face away to hide his smile but Tommy laughed at his cousin, who sputtered for a moment, unsure of how to carry on. Finally he turned to Slaughter and said, "Bill, reckon you'd better tell this lady why we're here."

When Agent Slaughter turned back, his smile was gone. There was a hard look in his eyes and a set to his jaw that made Tommy a bit nervous. For one thing, their primary purpose for being there was to gather information. For another, it's not necessarily a great idea to take the offensive with someone who has a rifle trained on you, even if the rifle looks like it's been left out in the rain for several years.

"Ma'am, I'm a special agent for the Stock-Raisers' Association, we're here on official business. I'd appreciate it if you'd put down that gun."

"I bet you would," the woman said with a sneer. "You're one of them sumbitches who hung my daddy. I oughta shoot you right now."

Now Tommy was really spooked. With a subtle move, he nudged his horse, Rusty, to ease over a bit. Rusty, his cousin, noticed and did the same with his horse so they were spread out more. He'd never imagined this visit might lead to a gun battle, especially with a woman. He looked over at Slaughter and what he saw made him more nervous. His eyes were blazing and his hand was moving bit by bit towards his pistol.

"You better keep your hands up high and away from that gun you're reachin' for." The voice came from the shadows of the porch. A moment later a woman, younger than the other, stepped into the sunlight. She was wearing a pair of pants that were several sizes too large for her with a length of baling twine through the loops to hold them up. She was aiming a pistol at the Stock-Raisers' agent. Like the weapon carried by the first woman, her pistol was old and tarnished but that didn't provide much comfort. "I'll blow a hole in you if you move your hand any closer."

The image of Nathan Averill flashed through Tommy's mind. He couldn't imagine the old lawman shooting it out with two women whom they'd only come to talk with. It made no sense. He would have remained calm and gone ahead with the plan to talk.

"Reckon we all oughta calm down just a bit, don't you think?" He stared hard at Slaughter. "Bill, there's no need for things

149

to get out of hand here."

The man had been holding his breath but now he exhaled in a rush. "You're right, Sheriff Stallings. I don't like having a gun pointed at me though."

"Nobody does," he said with a chuckle, trying to lighten the mood. "Reckon they didn't like their daddy bein' hung neither though." He turned toward the women with a smile on his face. "I heard about your daddy, ladies. I know that must've been hard on y'all but Agent Slaughter wasn't working for the Stock-Raisers' when that happened. It wouldn't be fair to blame him for that."

"Didn't seem to me like anybody was interested in what was fair when they hung Daddy," the woman with the Winchester said. "Didn't even give him much of a trial. Just took him out and strung him up."

"Your pa was caught red-handed stealin' cattle, lady," Slaughter said. "That's a hangin' offense. I don't see what's unfair about that." The woman bristled.

Speaking in a loud whisper out of the corner of his mouth, Tommy said "I got this, Bill. You can help by stayin' quiet and not throwin' kerosene on the fire." He focused on the woman in front of him. "Ma'am, you may be right about your daddy, but there's nothin' we can do about that right now. We got somethin' else we wanted to ask you about. We're just lookin' for a little information, that's all."

"If you think you can smooth-talk me, stranger, you'd better think again." The woman glared at him. "I wouldn't give you a sip of water if you was dyin' in the desert. I sure as hell ain't gonna give you any information. Now y'all get off our property or we'll shoot you for trespassin'.'"

He didn't bother to look in his cousin's direction. He knew he could count on him to be ready for whatever came. Instead, he looked at Bill Slaughter. The man continued to look like he was ready to shoot it out with the women. Tommy couldn't see any way that could turn out good, no matter who survived the battle. He thought of Nathan Averill and contemplated what he might do in such a situation.

"Sure ain't lookin' to get shot, ma'am," he said. "Sorry to have troubled you, we'll be on our way."

Slaughter glared at him, insisting with his eyes that Tommy take a different course. Shaking his head, he jerked it back in the general direction they'd come. "Come on, Bill, let's head on back."

He wasn't sure Slaughter was going to

comply with his direction. The agent sat there for a long moment, glowering at the woman, then he reined his horse around and began to ride away. As Tommy rode in beside him, he snarled, "What in the hell are you doin'?"

"Not yet," Tommy whispered. "Wait till we're away."

They rode in silence for ten minutes, putting some distance between themselves and the dilapidated ranch house. He could feel Slaughter fuming.

"All right," he said. "Let's talk."

Slaughter exploded. "I said what in the hell are you doin'? We came to get information from those women and instead, they gave us disrespect. And you just let it slide."

"So you want to shoot 'em because they didn't show enough respect? Where I come from, that ain't the way a lawman operates." Tommy shook his head. "Besides, we got some information."

"What information is that?" Slaughter was still fuming.

"We know they're still plenty hot about their daddy bein' hung for one thing. We know they're holdin' a huge grudge, for another. We dang sure know they're mighty feisty. Maybe they learned a thing or two about cattle rustlin' from their daddy."

At that, Rusty snorted. "Right, cousin, those ladies are dangerous bandits. Reckon we done found our cattle rustlers."

Slaughter didn't join in the laughter but his expression eased up a bit. "You're not sayin' you think those women are rustlin' cattle, are you?"

He shrugged. "Well, I don't know but I am sayin' that we might want to consider the prospect. They have the know-how and they sure 'nuff got the right attitude."

"They were both rough as cobs," Rusty said, "but I can't believe we're huntin' lady cattle rustlers. That don't make sense."

Tommy could see he was getting nowhere with his cousin and the agent. Heck, they might even be right, he might be on a wild-goose chase. Still, he wasn't ready to give up on the idea. He did figure, however, that there wasn't much point in continuing to discuss it.

"Maybe not," he said. "Let me know if either of you boys comes up with a better idea."

They rode along in silence for a while, then Rusty laughed again. "Lady cattle rustlers. What's the world comin' to?"

My dearest Mollie,
Oct. 11, 1886
I hope you are doin good, I miss you a great deal. Me and Rusty and that Slaughter fella thats agent for the cattle growers assoseashin went to talk to some ladies whose daddy was a rustler but he got hung. They werent to allfired happy to see us I can tell you that. I thought Slaughter was gonna get in a gunfight with them but he calmd down. He's kind of a hothead which I know made you laff comin from me but he is anyway. I think maybe these ladies got somethin to do with this cattle rustlin but Slaughter and Rusty laffed at me. They dont think a woman could be a rustler. I dont know. What do you think. Did I menshun I miss you. I sure do. I better go now, I got to get some sleep. Aunt Martha will post this tomorrow along with the one I wrote yesterday.

Youre lovin husband,
Tom Stallings

VI

The next morning at breakfast, Tommy handed his Aunt Martha the second letter he'd written to Mollie. As he did, he felt a pang of sadness. The past few months had been a rough patch for him and his lovely bride. More than anything, he wished he could hear her lilting Irish brogue as she teased him about one thing or another.

"I'll take this letter to town with the one you gave me the other day," Aunt Martha said. "I'm sorry I didn't get around to it yesterday but I didn't have time to make that ride to town. Reckon it worked out all right though since you got this letter to go with the other one." She smiled. "That wife of yours must be somethin', Tommy Stallings. I remember I used to near 'bout have to put a gun to your head to get you to write your lessons back when you was livin' here and now you're writin' two letters in three days."

He shook his head and laughed. "You're right about that, Aunt Martha. I still don't much like writin' but I do miss my Mollie somethin' fierce." He paused for a moment and thought, then he continued. "Aunt Martha, can I ask you a question?"

"Reckon you just did," she said with a grin. "You got another question for me to go with that one?"

"I do," he replied. "One thing I miss about Mollie is that she helps me look at things from a woman's point of view, which ain't somethin' I'm accustom to doin'."

"And since she ain't here, you want to run somethin' past me to see what I think?"

"That's it," Tommy said. "Do you mind?"

"Not at all, honey. Let's hear it."

"All right," he said, a note of uncertainty in his voice. "I got to warn you, when I brought this up with Rusty and that Slaughter fella, they laughed at me."

"I can't promise I won't laugh, too," she said. "Still, if it's important, don't let that stop you."

"Do you think a woman could be a cattle rustler?"

" 'Course she could," his aunt said without hesitation, cocking her head and giving him a strange look. "Why are you askin' me somethin' like that?"

Tommy explained their interaction with the daughters of Jim Sully the previous day and how he'd come away with some suspicions about their possible involvement with the rash of cattle thievery.

"I know Annie and Jennie Sully," Aunt Martha said. "Known 'em since they was little girls." She nodded as she thought about his question. "They were both sweet little things back in those days. I think they changed once their daddy got strung up."

He laughed. "They might've been sweet when they were little but they were mean as

156

rattlesnakes yesterday. I thought them and Agent Slaughter were gonna have a shoot-out right there in front of me and your baby boy."

"That's what I mean," Aunt Martha said, nodding. "They're bitter and to tell you the truth, I can't blame 'em all that much."

"Why's that?"

"I think them Stock-Raisers' boys got a little ahead of themselves hangin' Jim Sully."

Tommy frowned. "You don't think he was rustlin' cattle?"

"Oh, I know he was stealin' cows," Aunt Martha replied. "I also know that he was goin' through some hard times. We were comin' out of a drought and he was desperate to feed his family. Those two little girls' mama had died and things were mighty rough. I ain't sayin' he was right for thievin' but I don't believe they should've hung him. Seems like there could've been somethin' else they might've done instead."

"Speakin' of hard times, it don't look like things have gotten too much better. That's a pretty raggedy lookin' spread they're on."

"I expect you're right. It ain't easy makin' a go of it out here on these plains. I'll tell you one thing though, if they're tough enough to give it a go at ranchin', they'd be tough enough to try their hand at cattle rustlin', too."

He scratched his head. "I don't doubt that they'd be tough enough, Aunt Martha, I'm just havin' trouble thinkin' about lady cattle rustlers." He laughed. "I tell you what, they were sure itchin' to get into it with Bill Slaughter. I tried to tell 'em he wasn't even workin' for the Stock-Raisers' Association when their daddy got hung but they didn't want to hear it."

"That should tell you somethin' right there," his aunt replied. "And I don't know why you can't imagine lady cattle rustlers, we sure 'nuff do most of the other jobs out here on the plains. You've seen me work cattle with your uncle. You know I can do it all. I can rope 'em, flank 'em, and I can cut 'em."

Tommy chuckled. "That's a fact. Maybe you're right, I do need to keep my mind open to the possibility. Gonna be hard convincin' Slaughter and your hardheaded son though."

"If they won't listen to you, send 'em around my way, I'll straighten 'em out."

"I don't doubt that you would, Aunt Martha." He hesitated and then continued. "I want to tell you again how sorry I am for the way I acted all those years ago. You and Uncle Joe were never nothin' but good to me. I acted like a lowlife cur."

His aunt's eyes misted over and she wiped them with the sleeve of her dress. "Tommy, what happened to your daddy, mama, and little sister was horrible. Don't forget that your daddy was Joe's little brother. It tore us up and we could see it ate at you somethin' fierce. We couldn't figure out how to help other than feed you and give you work to do."

He got a little bit choked up and it took a moment before he could speak. He cleared his throat and said, "You and Uncle Joe did fine, I'm the one who let you down."

"No you didn't, Tommy Stallings," Aunt Martha said. "You came back and I can see you've turned into a fine man. I'd love to meet that pretty Irish bride of yours."

"I'd sure like that too, Aunt Martha," he said. "Maybe I'll bring her to Texas and let you meet her."

"I can't think of anything I'd like better," she replied.

They stood there for a minute, both of them feeling a little awkward but good all the same. He broke the silence. "Reckon I better get on back out there and see if I can catch some cattle rustlers." He grinned. "Heck, maybe I can even catch some lady cattle rustlers."

VII

"If you think them young ladies are ridin' around at night dressed up like scarecrows and stealin' people's cows, you're even dumber than you look." Rusty shook his head in disgust.

"That's pretty funny comin' from a fella with a big red bird's nest on his face," Tommy shot back. "Maybe you'd like to tell your ma what a dumb idea it is. She sure didn't seem to think so."

His cousin shrugged his shoulders. "Ma's got some funny ideas, you know that. I ain't about to try to argue with her. You know good and well you'd have better luck changin' a fence post's mind."

"I don't believe fence posts have minds, cousin," Tommy said in a smug tone. He felt like he'd gotten the best of this exchange. "Anyway, I don't know why you're not even willin' to consider the idea."

"It just don't make sense, that's why. You ever knew a lady cattle rustler before?"

He considered his cousin's question. "Nah, I reckon not but that don't mean it couldn't happen."

"Pigs could sprout wings and fly away, too, but that don't mean it's gonna happen."

He began to reevaluate whether he'd gotten the best of this exchange with his cousin. He sighed. "Maybe you're right. I ain't sayin' you are but I reckon you could be. I won't give up on the notion without askin' around a bit but I'll try to keep my mind open to other possibilities. Maybe you should, too."

Rusty snorted. "You bet, cousin. You keep thinkin' there's lady rustlers. I'll keep lookin' up at the sky waitin' to see some flyin' pigs."

Tommy wasn't sure where to start with checking up on the Sully girls. Heck, he wasn't even sure if he should start. Much as he hated to admit it, in all likelihood, his cousin was right. Who'd ever heard of lady cattle rustlers? Still, there was something about them that left him with the feeling that they might just be the first ones. He figured he should talk with Agent Slaughter about the idea since it was his official investigation. Rusty had told him the Stock-Raisers' folks had a little office in Oneida so he saddled up and headed in that direction. It would take him a couple of hours to get there and that would give him some time to think this thing through.

He arrived in Oneida right around noon

with no more answers and several more questions in his mind. One of his questions was how to figure out where in the heck the Stock-Raisers' Association office was. He was a semi-trained investigator though and he was pretty confident he could find the answer to that particular quandary. He asked a stranger on the street to direct him but the man had no idea what he was talking about. It took three more tries before he found someone who could tell him but he got to the bottom of it. Now if only he could solve the rest of the cattle rustling mystery with as much ease.

Following the directions the stranger gave him, Tommy located the Stock-Raisers' office, which he identified by the sign on the door that said "Stock-Raisers' Association." Dang, he was on fire with this investigating business. He dismounted and tied Rusty, his horse, to the hitching rail outside the office. He knocked on the door but there was no response. He opened it and called out a howdy so Slaughter didn't spook and shoot him. There was no response.

Just his luck. He'd ridden all the way here and the agent was not in his office. Now he had another mystery to solve. Since he was on something of a roll with this investigating business, he figured he could puzzle it out. As he started to ponder the where-abouts of the man, his stomach growled and he realized he was hungry. It took only a brief moment before he recognized that as a clue. If he was hungry, that meant it was lunchtime. Figuring that Bill Slaughter's stomach operated about the same as his did, he suspected he might be looking for a meal as well.

Although Tommy didn't remember much about Oneida, most towns had a limited number of places to eat. Most of the time, you had your restaurant and you had your boarding house. A third option might be the saloon. He figured the agent would need a place to stay while he was in the area investigating the rustling. That made the boarding house the most obvious place to start looking. He set out to track down Bill Slaughter.

He didn't even need to ask anyone's help to find the boarding house. He spotted the only two-story building in the town. The top floor would be where the guests stayed and the bottom floor would be the dining room. He marched over to the place, feeling pretty cocky. This investigating thing was not all that hard. Sure enough, there was a sign over the door that read Campbell's Boarding House. He walked in and once his eyes adjusted to the change in light, he spied Slaughter sitting at a table by himself in a corner. He looked up, spotted Tommy, and hailed him to come over.

"Sit yourself down, Stallings," Slaughter said. "I'm enjoyin' some of this fine stew they're servin' here. You hungry?"

He eyed the stew. "What's in it?"

Slaughter laughed. "I ain't sure. It's some kind of meat but I couldn't tell you what animal it comes from. I been eatin' here since I first come to town though and I ain't died yet. It don't taste all that bad."

Tommy shrugged and sat down at the table. A middle-aged woman stopped by on the way back to the kitchen, her arms loaded with plates. "You want some stew, cowboy?"

"You got anything else?" He wasn't sure he could stomach a meal where the ingredients were a mystery. He had too many mysteries to solve already in his life.

"Yep," she said. "You got two choices . . . stew and nothin'. Nothin' is free, stew costs fifteen cents. Coffee's free."

Shaking his head, he said, "Reckon I'll take the stew and coffee. Nothin' ain't very fillin'." She walked away chuckling.

"Don't reckon you came to town for the stew so you must've wanted to talk to me,"

Slaughter said with a grin. "You find out anything?"

"No, not really," Tommy replied. "I been thinkin' about our visit to the Sully girls the other day and I wanted to talk some more with you about it."

At the mention of the Sully girls' names, the agent's eyes blazed. "Danged uppity hides, I thought about shootin' both of 'em just for bein' so ornery."

"Like I mentioned before, Bill," he said, "bein' ornery ain't illegal. A lawman can't go gunnin' somebody down just cause he don't like the way they're actin'."

"Yeah, well, people like their daddy gunned my daddy down. You takin' the side of the outlaws?"

"No, Bill," Tommy replied, trying to keep the tension out of his voice. "That's kind of my point. Gunnin' people down is pretty much against the law unless they're shootin' at you first. Those young ladies weren't shootin' at us. If we'd shot 'em, that would make us the outlaws."

"Well, they sure had their guns pointed in our direction. I'm just sayin' it made me mighty hot."

He wanted to have a successful working relationship with the agent so he tried to lighten the tone of the conversation. "It didn't make me feel all that good either, to tell you the truth. The fact that they seemed a bit trigger-happy is a part of what I wanted to discuss with you, in fact."

"What about it?" The man still seemed annoyed.

He hesitated. "This might sound a little bit off the wall to you."

"Just lay it out there," Slaughter said, frustration evident in his voice. "If you got any ideas at all, it's more than I got right now."

"All right," he said. "I know those girls' daddy was a cattle thief. I just wonder if they might have decided to enter the family business is all."

Agent Slaughter shook his head. "You ain't still thinkin' they might be the cattle rustlers we're lookin' for, are you?"

Tommy felt his face getting hot, a combination of embarrassment and irritation. "As a matter of fact, I am sayin' it's somethin' we might should consider, yeah."

Slaughter laughed out loud. "Well if that ain't the silliest thing I ever heard. Lady cattle rustlers."

His embarrassment was gone and the irritation was turning to anger. "You got any better ideas? Never mind, don't answer that. You already said you didn't."

"No need to get mad, Stallings," the agent said, holding up his hand. "It's just seems like a pretty far-fetched notion is all. How many lady cattle rustlers you ever heard of?"

Tommy had had enough. He stood up and tossed fifteen cents on the table. "Like I said, you got nothin'. This may be far-fetched but it still beats nothin'. I'll check into the Sully girls, you keep chasin' nothin'." He turned and walked out of the boarding house.

As he rode back toward his uncle's ranch, Tommy fumed. He knew his idea was a long shot but both Slaughter and his cousin were acting like it was out of the realm of possibility. In addition, they were acting like they thought he was an idiot for coming up with the idea.

The thought of his being an idiot reminded him of his lovely Irish wife, who sometimes referred to him as an *eejit* . . . the Irish slang word for idiot. It was times like this when he missed her the most. He could talk with her about what was on his mind and she would always tell him straight up what she thought. Even when she disagreed and called him an *eejit,* he knew she did it with love in her heart. He didn't believe she would think he was an idiot for considering the Sully girls as suspects.

As he contemplated his next moves, he gave some consideration to making another trip out to the ragged piece of land that the Sully girls owned. He thought he stood some chance of getting a more hospitable reception if he didn't take Agent Bill Slaughter along. The man wasn't levelheaded when it came to dealing with suspects. Nathan Averill had taught him to give folks the benefit of the doubt. You might suspect someone of wrongdoing but that didn't mean you were right. You needed evidence to support your suspicions. And you sure didn't get into a raging gun battle with someone because you didn't like the way they talked to you.

It was too late in the day to make the trip to the Sully place and get back home before dark so he pointed Rusty in the direction of his uncle's ranch and kicked him into a lope. As always the horse was willing to give him what he asked. Right now, Tommy wasn't so sure about Rusty, his cousin. He could understand his being skeptical regarding the notion that the Sully girls were rustlers but it seemed to him that after all the hurrahin' was done, his cousin should back him up. He hoped that would be the case; that's what family did. He also hoped he wasn't on some sort of bootless errand.

Uncle Joe shook his head. "You think the Sully girls are doin' what?"

Tommy's face turned crimson. He scowled at Rusty who had obviously filled in his father on his suspicions. "Well, sir, there's a pretty good chance they know a bit about cattle rustlin'. From what I heard about their daddy, he was pretty full of zip back in the day when it come to stealin' folks' cows. You don't think it's possible that they decided to follow in his tracks?"

"If that ain't the most asinine notion I ever heard, I don't know what is," his uncle replied. He sat back in his chair and laughed. "They're girls, Tommy. Girls don't rustle cattle."

Aunt Martha slammed down the pitcher of buttermilk from which she was about to fill up her husband's glass. The table shook and some buttermilk slopped out on the tablecloth. She gave her husband a fierce look. "If you don't stop brayin' like a jackass, I might just pour this buttermilk on your head."

Uncle Joe shook his head in confusion. "What's got into you? I was just sayin' there ain't no way those little girls were the cattle rustlers that's been plaguin' folks for the past six months. Any fool could see that."

He could see from the set of her jaw and the fire in her eyes that his aunt had not taken her husband's comments well, most especially the last one. He was wishing he was somewhere else other than at the dinner table. He glanced at Rusty and saw that he, too, was looking for an escape route.

Aunt Martha stood up. "I, for one, could see the possibility that those 'little girls,' as you call 'em, could be smart enough and tough enough to rustle cattle." She fixed her husband with a defiant stare. "Are you callin' me a fool?"

Far too late, Uncle Joe realized the dangerous ground he had trod upon. He did his best to walk backwards away from the quicksand.

"Well a'course not, sweet pea," he said.

Tommy glanced at his cousin and saw that his jaw had dropped almost to the table. He assumed that he'd never heard his father refer to his mother as "sweet pea" before. Tommy took that as a sign of how desperate his uncle was to find a graceful way to exit the perilous situation. He looked back over to his Aunt Martha, trying to gauge how effective the "sweet pea" defense had been. Judging from her expression, it wasn't working.

"Don't you 'sweet pea' me, Joe Stallings," she said. "You near about called me a fool. If you think you can get out of that by tryin' to sugar talk me, then I know who the real fool is." She turned and walked toward the bedroom. Turning back, she said, "Supper's over. You three yahoos can clean up." She went into the bedroom and slammed the door behind herself.

Uncle Joe gazed after his wife, then turned a bleak stare on his son and nephew. "Thanks a lot for pullin' me into this mess." He shook his head in disgust and stood up. "You two can clean up, I'm goin' out to the barn. Think I'll slop the hogs. Least they appreciate me."

Tommy and Rusty watched him walk out the door. They looked at each other. His cousin shrugged.

"I'll wash, you dry."

My dearest Mollie,
Oct. 12, 1886
I know I just wrote you yesterday but I miss you somethin fierce and I sure wish I could talk to you. I'd give about anything to here the sound of your voice. I wish I coud find out what you think about my idea that those ladies I told you about mite have been stealin cattle. Rusty and that Slaugh-

ter fella think I'm loco and Uncle Joe got in a lot of trouble with Aunt Martha cause he said only a fool would think that. She sort of thinks it so she gave him what for cause he pretty much called her a fool though I don't think that was what he intended. Nether one was very happy. I dont know when I can post this letter but Ill do it soon as I can.

Youre lovin husband
Tom Stallings

VIII

Tommy got up early the next morning and saddled up Rusty, the horse. He was hungry but he didn't want to wait around and try to explain to Rusty, his cousin, what he hoped to accomplish by visiting the Sully girls again. Truth be told, he didn't want to hear any more hurrahing from his cousin either. He figured he could skip breakfast and make do with chewing on some jerky while he rode out to the little scraggly ranch. He hoped to be back home by noontime unless the girls shot him for trespassing, in which case he figured he wouldn't need a meal.

As he headed out in a long trot, he considered his strategy. He hoped that not having

Agent Slaughter along to antagonize the ladies would make it possible for him to ask them some questions without getting shot. While he did have suspicions about their involvement in the rash of cattle thievery, the original question they'd hoped to get an answer to was whether or not there were men who had ridden with Jim Sully back in the day who still might be around and might have renewed his rustling campaign. He thought that might be a safer topic with which to start the discussion.

If he was able to establish a friendlier tone with the Sully girls, one that didn't involve their threatening to shoot him, he hoped he might be able to look around a bit. While he doubted that they would give him a tour of the ranch, he thought that if he could gain a measure of their trust, they might let down their guard a bit. If so, he might then be able to slip around and look for evidence of foul play.

After that thought ran through his mind, he had to laugh at himself. He sounded like a real sneak. He figured that was something that came with the territory when you were dealing with suspicious people though. If the ladies were, in fact, the culprits, he doubted they would break down and confess to him just because they were overwhelmed by his charm, even though he could be mighty charming.

When he was seventy yards or so from the ranch dwelling, he hollered, "Hallo the house." He figured he'd be better off not coming up on the girls sudden-like. Given their attitude the previous visit, he thought surprising them might prove fatal. Once again, the older girl, Annie, came out front. Once again, she had the rusty old Winchester, which, once again, she pointed straight at him.

"Mornin' Miss Sully," he said in the friendliest voice he could muster, given that his mouth was suddenly very dry. Having a rifle, even an old beat-up one, pointed at a fella didn't make it easy to be sociable. "I was hopin' maybe to visit with you and your sister a bit this mornin'. You mind if I step down?"

"I do mind, you lop-eared galoot. You stay put in that saddle or I'll blow a hole in you."

With no hesitation, he held his hands up high, hoping it was obvious he wasn't intent on being belligerent. "Whatever you say, ma'am. I ain't lookin' for trouble, I just wanted to talk a bit."

"What did you not understand from our short chat the other day? We got nothin' to say to law dogs, do we, sis?"

Tommy had an eerie feeling that he was reliving the events that had occurred two days before. The other Sully girl, Jennie, once again stepped off the porch and pointed her ragged old pistol at him. She was wearing the same britches that were several sizes too big for her and she didn't look any more welcoming today than she did then.

"Ladies, like I said, I ain't lookin' for trouble. I'm just tryin' to find out who's behind all this rustlin'. It's been goin' on around these parts for a number of months now. It's hurtin' small ranchers, folks like yourselves, and we're hopin' to put a stop to it. Surely you can understand that."

Annie Sully sneered at him. "You think me and Jennie give two hoots in hell about them small ranchers? Where were those folks after they hung our daddy? Where they been the last five years while we was tryin' to scratch out a livin' on this rock pile of a ranch? They don't care nothin' about us and we don't care nothin' about them. Now if you don't want to get shot, you'd best turn that ugly pony around and light out from here pronto."

He could tell Rusty's feelings were hurt by her callous insult. He wasn't sure why she had to drag the horse he rode up on into the discussion. It didn't seem like a good time to bring that up though so he didn't.

"Well, I reckon if that's the way you feel, I won't take up any more of your time. I was hopin' maybe you'd be willin' to help out."

"Annie, I believe he's even dumber than we thought he was the other day," Jennie said to her sister. "I'm half a mind to shoot him just for bein' so dumb."

Well now they'd not only insulted his horse, they'd insulted him, too. Apparently, his charming ways weren't anywhere near as persuasive as he'd thought they were. With two weapons pointed at him though, he didn't feel like he was in a strong position to protest.

"All right, I can take a hint," he said as he reined Rusty around. "I won't bother you anymore." As he rode off, he couldn't resist hollering back over his shoulder. "My horse ain't ugly though."

He probably shouldn't have done that. He saw Annie raise her Winchester to her shoulder. That was enough for Tommy. He spurred Rusty and he responded like a champion by breaking into a gallop. Apparently his horse had figured out well before he had how inhospitable these women were. He heard a gunshot but didn't feel the burn of the bullet so he kept on going. He didn't know if she was trying to hit him or put a scare in him. If it was the former, she'd failed. If it was the latter, she'd succeeded. He didn't slow down until he was a good half mile over the rise.

Tommy was conflicted on the subject of whether to tell his cousin about his visit to the Sully place. He really wasn't in the mood to hear more teasing but the fact was, Rusty was working with him on this investigation and he figured he owed it to him to keep him informed. He decided he could leave out a few of the more sensitive details and just tell him the high spots. On reflection, he couldn't think of any high spots. Oh well. He decided he'd tell him that they had refused to talk with him, which left him at a dead end.

"Them's the two meanest girls I ever seen," Rusty said after hearing his cousin's somewhat watered-down version of his trip to visit the Sully sisters.

It occurred to him that Rusty didn't know the half of it, which was fine with him. "They sure 'nuff are. I don't know if they're hidin' somethin' or if they're mean as a couple of rattlesnakes who just shed their skins."

His cousin gave him a suspicious look. "Your old ugly roan horse looked like he'd been pretty lathered up when you got home. You sure you're tellin' me the whole story?"

"Yes, I'm tellin' you the whole story," he snapped, "and Rusty ain't ugly." He frowned at his cousin. "Leastwise, my horse, Rusty, ain't ugly. Can't say much about others who might be named Rusty."

"Now you're just bein' mean, Tommy," Rusty said with exaggerated patience. "You're also not answerin' my question. How come your horse was all lathered up?"

Throwing up his hands, he said, "All right, here's the story. Them girls run me off their land like a scalded dog. They called Rusty ugly, me dumb, and they took a shot at me as I rode away. Are you happy now?"

"Hell, no, I ain't happy, Tommy," Rusty replied. "You may be hard to get along with but I don't want no one shootin' you." He frowned. "Why do you figure those girls were so ornery towards us? I know Slaughter was kinda spiteful towards 'em but you and I weren't nothin' but affable."

Tommy nodded. "I know, I been thinkin' about that. I know you think I'm loco for considerin' they might be the rustlers we're lookin' for but they sure do act like they're hidin' somethin'."

"You're right, I do think you're loco for believin' they're cattle rustlers. That don't mean you ain't right about them hidin' somethin' though." His cousin scrunched up his red-bearded face as he considered the possibilities. "Wonder what it is."

"I wish I could find a way to take a look around their place. Whoever's stealin' these cattle has got to be keepin' 'em somewhere. To look at their run-down outfit, you'd know them girls wouldn't have more than a few head of cows. If we found a bunch of cattle penned on their property, you might have to change your opinion about me bein' loco."

"Oh, I'd still probably think you're loco . . . hell, you are . . . but I might come around to your way of thinkin' about the Sully girls," Rusty said with a grin. "I don't know how we can nose around their pile of rocks without gettin' shot though."

Tommy exhaled in frustration. "Me neither. I'm gonna keep thinkin' about it though. I'll let you know if I come up with an idea."

The moon was nearly full, which made visibility good. The outlaws could see their quarry. This job seemed almost too simple. No rail fence to tear down, just a few

179

strands of barbed wire to snip and away they would go with the cattle. The rustler in the lead dismounted, took out a pair of fence cutters, and went to work on the five-strand fence. In minutes, there was a clear path between two fence posts.

The second rider moved in and worked around to the back side of the bunch of cattle, pushing them towards the opening. The first rider mounted up again and moved out of the way, waiting to pick up the group after they were clear of the downed fence. The cattle were agitated going through an unfamiliar opening, which made it difficult to get an accurate count as they moved through the gap. Once they were out in the open, they settled down and they tallied up what they had. Seventeen head. Not a bad haul. With the addition of this lot to what they'd stolen so far, they had a good herd to head on up to the Indian Territory. They could get a good price up there and that would go a long way towards easing the financial strain they were trying to alleviate. Sometimes this all seemed too easy.

A shot rang out. Instinct kicked in and both riders ducked, although they had no idea from which direction the gunfire was coming. A voice rang out.

"You get out a here, you rustlin' sons a bitches! Beat it or I'll fill you full a lead."

Neither outlaw needed any more encouragement. They both lit into a gallop and headed over the rise towards the northwest. The rifle bearer fired off three more shots in their direction but he wasn't trying very hard to hit them. He wasn't a killer but he didn't appreciate folks trying to steal what was his. He walked over and inspected the cut fence, cursing as he looked at the damage. There were a few hours of work he hadn't planned on doing when the sun came up. Just what he needed, more work.

IX

Tommy rode in to Oneida with the intention of posting his last letter to Mollie. He didn't know if she'd received the two his Aunt Martha had posted a couple of days earlier and he wasn't optimistic that he would ever get a reply. It made him feel better to write down his thoughts and feelings and send them to his wife though. He figured that was worth something.

The man who owned the mercantile was also the postmaster for Oneida. Tommy figured he might pick up a few supplies while he was in town. His aunt made the finest biscuits in the panhandle of Texas and she was low on flour. He also thought he might pick up some Arbuckle's coffee. He didn't know if she was running short on coffee but you could never have too much Arbuckle's on hand.

When he got to the mercantile, he tied Rusty to the hitching rail out front and walked in. It took a moment for his eyes to adjust to the dim light inside, then he started looking around on the shelves for the items he needed.

"Can I help you find something, son?" An older gentleman wearing a pair of glasses, and a shirt, tie and vest, came up to where he was standing. Tommy didn't recognize him.

"Thank you, sir," he said. "I'm pickin' up a few items for my Aunt Martha and I need to post a letter, if it ain't too much trouble."

"No trouble at all, son, that's what I'm here for." He looked at Tommy for a moment. "Your aunt wouldn't be Martha Stallings, would she?"

"One and the same," he replied with a smile. "I ain't sure the world is ready for more than one of my Aunt Martha."

The man laughed. "She's a pistol, that's for sure. She was just in here day before yesterday posting a couple of letters. You kin to them folks?"

"Yes, sir," he nodded. "They're my aunt and uncle. I lived with 'em for a while until about five years ago."

"I came to town around four years ago, that's when I bought this here mercantile," the man said. "I heard about you. You were that boy whose folks got killed by those savages."

Tommy felt a stab of grief, which surprised him. He thought the pain of that loss was well behind him. It appeared that it was not.

"Yes, sir, that's me. I lived with 'em for almost seven years."

"It's coming back to me now. Pardon my manners, I'm Fred Carlisle, the owner of this place."

Reaching out his hand, he said, "Tom Stallings, pleased to meet you."

"Where you been since you left?" Carlisle seemed interested in getting to know him.

"I been out in the New Mexico Territory for these past five years."

"What'd you do out there, if you don't mind me asking?"

"I don't mind," Tommy said with a smile. "I cowboyed for a time, then I got into the lawman business. I was a deputy and then acting sheriff in Colfax County up in the northern part of the territory."

"What brings you to these parts?"

"My cousin, Rusty . . . you might know him . . . came out to visit me and told me Uncle Joe and Aunt Martha needed my help. I expect you've heard about that rash of cattle rustlin' that's been goin' on now for months."

"I do know Rusty," Carlisle replied. "Nice boy though that red bird's nest of a beard on his face looks plum ridiculous. And yep, I heard about the thievery. Somebody should do something about that."

"There's folks takin' a stab at trackin' those outlaws down. You're bound to have run into Bill Slaughter, the agent for the Stock-Raisers' Association, he's stayin' over to the boarding house."

The man made a face, which Tommy wasn't sure how to interpret. "I've crossed paths with the young man a time or two," he said. "I'm not sure he's the man to get that job done."

Although he wasn't interested in having a discussion on the merits and qualifications of Bill Slaughter, Carlisle's reaction caught him by surprise nonetheless. It occurred to him, though, that since this man seemed to have been on the scene in Oneida for quite some time, he might have knowledge of the Sully girls that could be helpful.

"Mr. Carlisle, you seem to know a lot of the folks around these parts," he said. "I got a question for you. Do you know the Sully family? The Sully girls still live on the little ranch their pa left 'em. I understand he was hung for cattle rustlin' a while back."

Carlisle nodded. "I knew about Jim Sully and I know the girls. Don't see them much because they almost never come to town. Why are you asking about them?"

"Just curious," Tommy said. "We had hoped to talk to 'em to see if they knew of any old-timers who had ridden with their pa back when he was stealin' cows. Tryin' to get some kind of idea who's responsible for all this thievery."

"Well, I can answer part of that question," he said. "I heard Jim Sully only rode with two other boys. I met them once. They were kind of wild but not real dyed-in-the-wool desperados. They'd all fallen on hard times due to the drought. I don't think they really wanted to be cattle rustlers, they were just trying to get along." He sniffed in indignation. "I know it was before my time but I didn't really hold with them hanging those boys. Thought maybe they deserved some time in jail but not being strung up. That gang of cattlemen were bloodthirsty if you ask me."

"So you don't think there's anybody left who might've learned the trade from Jim Sully and decided to take it up again?"

"I got no idea who it could be," Carlisle said.

He hesitated, then decided to plunge ahead. "What about the girls?"

Carlisle looked puzzled. "What about the girls?"

"Any chance they might be the rustlers?"

Carlisle's eyes bugged out. He shook his head and threw it back as he guffawed with laughter. It took several moments before he could speak.

"You think the Sully girls are cattle rustlers?" He chuckled some more and shook his head. "All I can say is lawmen must have some strange ways out in that New Mexico Territory."

Tommy felt his face grow hot and knew that it was flaming. He sure was having trouble finding any takers for his notion that the Sully girls were the desperados they were looking for. He figured his conversation with Fred Carlisle had come to an end.

"How about I pay you for the flour and coffee, Mr. Carlisle, and get this letter posted. I've taken up enough of your time today."

Carlisle walked over to the counter, chuckling and shaking his head as he went. "Lady outlaws, if that doesn't beat anything I ever heard."

X

"Why on God's green earth would I do somethin' silly like that?" Bill Slaughter looked at him like he'd lost his mind. "If I ask Sheriff Carter for a search warrant to the Sully place, he's gonna ask me what I need it for. I ain't gonna be the one to tell him we think those cantankerous girls are cattle rustlers. He'd laugh me right out of town."

Tommy's pride was already stinging a bit from his conversation with Fred Carlisle at the mercantile. He'd ridden out to meet up with Rusty and Slaughter and almost immediately, he was being ridiculed again. He felt his temper rising and struggled to control it. If someone had asked him the previous week if he believed women might engage in rustling cattle, he would have laughed in that person's face. Now, however, he wasn't so sure and the more people scoffed at his idea, the more stubborn he got about pursuing it.

"What would it hurt to take a look around their place? If we don't find anything, you

187

can laugh *me* right out of town. On the other hand, there might be somethin' there to see. Who would be the one to look silly if we neglect to check it out and miss somethin' important?"

"I'm tellin' you," the Stock-Raisers' agent said, chuckling as he spoke. "That's the most ridiculous notion I ever heard." Rusty joined in the laughter, which drew him a dirty look from his cousin.

"So, you got a better idea?" He was getting pretty fed up with being the butt of teasing by Slaughter and his cousin. "You don't want to even think about what I'm sayin' but I don't hear neither of you proposin' anything better."

"That's where you're wrong, Mr. New Mexico lawman." Although he smiled when he said it, Tommy got the feeling he was only half-joking. As usual, there seemed to be an edge to whatever the man had to say. "I do have an idea."

"Well let's hear it then."

"All right, here goes. Whoever's doin' this seems to have some kind of a system," Slaughter said.

"What do you mean by that?" Rusty had a confused look on his face.

"I mean if you pay attention to what they've done, you'll see that they do some things the same. For example, they never hit the same ranch twice in a row."

"They dang sure hit my folks' place twice," Rusty responded, his voice loaded with indignation.

"But not in a row. In between those two times, they hit other ranches." Slaughter was animated now. "That's my point exactly."

"I don't see your point."

"I'll spell it out for you," he said. "Who did they steal from last?"

Tommy remained silent as he listened to the exchange between the agent and his cousin. He needed a moment to get his temper in check. The man's attitude was downright belligerent. He waited to see how his cousin would respond.

"Heck, I don't know," he said. "I can't remember all that kind of stuff."

"Well, I can," Slaughter said. "It was Nathan Roberts's place. Before that, it was John Steele's."

"So what?" Rusty was getting frustrated.

"So we look at the last four or five ranches that have been raided. Then we think about who's left over that hasn't been hit in a while. Whoever that is, that'll be where they go next."

Tommy decided it was time to weigh in. "Reckon that makes some sense all right.

But let's say we get a notion of what ranch they might rob next. What do we do then? We can't just spend every night watching that ranch. They might hit it next week or it might be next month."

"Maybe you can't but I can," Slaughter responded. "We ain't gettin' nowhere with what we're doin'. And I'll say to you what you said to me. You got a better idea?"

He thought for a minute. "Nope, guess I don't." He looked at his cousin. "What about you?"

Rusty shrugged and shook his head. And that's how they came to spend the next four nights at the Sawyer place.

"Would you get off me?" Tommy gave his cousin a none too gentle shove. Rusty had fallen asleep again and slumped over against him. Tommy was already out of sorts due to a lack of sleep and had little patience with his drowsy cousin.

"Sorry," Rusty mumbled. "I can't help fallin' asleep. This is the fourth night we been up. I can't keep my eyes open."

They were behind a mesquite bush that afforded them cover as they watched the pen that contained seventy-five head of cattle. Their horses were concealed in a wash about a hundred yards further away from where the men were staked out. As Rusty mentioned, they had been in this spot the previous three nights with no sign of the outlaws. So far, it looked like the fourth night would be no more productive.

"Would you boys be quiet," Slaughter whispered in a hoarse voice. "Anybody who was plannin' on stealin' cattle would hear you before they got within a mile of this place."

"Well I doubt that's gonna be a problem 'cause I don't reckon there's any rustlers within ten miles of this place," Rusty said, making no attempt to hide the irritation in his voice.

"You don't know that," the agent said.

Tommy had gone along with Bill Slaughter's plan to lay in wait for the rustlers. It didn't seem like a great idea to him but the only alternative he had to offer was to go search the Sully girls' ranch to see if they could find some of the stolen cattle, and the agent wouldn't go along with that.

"Rusty's got a point, Bill," he said. "This is the fourth night we been here and we ain't seen nothin'. We got a full moon tonight. I doubt anybody's gonna steal cows on a bright moonlit night like this."

Rusty jumped back in the conversation. "Dang right I got a point," he blustered. "I

191

reckon . . ."

"Quiet," Slaughter whispered in a hoarse tone. "I hear somethin'."

The two shut up straightaway. Slaughter pointed to the northwest and they all focused their attention in that direction. The land went up a bit, not even enough to be called a hill. They could hear a horse nickering but they couldn't see the rider or riders. Tommy felt his stomach muscles tighten, a feeling that was not unfamiliar to him. He'd been in situations like this before and he knew that he needed to steady his breathing and relax his hands and arms. If it came to a fight, you couldn't shoot straight if you were all seized up and breathing heavy.

Slaughter pointed again and Tommy saw two riders come over the rise. He blinked and stared. Up to that moment, he'd taken the talk of "scarecrows" as just that . . . talk. Under the light of the full moon though, he saw that the riders' heads were covered by some sort of material, perhaps a canvas bag. Danged if they didn't look like scarecrows.

Slaughter leaned over and whispered in his ear. "Should we take 'em?"

Tommy leaned back and said, "Not yet, they ain't done nothin' wrong. It ain't against the law to dress up like a scarecrow.

Wait till they do somethin', then we'll get 'em."

Agent Slaughter nodded. He could feel the tension coming off the agent in waves and he was concerned that when they made their move to take the outlaws, Slaughter would get out of control. Tommy had killed men before but he didn't want to do it unless there was no other choice. He feared Agent Bill Slaughter had no such reservations.

The scarecrows rode past where they were hiding and headed in the direction of the pen. Once they were past, Tommy motioned to the other two to come closer. He whispered, "Let's spread out so they'll think there's more of us when we make our move. Bill, you go right, Rusty go left. I'll come up behind them. Make sure you don't wind up straight across from each other. If there's any gunplay, we sure don't want to shoot each other." As they nodded, he spoke again. "Wait for my signal. Let me take the lead."

"Hell, you ain't even a lawman in these parts, Stallings," the agent complained. "Why are you takin' the lead?"

He stared a Slaughter for a moment and then asked, "You ever done this before?"

Slaughter fumed for a second and then

replied, "No, I ain't."

"I have," he replied. "That's why I'm takin' the lead."

He thought for a minute that Slaughter might continue to challenge him but then the man nodded, drew his pistol, and moved off to the right. Next, he glanced over at Rusty, who gave him a grin and then moved off to the left. Tommy waited until the two were in position before he also drew his pistol and moved toward the pens with all the stealth he could muster.

In the meantime, the two rustlers were still mounted and appeared to be studying the wire between two posts. He could hear them talking but couldn't make out what they were saying. He looked to his right and saw Slaughter spread his arms wide in a gesture that seemed to be asking for direction. Tommy held up his hand to indicate that they should wait. He looked around to see where his cousin was and in the bright moonlight, he saw Rusty flash a thumbs up signal.

Although the outlaws were engaged in what appeared to be a cattle rustling attempt, Tommy hoped, if possible, to wait until they dismounted to cut the barbed wire down and started moving the cattle out of the pen so there could be no question as to their intent. He realized that they would need to get closer in order to apprehend the criminals. He wanted to at least get close enough that the outlaws could see they had no chance to attempt a getaway without being shot out of the saddle.

Tommy could see that both Slaughter and Rusty were watching him with great care. Once again, he held up his hand but began easing forward. He hoped they understood that he wanted them to go slow. To his relief, he saw them both move in toward the outlaws. The cattle were becoming restless and the clamor they made covered any noise the three of them were making as they snuck up on them.

Advancing slow as molasses on a cold morning, Tommy and the others were able to get within ten yards of the rustlers. Glancing to his left and right, he determined that they were in the positions they needed to be. The outlaws showed no sign of dismounting and Tommy didn't feel like he could wait any longer. Again, he signaled so Slaughter and Rusty could see that he wanted them to stop where they were. When they did, he took one more step forward and spoke in a loud voice.

"Hold on there. Get down off your horses right now."

One of the rustlers whirled around. Seeing Tommy, the rider reached in the direction of the rifle in a scabbard on the saddle.

"Stop now," Tommy yelled. "You touch that gun, I'm gonna shoot you."

The rider stopped and then raised both hands to shoulder height. Without taking his eyes off the scoundrel, he said to the other one, "You, too. Hands up right now." The rider complied. "Y'all climb on down off them horses now." Both outlaws obeyed.

"Come on Stallings," Bill Slaughter yelled. "Let's shoot 'em before they start a gun battle."

"Nope," he said. "We're not shootin' anybody right now."

"Are you loco?" Slaughter waved his pistol in the air. "What if they draw on us? They could do it in a split second."

"If they do that," Tommy said in a firm voice, "then we'll shoot 'em. Not before."

"You takin' sides with outlaws again?" The anger in Slaughter's voice was palpable.

"That's exactly what I'm not doin', Bill," he replied. "If we was to gun these varmints down with their hands raised, it would be cold-blooded murder. That's what outlaws do and I'll have no part of it."

"Nobody would know," Slaughter said. His voice was shrill. Tommy figured that's what bloodlust sounds like.

"Rusty and I would know," he said. "You plannin' on shootin' us, too?"

Slaughter hesitated. "Nah, I ain't gonna shoot you. You're wrong though. These cattle-thievin' dogs ought to be shot down where they stand."

"No," he replied with more patience than he felt. "They should get a fair trial. If they're found guilty, they should get whatever the law decides they got comin'. Might even get hung but not till the law decides. Not you. Not me. The law."

The agent stared at him for a time and then turned away. "Whatever you say, Stallings. We'll see what the real sheriff has to say when we get these scoundrels to town."

"That we will," Tommy said. He called to Rusty, "Run fetch your rope, cousin. We're gonna tie these thievin' poltroons up." Turning his attention back to the two rustlers, he said, "I want you to sit down back to back right there in the dirt." When they hesitated, he barked, "Do it now. I got a pard that wants to shoot you. You best do what I tell you or I might not be able to stop him."

Whoever the rustlers were, they weren't stupid. They immediately sat down where they stood and scooted together until their backs were touching. They waited there for a few minutes until Rusty came running back with his rope.

"Disarm those varmints and then tie 'em up," Tommy said. "Wrap your lariat around them and use your piggin' string on their hands."

Rusty took the outlaws' pistols and tossed them in the direction of where the other two stood, then he followed directions to the letter, pulling his rope tight so their arms were pinned in front of them. He tied a strong knot on the side and then set to tying their hands. When he was done, he stood up, stepped away, and smiled at his cousin.

"Don't reckon they'll get out of those knots any time soon," he boasted.

"I don't want to disappoint you," Tommy said, "but you're gonna have to do it again when we get 'em loaded up on their horses to take 'em to town. This is just temporary so we can get a good look at 'em."

His cousin shrugged. "That's all right, now that I practiced, I'll tie an even better knot the next time. I sure am curious to see who these *cabrónes* are."

"Reckon we all are," he said. "You want to do the honors, cousin?"

"Don't mind if I do," Rusty said. He stepped back over to the outlaws, took off their hats, and set them down in the dirt.

Then, grasping a mask in each hand, he pulled them off to reveal the identities of the rustlers. He stumbled back in shock. All three cowboys were speechless. Bill Slaughter found his voice first.

"I'll be damned." He shook his head and turned to Tommy. "Looks like you were right."

Even though he'd pushed the notion that the Sully girls might be the rustlers they were looking for, Tommy realized that, in fact, he hadn't believed it until now. He couldn't discount what his eyes were telling him though. They'd just caught Annie and Jennie Sully in the act of stealing cattle.

Rusty stepped over to where the girls were sitting. He seemed befuddled and bothered. "What are you girls thinkin'? You could have got shot. Hell, you might get hung now." He was so disturbed that he repeated himself. "What were y'all thinkin'?"

Jennie sneered at him. "I'm thinkin' you're an ugly redheaded polecat, Rusty Stallings. If you don't back off, I'm gonna spit right in your face."

The redhead took a step back, shaking his head in shock and bewilderment. "That ain't no way for a lady to talk, Jennie. And this ain't no way for a lady to act."

Her tone changed. In a reasonable voice,

she said, "Come here a little closer, Rusty, I need to tell you somethin'." He stepped in closer and she spit in his face.

"Dammit," he yelled, jumping back and wiping his face. "What's the matter with you? You need to learn to act right." He stared fiercely at the girl. Tommy could see that he was beside himself with fury and wanted to say something hurtful. "You need to get you a pair of britches that fit, too. You look plum ridiculous."

Jennie Sully snickered and said back over her shoulder to her sister, "Would you look at that, Annie. I'm gettin' fashion advice from a fella with a bird's nest on his face. Don't that beat all?"

Rusty threw up his hands and walked around behind where Tommy was standing. "I give up," he muttered. "I got nothin' more to say."

Agent Slaughter had been watching the exchange. Now he spoke up. "Stallings, we caught 'em red-handed. You saw it; they were stealin' those cattle when we got the drop on 'em. I say we string 'em up right here and now. That's what you get for rustlin' cattle in Texas."

"No, Bill, we ain't gonna string 'em up. That's not the way real lawmen act. I don't care whether you're in Texas or the New

Mexico Territory . . . you shouldn't act that way even if you're from Oklahoma."

Slaughter said something under his breath that Tommy chose to ignore, then he asked, "What do you propose we do with 'em then?"

"I propose we take 'em into Oneida to the sheriff so he can lock 'em up. What happens after that will be up to a judge." The agent fixed him with a baleful stare but Tommy was steadfast. "That's the way it's supposed to be done, Bill, and that's the way we're gonna do it."

"You reckon Sheriff Carter's gonna be waitin' in his office in the middle of the night on the off chance somebody might bring in some cattle rustlers?"

He was fed up with Slaughter's attitude. "Bill, if you ain't got nothin' helpful to say, I'd appreciate it if you'd just not say anything," he said with an edge of irritation in his voice. "Of course the sheriff won't be there. We'll wait there outside his office until morning and turn over custody of these ladies when he gets there."

Slaughter muttered some more under his breath but then said, "All right. I don't know who put you in charge of this investigation but I can see you and your cousin are bound and determined not to do it my

201

way. So be it. I wash my hands of the whole thing." He threw up his hands and walked away toward where their horses were tied. Looking back over his shoulder, he said, "Let me know when you're ready to ride."

Tommy recalled that when he first met Bill, he'd thought he might come to like him. He had changed his mind. Turning to his cousin, he said, "Follow Bill to our horses and bring 'em back, then we'll get these ladies on their horses and head to town. I'll keep 'em covered, you can tie their hands behind their backs and boost 'em up."

"Why do I have to be the one to boost 'em up?"

" 'Cause I'm the sheriff and you're my deputy, that's why," Tommy replied.

Rusty pondered that for a second. "That don't make any sense, cousin. We're in Texas now and you ain't a sheriff. That means I ain't your deputy nor no one else's."

He shrugged. "The last time we were lawmen, you were my deputy. That's the way it stays until there's some official change in our ranks." He grinned. "Besides, that little one seems to like you. I doubt she'll mind you givin' her a boost."

Rusty rolled his eyes. "That's just too silly for me to even say nothin'. You realize that, don't you?" Tommy continued to grin at his cousin.

With some difficulty and a good deal of profanity, they got the women on their horses, tied lead ropes to each one, and headed to Oneida to wait for the dawn and the arrival of the sheriff.

They reached their destination as light began to appear on the eastern horizon. Tommy wasn't sure what time the sheriff might show up so he got his prisoners down from their horses and once again had them sit back to back while Rusty tied them up. No one seemed inclined to talk so they settled in to wait. As the sun came up, citizens began to walk the streets of Oneida heading to their places of business or running errands. People gaped at the sight of the two women seated and tied up but no one dared to come over and ask what they were doing. Tommy saw a man walking up the boardwalk in their direction and thought it might be Sheriff Carter. He checked his pocket watch and saw that it was right at 8 a.m.

As the sheriff got closer, they could see that he was looking at their little band with curiosity. He recognized Agent Slaughter and walked up to him.

"Mornin', Bill. What exactly is it that you're doin' here?"

"Mornin', Sheriff," Slaughter replied. "We caught them cattle rustlers that's been botherin' everybody for all these months. We brought 'em in for you to lock up."

Carter glanced down at the women and then back up to Slaughter. "Well, where are they?"

Slaughter shook his head in exasperation. "This is them, Sheriff. These are your rustlers."

The sheriff, in turn, shook his head in confusion. "Them's the Sully girls, Bill. It's their daddy who was the cattle thief." Glancing down, he doffed his Stetson and said, "Mornin', ladies." Turning back to Slaughter, he continued. "So where are the rustlers?"

Tommy stepped forward. "What Bill's tryin' to tell you, Sheriff, is that the Sully girls are your rustlers."

Sheriff Carter turned to him and said, "And who the hell might you be?"

Jennie Sully snickered.

"I'm Rusty Stallings's cousin, Tom, from the New Mexico Territory. I was a sheriff out there but I come to Texas to help out my Uncle Joe and Aunt Martha."

Carter nodded and turned to Rusty.

"Mornin', Rusty, how's your folks?"

"Passable, Sheriff," Rusty replied. "Doin' better now that we got these rustlers tracked down and caught."

The sheriff nodded again and turned back to Bill Slaughter. "So you're all sayin' these little ladies are the dangerous desperados that's been stealin' everyone's cattle. Do I have that correct?"

"Yes, sir," the agent replied with mounting enthusiasm. "We caught 'em red-handed in the act of stealin' Fred Sawyer's cows. I been tryin' to tell these two boys that in Texas, we string up cattle rustlers. We saw 'em do it, Sheriff. I say we're within our rights to hang 'em this very mornin'."

The sheriff took a deep breath and shook his head. "No, Bill, we ain't hangin' no one this mornin', least of all these ladies."

"Then what are we gonna do, Sheriff?" Slaughter was becoming agitated.

"Well, 'we' ain't gonna do nothin', Bill. You done your job as an agent for the Stock-Raisers' Association. You brought me two suspects . . ." Sheriff Carter stopped, looked over at the Sully girls, and shook his head. "You brought me two suspects you say were stealin' cattle. Your job is done here." He turned to Rusty and said, "Why don't you help me get these ladies up on their feet and escort 'em inside to the jail cell." Turning back to Slaughter, he said, "That's what I'm gonna do. I suggest you go get some breakfast and then go to bed. You look like hell."

"I sure wish you didn't have to run off, hon," Aunt Martha said to her nephew. "I just feel like I'm gettin' to know you again and then you go and take off."

After handing the Sully girls over to Sheriff Carter, the two had eaten a substantial breakfast at the boarding house in Oneida before heading back to the ranch. They'd had a tough job keeping their eyes open until after suppertime, although Tommy had to admit that he perked up when his Uncle Joe ate crow about being wrong about the lady rustlers. Tommy hadn't made too much of a fuss but Aunt Martha certainly did. He had a feeling his uncle would be hearing about his derogatory comments for quite a time to come.

"I wish I could stay, Aunt Martha," he said, "but I got to get back to my wife." He intended to say more but the words got caught in his throat as he thought of his bonnie Irish bride. He'd been away too long. When he could speak again, he said, "She's been far more patient with me than

I deserve but she is human. I don't want to stay away any longer and take the chance she'll decide I ain't worth all the trouble."

Aunt Martha started to tear up. She reached out and pulled him close in an embrace. When she stepped back, she said, "She sounds like a pretty sharp young lady. I reckon she won't give up on you. We never did."

Now Tommy's eyes misted up. Dang that West Texas dust. "And I'll never forget that, Aunt Martha. Lord knows I didn't deserve the patience you and Uncle Joe have showed me." He turned to face his uncle. "Thanks, Uncle Joe, for lettin' me come back home. And thanks for takin' me in after my folks got killed. I don't reckon I ever thanked you for that."

Uncle Joe appeared to be having trouble with the West Texas dust as well. He wiped his eyes with his sleeves. "I cared about my brother and I cared about his wife. I don't tell people that often enough."

Aunt Martha snorted. "You don't tell people that ever."

Uncle Joe ignored her. "Reckon I'm sayin' I care about you too, Tommy. You're welcome home any time you feel like comin'."

He shook his uncle's hand and hugged his aunt one more time. He turned to his cousin and said, "You want to grab my war bag and carry it out?"

"How come you're always tryin' to get me to do the unpleasant chores for you? You wanted me to load them lady rustlers on their horses and now I got to carry your gear?"

Tommy started to argue with his cousin until he saw that he was grinning. "Somebody's got to make you feel like you're needed, cousin. Reckon the job just falls to me more often than most."

They walked outside to where Rusty, the horse, stood waiting. He looked at his horse and then looked at his cousin. "Yep, there's a definite resemblance there."

Rusty shook his head and rolled his eyes. "You ain't gonna get a rise out of me on that one, cousin. That's a mighty fine horse you got there. I'm proud that he's named after me."

Tommy laughed and reached out to shake his cousin's hand. He was surprised when Rusty pulled him into an embrace. It only lasted for a few seconds and when he pushed Tommy away, Rusty gave him a light manly punch on the shoulder.

"I ain't certain when I'll see you again, cousin," Tommy said. "I hope it won't be too long though. I got no idea what me and

Mollie are gonna do now. Hell, maybe we'll just pick up and come to Texas."

"We'd like that," Rusty said. "I know Mama would love Mollie. Pa and I could use some help around here, too. I hope you'll consider it."

He nodded. "We'll talk it over. Are you ever gonna shave that bird's nest off your face? That might make the difference as to whether or not Mollie would be willin' to be around you."

Once again, Rusty shook his head and rolled his eyes. "I would shave it off right now but then you'd have nothin' to hurrah me about."

Tommy had to laugh at that. Then he put his foot in the stirrup and climbed up on old Rusty, the horse. He waved and then headed West towards the New Mexico Territory and his Mollie.

Dear Cousin Tommy,
Nov. 14, 1886
I hope this letter finds you and your Mollie doing good. Give Mollie a hug from me and tell her I know she likes me better than you. Ha ha. Ma and Pa say howdy. Ma says she loves you and Pa says you turned out better than he thought you would. I thought you would want to know

what happened to the lady rustlers. I know you had to leave right away to get back to your wife but you missed the fun. Agent Slaughter wanted to string them up without a trial which you knew. The sheriff would not have it though and said they would wait til the circuit judge got there. The girls cooled their heels in the jail for a week until the judge arrived. You should of seen them when they went into court, you would not have recognized them. Last time you saw them, they was rougher than a cob but they was neat and clean and brushed when they saw the judge. He looked at them and asked where the cattle rustlers was. Slaughter liked to had a fit. He tried to convince the judge that they was guilty but the man said he did not think perty ladies like them would do nothing like he said they had done. He said even if theyd done a few things wrong, there was not a good place to lock them up anyhow. He told the girls they better behave themselves and let them go free. They cleared out and no one has seen them since. Slaughter left also without so much as a thank you. Like I said I do not know where the girls went so you best keep your eyes peeld out there in the New Mexico territory. You never know when some scarecrows might show up. Ha ha.

Your cousin,
Rusty Stallings

ABOUT THE AUTHOR

Jim Jones is the author of five novels set in northern New Mexico in the late 1800s: *The Lights of Cimarron, The Big Empty,* and the Jared Delaney series, including *Rustler's Moon, Colorado Moon* and *Waning Moon.* His songs and books are about the West . . . cowboys, horses & cattle, cattle rustlers, the coming of the train . . . songs about people and land, rivers and mountains, the beauty of the Western sky.

■ ■ ■ ■

A JAKE SUMMERS
WESTERN MYSTERY

COLD THE BITTER HEART

PHIL MILLS, JR.

■ ■ ■ ■

I

The roar of discontent from inside the bank office bore no semblance to civilized discord. Like two rabid dogs fighting over a flesh-covered bone, those behind the bank owner's closed door fought verbally, bordering on the precipice of actual physical entanglement.

An argument involving at least two as yet unknown participants raged. The thin office walls were no match for the shouts from the other side. Everyone within earshot could hear each word.

Jake Summers stepped into the lobby of the bank and became indirectly involved in the verbal engagement. Someone he assumed to be Gabriel Swanson, president of the Chugwater bank, and at least one other man were involved in a heated exchange.

The bank's only employee, a timid young man named Morgan Davis, stood mesmerized inside his teller cage . . . his blue eyes framed by wire-rimmed glasses showing signs of primeval fear and concern. Although he acknowledged Jake's arrival with a simple nod of his head, he made no effort to offer his services.

The office door flung open and the fight spilled out. No longer buffered by the closed door, Jake witnessed Swanson arguing with Robert Baxter, the forty-six-year-old owner of the T Bar 7 Ranch west of Chugwater, Wyoming.

"I'll find the money somewhere you arrogant jerk," shouted Baxter. "You can't stop me. All the business I've given this poor excuse for a bank and now you deny me a few dollars."

"Robert!" exclaimed Swanson.

"I've made you a rich man," Baxter interrupted. "Without me and the other cattlemen in this country, you wouldn't have a pot to piss in and you know it."

"Robert, let me explain. Come back into my office and let's talk."

"I'm done talking," yelled Baxter as he turned toward the bank lobby. He walked past the speechless teller who stood immobilized, the young man's forehead spotted with droplets of sweat. His shirt collar was soaked. Baxter spotted Jake, but offered no sign of recognition as he hurried toward the front door. His boots pounded on the bank's wood plank floor.

"Wait," called Swanson who followed Baxter into the lobby. "That's exactly my point. I represent a lot of cattlemen in this area. They depend on this being open range country. If I loan you money for barbed wire, the others will have my hide. Can't you see my point?"

"I don't give a rat's ass about everyone else," said the angry Baxter as he turned back to face the banker. "I've got a ranch to run."

"But why barbed wire? You've got along fine for years sharing that grass with everyone," said Swanson. He hesitated when he realized Jake was listening. "Think about your neighbors like Summers here."

Baxter glanced at Jake and said, "It's nobody's business what I do on that ground. Besides, I'm running fence up along Horse Creek. That's nowhere near the Meadows place and Summers here," he said, as he waved his left hand in Jake's direction.

"Robert, that's open range country. Your neighbors won't take kindly to any fences, much less barbed wire out there. You're asking for trouble. Somebody's going to get hurt before it's over. I'm trying to talk some sense into you. Things are going to get ugly and unhealthy for you and everyone else."

"Is that a threat?" Baxter yelled, taking a step back toward Swanson. The rancher's face was red and his hands were clenched. The blood vessels on each side of his forehead bulged.

"Easy now," Swanson implored while taking a step back, raising both hands palms out to fend off a possible physical attack.

Jake feared he might need to intercede if things continued escalating toward actual fisticuffs.

Baxter hesitated, then turned and stomped out the bank's front door. Each footstep echoed on the plank walkway outside with a thud.

Swanson turned to face Jake. "Sorry you had to hear all that, but probably best you did. If something should happen to me, you know where to look first. Once cattlemen like Baxter start talking fences, it won't be long until wire crisscrosses this entire territory. God forbid it be barbed wire."

"You may be right," said Jake. "I'm worried about Baxter. I thought he would explode and have a heart attack."

"The man has anger problems," continued Jake. "Honestly, I don't see how he keeps any hands. His foreman, Austin Freeman, is as bad, especially after a couple drinks."

Swanson nodded in agreement. "Makes you wonder why his wife and two girls stay with him." He hesitated, "Then again, maybe his wife stays for another reason. Rumor is she's kinda fond of Freeman, or so I've heard."

"You implying something?" asked Jake.

"No, just a rumor."

"Well, I'm not into rumors," said Jake. "They probably get along better than we realize. Takes all kinds."

"He ever talks to me like that again and we'll have more than words," said Swanson. "I'll be happy to oblige him if he ever wants to get into a real fight."

Swanson frowned and turned back toward his office. *Nobody talks to me that way. One day that man will get his comeuppance. Mark my words.*

"I don't see you getting into a gunfight with him," said Jake. "Or a bare-knuckle brawl for that matter."

"Oh, there are ways to take a man down," noted Swanson, stopping to turn back and face Jake. "There are ways . . . many ways. Now, how are things out at your place? How is Miss Sarah and that young'un of yours?"

"That boy is growing like a bad weed and twice as troublesome. And Sarah is fine. Thanks for asking," smiled Jake.

"How old is that boy? What's his name again?"

"Cody . . . John Cody Summers and he's four," said Jake. "You ready to take some of my money? Sarah and I want to pay down on that stock loan we borrowed last fall. We've had a good crop of calves and our yearlings brought top dollar in Ogallala recently."

"That's wonderful. You, Miss Sarah, and young Mr. Cody are making things work out there."

Their conversation was interrupted by the sound of shouting on the street. From the window, they saw Baxter motioning in the direction of another rancher, Justin Riley, owner of the Sybille Creek Ranch northwest of Chugwater. Riley ranched not far from Jake and Sarah's Meadows Ranch.

Baxter held a Winchester Model 1873 lever-action repeating rifle in his hands and it was aimed at the unarmed Riley. Baxter's foreman, Austin Freeman, stood alongside holding a Henry breech-loading lever-action 1860 rifle.

Swanson and Jake hurried outside. They heard Baxter shout, "Tell that no-account son of yours to stay away from my daughter. If he doesn't, I'll be forced to stop him myself."

Behind Riley and on the opposite side of the family's buckboard stood the two Riley brothers, Nelson and Vincent. They had been loading supplies from the general store. Neither man moved. The twenty-two-year-old Nelson just smiled. The younger of the two brothers, he had long blond hair and rugged, bronzed features most young women found attractive. His twenty-six-year-old brother Vincent stood a few feet away. He had a well-trimmed beard that matched his tasseled brown hair. Both wore sweat-marked, gray felt hats and carried Colt .45 revolvers in holsters tied to their legs.

Nearby in the store doorway, Justin's wife of thirty years, Barbara, stood holding several packages. She was frightened and it showed in her trembling hands. Next to her was their seventeen-year-old daughter, Elizabeth.

"Put the rifle down, Baxter. I'm taking my family home. You are out of control. We're leaving."

"I've warned you," shouted Baxter. "You hear that, boy," pointing at Nelson. "Stay away from my daughter. I know you've been sneaking around behind my back and I won't have it. No more!"

Nelson Riley stepped around the buckboard and stood next to his father. "You talking to me?" His right hand rested on the dark handle of his holstered pistol.

"Keep your mouth shut, boy," exclaimed Riley. "I'll handle this."

"I can take this old man," said the younger Riley. "He can't tell me what to do or not do."

"I said keep quiet, boy. Let me handle this."

Baxter raised his rifle for emphasis and leveraged a .44-40 cartridge into the chamber. Then he repeated, "Stay away from Catherine."

Meanwhile, Freeman stepped closer, his Henry rifle ready. "Easy, boss. They're leaving." Freeman stared at the boy for any sign of gunplay. "Everyone is watching."

Baxter spoke without turning to his foreman, "You really think I give a tinker's damn whether anyone is watching or not? That loser son of his better stay clear of the T Bar 7 and my girls or he may end up dead."

"Be careful how you talk about my family, Baxter. We haven't done anything to you," said the elder Riley.

"You and that boy of yours have been told!" said Baxter.

"Let's go home," suggested Freeman.

"They heard you. Let's ride."

Baxter lowered his rifle and backed away but kept his bloodshot eyes on Riley and his family . . . especially the younger son. "I won't say it again," he spoke again like a dog getting in one final growl. He went to his horse tied in front of the bank, mounted, and roughly wheeled the bay gelding toward home.

Swanson and Jake watched before starting back inside the bank. Behind him Jake heard the elder Riley tell his family, "Finish loading up. It's time to go home."

Jake watched the Riley family leave in the opposite direction, thus avoiding a second confrontation somewhere outside of town. He felt a cold breeze blow against his cheek and he shivered. He grasped the irony of Wyoming's often biting cold weather matching the bitter mood of the angry rancher.

II

Rusty hinges on the T Bar 7 barn door moaned in dry torment as Austin Freeman slowly pulled it open and stepped inside. His senses were greeted with the strong smell of moldy, old hay and horse manure. As his eyes became accustomed to the dim light, he hesitated, searching the dark shadows for movement. He didn't have to wait long.

Ruth Baxter quietly stepped from the nearest horse stall and without speaking was gathered into the foreman's willing arms. The thirty-seven-year-old wife of the territory's most volatile rancher embraced Freeman and held him tightly.

Baxter had met the woman nineteen years earlier on a cattle buying trip to Denver. After some determined persuasion she'd agreed to marry the outspoken rancher who was nine years older. Together they had two free-spirited daughters, seventeen-year-old Catherine and sixteen-year-old Virginia.

The man demanded a cult-like loyalty from his family and all who worked on the T Bar 7. Failure by hired hands to follow his demands was met with defiant retaliation, including death. Family members were subjected to verbal abuse with threats of physical punishment. His wife and daughters were not allowed in Chugwater without him. He claimed it was for their own safety and protection. Others simply called it an unhealthy combination of control and jealousy.

"What happened in town today?" Ruth asked, taking a step back but staying within arm's reach.

"First things first," whispered Freeman as he stepped forward to kiss her.

"Please, not now," she exclaimed, pulling away. "Robert came home fighting mad. And like he normally does, he took his anger out on me and the girls. He yelled at me and screamed at Catherine about that Riley boy. What happened?"

Freeman stepped back as rays of early evening light found their way through cracks in the barn walls, and he began explaining the sequence of events leading up to and including Baxter's confrontation with the Riley family. "He was like a rabid dog. I half expected him to start foaming at the mouth. I was shocked he didn't shoot someone. He told Riley to keep his son away from Catherine. He even threatened the boy himself."

"Nelson must be twenty-one . . . maybe twenty-two," whispered Ruth. "Catherine is only seventeen. She's so young. That boy is too old for her. We don't know anything about him. I don't trust him. I've told her that several times and we usually end up arguing."

"Well, whatever his age, he came close to getting shot today. The boy spoke up. Tried standing his ground in front of a crowd of townspeople. I'm sure it was more brag than bite. But Baxter was ready to shoot and claim some type of justification. Your prize of a husband made it clear to everyone within earshot the Baxter girls are off limits."

"That include me?"

"Especially you," smiled Freeman. "Besides you're already mine."

"Well, don't let Robert hear you say that or we'll both be dead. I'll be honest. I don't know how much more I can take," said Ruth as she began to tremble. "The verbal abuse. The yelling and screaming. I'm scared one day he will hit me. The man's insane."

A horse snorted in one of the stalls and both Freeman and Ruth Baxter were startled and turned to look. Both were fearful their nemesis might be nearby and listening.

"We need to be patient," said Freeman while looking over her shoulder, not convinced they were alone. "He keeps up with his tantrums and he's going to make someone mad enough to fight back," he continued.

"Tantrums? My god, they're more than tantrums. He goes into an uncontrollable rage. If you truly want us to be together we need to make it happen. I've had enough," she said.

"You know I want us to be together," he said as he reached for her shoulders. "You know how I feel."

"We need to do something and soon. And I mean soon. I can't and won't keep living like this."

"Don't do anything drastic," said Freeman.

He took the woman in his arms and started to kiss her but she pulled away and said, "Later, I gotta get back to the house before he misses me."

"When then?"

"I don't know. I think he's starting to suspect something. We need to be very careful."

"I know . . . but when?"

"Maybe this weekend, he'll be in Laramie for a cattlemen's meeting," Ruth whispered as she ducked under his right arm and went to the barn door.

"I don't know," said Freeman as he watched her. "He usually expects me to go with him to such things. I don't see him changing and leaving us here together."

Looking out into the evening twilight, she didn't see anyone so she slipped out and headed for the house. The sun had disappeared behind the Laramie Mountains, leaving the complex in semidarkness.

Freeman waited a few minutes before exiting out the barn's back door. He crossed through a horse corral and walked to the bunkhouse.

From a nearby stand of cottonwood trees, Catherine Baxter and Nelson Riley watched. They were in a position to see both exits so they saw the two leave in different directions.

"Father must be the only man in the territory blind to what is happening between my mother and Austin Freeman," she exclaimed. "Yet he threatens you and me. As long as he's around, you and I don't stand a chance for any happiness. He's so abusive and controlling. He doesn't understand we love each other."

"We'll be together soon enough," said Riley.

"Promise?"

"Yes, I promise," the young Riley answered. "Let's meet tomorrow up on Mule Creek where we met last Saturday. We'll figure out something. Until then we need to be patient."

"I don't know," said Catherine, turning away. "I'm tired of being patient. I want to be free to live my life. I need someone strong in my life who's willing to protect me. Someone with backbone."

Riley felt the sting of her comments and said, "You know I'd do about anything for you. I'm crazy about you. We just need a little time."

Catherine turned toward him and smiled, "You're my man. I know you would but please do something and soon."

"A few more days," said Riley.

The two young people embraced before Riley slipped into the darkness to find his horse. Catherine smiled. *Oh, I'm waiting. I'm even being patient, sweetheart.*

Catherine felt a sense of self-satisfaction and control. She could convince Riley to do about anything she wanted . . . even kill her father. As gentle raindrops drifted toward an eventual rendezvous with earth and she started for the house, she whispered, "Father, you're about to meet your well-deserved fate. Karma can be deadly."

III

Early the following Saturday morning, as the sun began climbing above the eastern horizon, several ranchers gathered in small groups in the street outside the Laramie hotel where for two days members of the Southeast Wyoming Cattlemen's Association had been meeting. The growing number of sheep in the area had become a major source of concern. Robert Baxter stood among them, loudly insisting all sheep owners be removed by force.

"The time for talk is over," Baxter shouted. "We've tried to persuade them to get out peaceably but they don't listen. They just keep coming. We need to use force, and shoot a few woolies if necessary to make it happen."

"You may be right," said Thomas Jackson Douglas, president of the cattlemen's association and owner of the Crazy Dutchman Ranch northeast of Morton Pass between Chugwater and Laramie.

"You know I'm right. And as president of the cattlemen's association, we expect you to provide some leadership," said Baxter. "What are you going to do?"

Douglas hesitated and looked at the small group of ranchers who stood nearby. Baxter was doing all the talking while they merely nodded in agreement.

"Give me a few days. I'll come up with a plan," said Douglas.

"Be damn quick about it," yelled Baxter as he looked around for support. "We elected you to represent our interests. I suggest you start doing just that."

232

"Wait a durn minute," said Douglas, his own voice rising. "Don't threaten me."

"Do your job!" Baxter called out as he turned to leave. He motioned for Freeman to follow.

Two other ranchers joined him as he began walking toward his horse. "Glad you said something," noted a rancher whose place was near Diamond, Wyoming.

"You know I'm right," exclaimed Baxter. "I'm tired of waiting while this country is overrun with those smelly animals."

Jake Summers had listened to the argument from the wood plank walkway in front of the hotel, but said nothing. *Not all sheep people are bad. You need to take time and get to know some of them. Cattle and sheep can live together. I've seen it. I've done it.*

Baxter wasn't finished. "In fact, I plan to pay one of them a friendly visit on my way home today."

"You and your foreman surely aren't going to try anything alone," stated another rancher from the Horse Creek area. "Let's wait and see what Douglas decides. Then we'll all go together."

Baxter and Freeman mounted their horses and started to leave. They spotted Jake and turned their horses. "Summers, we're heading your direction. Going to stop and see

Tellius Young. Why don't you join us? You should be involved. Some of us are starting to think maybe you don't mind woolies taking our range. How about it?"

"Not this time," answered Jake.

"Really?" asked Baxter. "Maybe I'm right about you."

"Believe what you want. I don't care what you think," said Jake. "I'm meeting Douglas for breakfast. I'm buying some heifers he's trying to sell. Maybe next time."

Baxter stared for a minute before turning his horse toward home. Freeman followed.

Jake watched them ride away. *That man worries me. He's always stirring the proverbial pot, starting a fight.*

"Damn sheep lover," uttered Baxter under his breath as they rode from Laramie.

"What? What did you say?" asked Freeman.

"That Summers. He lived with James Lincoln and his family a few winters back. He helped them with their sheep. I believe he's more sheepman than cattleman. We need to watch him."

A few hours later they crossed through Morton Pass where snow still covered much of the landscape at that elevation and then rode east toward Sybille Creek. Near a stand of cottonwood trees, Baxter pulled up and looked at Freeman. "I expect you to back me when we see Young. The man is nuts. I knew him before down in Colorado, but he's lost his mind. Now he's raising sheep. Maybe I can convince him to move out."

"I don't know," said Freeman. "Us riding in there alone doesn't make much sense to me."

"As long as you ride for me and take my wages, you'll do as I say. Like I said, I knew the old man years ago. He ran a few cattle back in those days. We'll be okay. You just plan on backing me if we can't reason with him."

Freeman started to protest but stopped short when Baxter glared at him.

Kicking their horses into an easy lope they rode along an unnamed creek bank full with snowmelt.

After riding two miles they rode into a valley surrounded on all sides by tree-covered mountains. The valley was only a half mile wide but stretched nearly two miles long.

"Hold on there," came a voice from some nearby trees. "Who are you? Why you here?"

As Baxter started to turn in the direction of the voice, a second person off to his left demanded, "Put your hands up. Both of you. We want to see your hands." The man remained hidden in the trees.

Baxter and Freeman raised their hands. "We're here to see Tellius. I'm a good friend."

Pedro Gonzales, a sheepherder who worked for Young, stepped in front of Baxter's horse pointing a rifle at the rancher. "How you know him?"

Baxter stared at the small, dark-skinned man. The man's brown eyes were buried deep in two sockets on his weathered face. "From the old days down in Colorado."

"I know you," exclaimed Gonzales, recognizing the T Bar 7 owner. "You're that cowman trying to run us out of here. We ain't bothering nobody in these mountains."

"You've got me all wrong. Where's your boss?"

"Right here, Baxter," came a voice from behind him. Baxter turned in his saddle and saw a tall, older man with a long, black beard sprinkled with gray walking in his direction. The man wore a black wool coat and carried an older Henry rifle.

"Tellius, my old friend," said Baxter as he started to dismount.

"Stay in the saddle," responded Young. "What the hell are you doing here? Why aren't you with your cows?"

"Why can't I pay my old friend a friendly visit?"

"We were never friends," stated Young holding, his own rifle at the ready. "What do you want?"

"We need to talk," said Baxter. "Can't we climb down and visit a spell?"

Young motioned for Baxter and Freeman to dismount. He told Gonzales to go check their back trail to see if the two men were alone. The second man known as Steely emerged from the trees with his own rifle also aimed at the visitors.

"We're alone. Go check," said Baxter, casting a wary eye on Steely.

"What do you want?" asked Young. "I'm busy. It's lambing season."

"I'll get right to the point. This is cattle country. Your sheep are ruining the grass up here and quite frankly I want to use this valley myself this summer. Temperatures will be cooler, the grass better, and there's plenty of water."

"I'm already here," stated Young. "Your cattle will need to spend the summer elsewhere."

"That's where you're wrong. I just came from a cattlemen's meeting in Laramie. We plan to have this ground and we'll use force if necessary to get it. Get my meaning?

237

There's not room enough in this territory for cattle and sheep. Oh, you'll leave all right or we'll help you leave," stated Baxter.

"I'm not going anywhere. Not without a fight. I suggest you ride back the way you came. Get out of here."

"Listen to me. I want you off this land within the next two weeks or I'll be back with enough men and guns to remove you."

Young pointed his rifle at Baxter and the rancher heard the click of the hammer on Steely's rifle behind him.

"One last time, I said get out of here," said Young. "Nobody rides onto my place and threatens me. I should shoot you along with your cur dog associate there. But I won't. Not this time. Don't ever come back. Get out of here."

Freeman started forward after hearing himself called a "cur dog," then hesitated and stopped. Steely was somewhere behind him. *No time for heroics.*

"You and I will meet again, I promise," said Baxter as he climbed into his saddle. "You can bet on it."

"You or your men come this way again and I'll shoot all of you. That's a promise. Now ride." Young fired a shot into the air, scaring Baxter's horse, which lunged sideways.

As Baxter and Freeman rode from the valley, they met the returning Gonzales, who stepped aside to let them pass. Baxter cursed and vowed to return in force. "I've got a score to settle with him myself," whispered Freeman.

Two hours later Baxter pulled up near Sybille Creek and dismounted. "Horses need a breather. Let them drink and rest a few minutes."

While the two horses drank cold water from the stream, Baxter pulled his Winchester rifle from its scabbard and turned to face Freeman. "I've got a problem and I don't like problems," he explained, pointing his rifle at Freeman.

"What's the matter with you?" exclaimed Freeman, uncertain about the turn of events. "Point that rifle somewhere else."

"No, I think I'll keep it right here."

"What are you doing?" asked Freeman. "What's the matter with you?"

"Tell me about you and my wife. How long have you two been going behind my back?"

"You're crazy."

"I said tell me about you and Ruth. I know she's been cheating on me and for a time I couldn't figure out with whom. The other night I watched her go to the barn

239

and a few minutes later you showed up."

"That was a coincidence," said Freeman, taking a step toward Baxter. "An accidental meeting."

"Like the devil it was an accident. I suspected something so I crept up to the side window and listened. All that stuff you were saying about me, I suppose that was coincidental as well? You both want me dead so you can be together."

"Okay, you arrogant jerk," exclaimed Freeman, realizing Baxter knew the truth. "She's tired of your abuse. We love each other. She hates you," shouted Freeman as he again took a step toward Baxter.

"Just what I thought. Well nobody can have her but me," roared Baxter, sensing Freeman was getting too close. He stepped backward but in doing so his foot slipped on a rock. He fell backward, twisting his ankle and dropping the rifle. Freeman pounced on it and aimed the Winchester at the ranch owner. The tables had turned.

"Ruth and I have waited a long time for this moment," said Freeman. "Finally . . . finally Ruth and I can be together. And the irony of you dying out here alone, killed by your own gun, what a tragic accident. What a pity."

"Wait a minute!" shrieked Baxter, lying

on the ground surrounded by patches of unmelted snow. He held up his right hand as if it would shield him. "Let's talk."

"What is it you are always telling people? There's been too much talk. Now it's time for action."

"You'll never get away with this," screamed Baxter as he tried crawling away.

Freeman smiled and said, "This is for Ruth, Catherine, Virginia, and everyone else you've abused, including me." He squeezed the trigger.

The explosion rocked the area, the sound reverberating off the surrounding canyon walls. Baxter screamed as blood and skin covered his torso. Most of Freeman's face was gone.

A shocked Baxter realized he was still alive. The rifle had misfired and exploded in Freeman's face, killing him instantly. Blood and skull fragments were everywhere.

The shock of nearly being killed rushed over him and then passed. He stood and tried regaining his composure. He realized the rifle had been tampered with . . . somehow plugged. *It was meant to blow up on me. First time I used it for something, I would have been dead. But who? Ruth? When? How? Couldn't have been Freeman. He would have known not to use it.* The details didn't much matter at the moment. *I'm still alive.*

Baxter limped toward the mangled and bloodied body of his foreman. Looking down at the corpse, he spat on the dead man. Then he brushed off remnants of Freeman's face still clinging to his clothing.

Baxter wasted no time gathering their horses, climbed into the saddle, and turned toward the T Bar 7 Ranch. It was getting late. The bloodied body of Austin Freeman was left on the cold ground for the wolves and vultures.

Baxter rode away realizing he would need a story to explain why Freeman hadn't returned with him from Laramie. *We got separated looking for somewhere to cross the creek. And Riley's Sybille Creek Ranch isn't far from here. Maybe I can turn this into something beneficial in a number of ways.*

His thoughts returned to his wife. *Ruth Baxter, you haven't seen me mad, not yet. Just you wait. You think things were bad before.*

IV

Light rain fell across the Laramie Mountain foothills as Tellius Young and Pedro Gonzales rode south in search of some ewes that had strayed from the main flock. Because it was lambing season, Young was concerned for their safety and that of any new babies. The ewes were found near a small, fast-moving stream inside a narrow box canyon. Snow still covered much of the canyon floor.

"Pedro, ease them back toward home. I'm going to go see Victor Bennington and maybe James Lincoln. Victor doesn't live far from here. I want to tell him what Baxter said. I'll try catching up with you. Otherwise, I should be back sometime after dark."

Bennington and his family kept nearly two thousand Churro ewes and wethers in a small secluded valley along Pole Creek, a few miles from the town of Iron Mountain. The man lived with his wife, Suzanne, and their two sons, eighteen-year-old Chester and sixteen-year-old Samuel, along with three Australian Shepherd dogs.

Bennington spotted Young striding from a stand of Aspen about fifty yards from a makeshift shed he used for lambing. He waved at his friend.

Young waved back and rode in that direction. The two boys, Chester and Samuel, stepped up beside their father and waited. Both boys carried rifles.

"Come on in and join us," said Bennington. "You look a mite wet and chilled.

Suzanne should have some hot coffee. You want a cup?"

"Sounds great," said Young. "Could use something warm."

"What brings you out this way?" Bennington asked as the two men went inside. The boys followed. "I'm guessing this isn't a social call, not with it being lambing season. Must be something serious."

Bennington motioned for Young to sit in an old rocking chair near a poor-drawing fireplace. A smoky haze filled the room with the smell of woodsmoke mixed with the pungent odor of sheep.

"Had a visitor today," explained Young. "Robert Baxter."

"Really?" asked Bennington, glancing at his two sons still holding their rifles. "Anybody hurt? Any damage?"

The mention of Baxter's name got everyone's attention. More than once he'd ridden into the Bennington valley and scattered their sheep. Bennington had vowed to shoot next time. Each visit had left the sheep owner angry. Baxter had also warned, "Move or next time we'll start killing your damn woolies."

"No. Not today. He claims several ranchers have decided to come force us out. They are joining forces. Thought you should know. If you see James and Martha Lincoln or any of our other neighbors up here, you might warn them. None of us are safe from Baxter or any of the other cattlemen around here."

"Thanks for the warning. We try to stay armed these days. Baxter's threatened us before."

"That man needs a good dose of arsenic," added Young. "His demise would benefit a lot of people."

"We've got plenty of arsenic. We use it for killing rats like him," offered Bennington, trying unsuccessfully to make a joke. "Not sure we have enough for Baxter though."

The younger Bennington, Samuel, looked at his brother before glancing at his father.

"We ain't moving, are we?"

"No, son, this time we'll stand and fight. We won't be run off."

"Neither will I," added a defiant Young. "Just wanted you to know."

"Thanks for the heads up."

"Well, I gotta head for home. Keep your guard up and let me know if you have any trouble. I'd suggest you and your boys stay armed," said Young as he got up to leave. "Don't forget to tell the Lincolns if you see them."

Chester was the first to speak. "Baxter and

everyone who rides with him needs to be shot. Maybe we'd finally have some peace."

"That's tough talk, boy, especially for someone who's only eighteen," said the senior Bennington. "We need to stay vigilant and calm. Let him start things. Our sheep are enough incentive to come riding down on us. We don't need to make things worse by provoking him."

Samuel looked at his outspoken brother and shook his head. "You hear that, Chester?"

Chester didn't answer but was clearly agitated. *Both his daughters hate him.* He gave his brother a look that said *keep your mouth shut.*

The bleating of sheep outside brought them back to the moment. There was still work to be done before dark. Baxter issues would need to wait until their daily chores were done. They went back outside and watched Young walking away.

At the same time, off in the distance, they all heard what sounded like a rifle shot. Bennington watched Young hesitate and look around before starting back toward home. One shot, then nothing. *Perhaps someone hunting.* Young disappeared into some cottonwood trees on the far side of the valley.

V

The same wind and rain followed Jake Summers along Sybille Creek, pushing him and his horse toward home. Two days in Laramie had been enough. He was ready to get home, and the Meadows Ranch lay another five miles or so up the creek. The wind tore at his back while the rain swirled around his face. The approaching night would be dark and wet with a threat of more rain mixed with possible snow flurries.

The thirty-year-old Jake was originally from Texas but had moved north at age eighteen with Harry Haythorn's last trail drive to Ogallala, Nebraska. He moved to the Judith Basin area of Montana. While there, he'd met and worked cattle with Tom Scott. Together, they'd moved to Wyoming where they continued punching cattle together.

Jake had met and married Sarah Meadows and they'd taken up ranching on her late father's spread known as the Meadows Ranch near Chugwater.

Without any warning, his thoughts were interrupted when he saw fresh horse tracks on the muddy and snow-covered trail. He reined up and took a closer look. *Looks like one . . . maybe two . . . horses. But where did they come from? Where are they going? I didn't pass anyone.*

Jake glanced to his left and saw only empty hills stretching southeast toward Chugwater. Off to his right and across Sybille Creek were swales and ravines leading back toward several shallow canyons before blending into the Laramie Mountain foothills. Nobody was in sight.

Without warning, Jake's horse shied and began dancing around, trying to turn away. The gelding's nostrils flared from both fear and surprise. He spotted a body lying motionless near a stand of cottonwood trees about ten yards off the main trail and close to the creek. The crimson red remains of the man's head lay scattered.

Nearby lay what was left of a Winchester 1873 rifle that appeared to have exploded when the trigger was pulled. Jake spurred his horse to move closer, and still horseback, he surmised the man had died when the rifle blew up in his face. *Who is this man?*

Jake dismounted, holding the reins of his nervous horse. As he stepped toward the dead man's body, something seemed familiar. Even though the man's face was disfigured and badly mangled, he recognized Austin Freeman's clothes and custom-made boots.

This is a long way from the T Bar 7. Looks like his rifle misfired and blew up. The barrel must have been plugged somehow.

Jake looked around for Freeman's horse. *Maybe I can lay him over the saddle and take him to Chugwater,* but the man's horse was missing.

Jake decided his only real option was to proceed on to the Meadows Ranch for a wagon and return for the body. After covering Freeman's body with his rain slicker and some rocks, he mounted his horse and kicked the gelding into a lope for home.

A happy Sarah met him as he rode into the ranch complex. She started to ask about his trip to Laramie but Jake wasn't smiling. "What's happened? You look upset."

"Found a body . . . Austin Freeman. Back down the creek about five miles."

"Oh, no!" she exclaimed as their four-year-old son, Cody, emerged from the barn. "What happened to him?"

"Papa," shouted the excited boy. "See what I —"

"Looks like he was shooting at something and his rifle misfired. It exploded in his face, killing him," explained Jake, not hearing his son. "Thing is, I saw him just this morning at the cattlemen's meeting. He was over there with Baxter and they left together. But

249

I didn't see any sign of Baxter or their horses. All I saw were some fresh horse tracks."

"Oh, my! What a way to die."

"Papa . . . papa," insisted the boy, running toward Jake.

"I wonder," said Sarah. "Doesn't make much sense. You think Baxter is okay?"

"I don't know. All I saw was Freeman."

Jake swept the boy into his arms and said, "I need to go back and get his body, then take him into Chugwater.

"How's my boy? You been taking care of your momma?" he asked while swinging the boy around. The boy squealed in delight.

"Somebody will need to go tell Robert Baxter his foreman is dead," said Sarah. "If he's still alive himself."

"I'll let Tom sort that out," stated Jake. "I'm worn out."

Tom Scott, Jake's longtime friend, was sheriff in Chugwater. He'd accepted the position on a temporary basis. That was four years ago, after he'd married a young woman from St. Louis named Molly Collins. Together, they had a four-year-old daughter named Abigail.

"Sounds like a tragic accident," Sarah added. "Want Cody and I to come along?"

"No, best I go alone. No sense in the boy

seeing Freeman's body. His face is a mess. Didn't recognize him but for the clothes and those expensive boots he wears. Besides it's going to be a long, cold night. May even snow."

"Okay, I'll fix you something to eat while you hitch the wagon. Come on, Cody, let's go to the house."

Jake unsaddled his horse in the barn and fed him some grain. He then hitched two horses to a wagon and climbed aboard. Sarah returned with some sourdough bread and beefsteak, along with some hot coffee. She also brought a wool blanket. "You sure this can't wait until morning?"

"No, I gotta get that body into town before the wolves find him. I covered him best I could. Getting dark. I'll stay in town tonight. I'll be home sometime tomorrow."

With a cold rain falling, Jake reached Chugwater after midnight. He went straight to the sheriff's office. Jake figured Tom would be home with Molly and Abigail but he assumed Eli Black, the deputy sheriff, would be in the office. He was correct.

"What the . . ." exclaimed the young deputy as Jake opened the door and stepped inside. Rainwater fell from his shoulders and began puddling on the wood plank floor. "Jake Summers. What are you doing in town on a night like this?"

"Found a body out along Sybille Creek close to my place. Believe it's Austin Freeman, foreman out at the T Bar 7."

The deputy and Jake went outside and removed the blanket covering Freeman's body. Jake explained what he'd found.

Black held up a lantern to see the body. "Sounds like a bad accident. Too bad since you believe it's Freeman. Looks like it could be him."

"That's what I figure," added Jake. "I can't figure why he'd be out in my direction. What would he be trying to shoot? Not likely he was hunting. I saw him with Baxter earlier in the day over in Laramie. They left together."

"Any sign of Baxter?" asked Black.

"No sign of anyone else. Just some horse tracks. Didn't see Freeman's horse either."

"Okay, I'll take care of him. You better get a room at the hotel. This rain is getting worse by the minute and starting to freeze. Hole up for the night."

"That's what I was thinking," laughed Jake. "I'll stop back first thing in the morning and talk to Tom. Take care of my horses and wagon, won't you?"

With rainwater running in small streams

down Main Street and still falling, Jake started for the hotel and a warm fire. He realized how tired he was. *Been a long, long day. A warm bed is going to feel mighty good.*

VI

Sometime before morning the rain died and the sun's early rays reflected off everything fresh and wet. Thin ice had formed in the shaded areas. Jake went to the café and found he was the first customer of the day. He ate a quick breakfast of bacon and eggs washed down with black coffee before heading to the sheriff's office.

"Guess I'll ride out to the Baxter place with the body and give them the news," Tom was telling his deputy as Jake walked into the small office.

Tom hesitated as he saw Jake come inside and gave his old friend a nod. "Eli, we'll let them bury him."

As Jake came up to them both, Tom turned and said, "In fact, Jake, why don't you ride along with me and tell me what happened. Maybe we could use your wagon?"

"Baxter may not be home yet," said Jake.

"What makes you say that?" Tom asked.

"Baxter and Freeman were at the cattle-

253

men's meeting in Laramie, along with myself and several other ranchers. They left early, but Baxter told me he planned to go see Tellius Young about those sheep of his."

"You mean that sheep guy up in Long Canyon?"

"Yes. He moved in there a few years ago with a couple thousand head. Baxter has been trying to run him out of that valley ever since. Without any success, I might add," smiled Jake.

"Baxter, along with a lot of other cattlemen," added Tom. "Ranchers hate sheep in this country, you know that. Jake, you're about the only cattleman that doesn't. But that hasn't stopped them from coming. More and more sheepherders every day."

Tom continued, "Was Baxter going alone? Why didn't Freeman go with him?"

"I have no idea. For all I know they were together. They left Laramie together, which makes it harder to understand why I found Freeman alone without his horse. I'm just saying Baxter may not be home yet," said Jake, shaking his head.

"I'll take that chance. Ride with me and we'll take Freeman's body. Maybe Baxter will be there and he can tell us why Freeman was alone."

Jake reluctantly agreed to go along, using

254

his wagon. The road to the T Bar 7 was muddy with snow and ice in spots. Jake handled the team and wagon while Tom rode alongside.

The morning air was crisp and cold, made worse by a steady Wyoming wind blowing down from the Laramie Mountains. Two hours later they pulled up in front of Baxter's large clapboard-sided home. His youngest daughter, Virginia, was the first to see them. She came outside and was soon joined by her mother, Ruth.

"Sheriff . . . Jake . . . what brings you out on this cold winter day? Surely, not a social call?" asked Ruth.

"Mrs. Baxter —

"Ruth . . . call me Ruth."

"Ruth, I'm afraid we've got some bad news," said Tom.

Jake sat on the wagon seat and watched. He said nothing.

"Oh, no, not Robert. What happened? How?" she asked without any visible emotion.

Jake watched Ruth, curious about her lack of emotion. *She thinks Tom is talking about her husband.*

"No, not Robert. It's your foreman, Austin Freeman," said Tom. "Apparently —"

Ruth Baxter gasped and had to grab a

wagon wheel to steady herself.

Jake saw her face turn white as she wiped what appeared to be a tear from her right eye.

Virginia took her by the arm and they went to the back of the wagon. Tom dismounted and joined them. Jake turned in the seat and watched.

"You sure you want to see him," Tom asked. "Apparently his rifle misfired and blew up in his face. He looks terrible."

"No, I want to see him," Ruth answered. She choked back her feelings while trying to remain calm.

Tom pulled back the blanket covering the body.

Ruth gasped, then stared blankly for several moments at what remained of the T Bar 7 foreman's face and his cold, stiff body.

"Is Robert here?" asked Tom.

The woman didn't hear the question, her gaze on Freeman's lifeless body.

"No, Dad's not here," answered Virginia. "Not back from Laramie yet."

"Either of you have any idea why Freeman would be over northwest of Chugwater? That's kinda out of the way for him coming back from Laramie. Any reason he'd be alone and not with Baxter?"

"No clue," answered Virginia. "Mother . . .

256

Mother, would you know?"

Ruth Baxter didn't respond. When asked again, she merely uttered a soft, "I don't know."

Virginia helped her distraught mother back into the house while Tom and Jake took Freeman to the bunkhouse. Three ranch hands accepted responsibility for the body.

As they turned back toward Chugwater, it was Jake who spoke first. "Didn't that seem a little peculiar to you?"

"What? What do you mean?" asked Tom.

"Back there. When Baxter's wife thought your bad news involved her husband she showed little emotion . . . almost like she expected him to be dead. But when she learned it was Freeman she nearly broke down."

"I don't know. Maybe," said Tom. "I didn't notice."

"And she didn't act all that surprised I found him so far from the T Bar 7."

"Why would she? Why would it matter to her where he was?" asked Tom.

"You don't suppose?"

"What?" asked Tom. "Suppose what?"

"The Riley ranch is only a few miles from my place. After that run-in between Baxter and Justin Riley in town a few days back, I wonder if maybe it had something to do with that young Riley boy? Just a thought," said Jake.

"If they were riding back from the Young place, they might have decided to follow Sybille Creek before turning south across Mule Creek and then ride this direction," said Tom. "Both of those streams are swollen with snowmelt right now. Would make crossing either of them difficult," he added.

"Maybe," added Jake.

"Probably."

"Where is Baxter?"

"Maybe they split up and went separate directions," said Tom.

"Where was Catherine Baxter?" asked Jake. "We didn't see her."

"Probably in the house. Who knows?" said Tom.

"Maybe my imagination," said Jake softly. "Just all seems a little strange to me."

"You need to go home and have some of Sarah's home cooking," laughed Tom.

A bald eagle soared overhead and screeched out a wild call of agreement. Jake glanced in his direction but remained deep in thought.

VII

On a ridge north of the T Bar 7 ranch complex, Baxter sat astride his horse watching the return of his foreman's body. Behind him was Freeman's saddled horse. Baxter had spent the night in what passed for a hotel in the small town of Iron Mountain west of his ranch.

The ranch owner waited until Tom and Jake left before riding toward home. He would feign ignorance of Freeman's death. He would tell everyone they got separated while looking for a place to cross the swollen Sybille Creek, each agreeing to ride on home if a crossing was found. It never crossed his mind someone might question why he had Freeman's horse.

Baxter rode to the bunkhouse and was met by one of his hands who informed him of Freeman's death. When he went inside, he found his wife standing next to the body with a linen handkerchief in her right hand. She'd been crying.

Ruth turned and saw her husband. His eyes were fixed on her and she felt a cold chill of panic and fear. *He knows. My God he knows about Austin and me.* She took a step back and bumped into the table on which Freeman was lying.

"My dear, why so sad?" Baxter asked sarcastically as he walked toward her, his voice taunting her. "After all he was only a hired man, a poor cowhand at that. Why the tears?"

Ruth hesitated, not knowing how to respond. "I . . . I thought . . ."

"You thought what, my dear? Such sadness for an ordinary cowhand. Don't be upset. He can be replaced. After all that's not me lying there cold and stiff and dead now, is it?"

Ruth started for the bunkhouse door but as she passed Baxter, he grabbed her roughly by the arm. "My dear, this isn't the end, in fact, it's only the beginning. You understand me?"

She yanked her arm free and whispered, "You bastard!"

Baxter laughed deep and hard. He looked around the room. They were alone. "Now . . . now, Mrs. Baxter, such ugliness. I'll tell you what. I'm hungry, why don't you go fix me something to eat like a nice little wife. We will talk soon . . . real soon. I'll be right along."

As Ruth stepped through the bunkhouse door, she glanced toward the horse corral and saw Baxter's bay gelding tied to the fence. She gasped when she also saw Freeman's saddled sorrel mare tied alongside.

Oh, my god, he was there. He was there when Austin died. Panic swept over her and she ran toward the house.

Catherine saw her coming and met her mother at the back door. "What's wrong? What's happened?"

Ruth pushed past her without speaking and went upstairs to her bedroom. She saw Virginia sitting in another bedroom brushing her long blond hair.

Catherine looked toward the bunkhouse and saw her father emerge and start toward the house. *Not again. Now what's he done to upset mother?* She retreated to the main living area and waited. She didn't have to wait long before her father found her. He glanced at his oldest daughter and asked, "Where's your mother?"

"Upstairs, she's —"

"I told her I was hungry. Since she won't do what I tell her, you will. Go fix me something to eat."

As Catherine started toward the kitchen, he called out, "First, get me some coffee. And be quick about it."

As Baxter removed his heavy coat, he noticed the dark, nearly black remnants of Freeman's splattered blood and skin still clung to his coat. *Need me a new coat. Need*

261

to go into town one day soon and get me one.
He tossed the garment on the floor and headed for the kitchen.

Taking his coffee, he stepped onto the back porch while Catherine hurriedly fixed him scrambled eggs and elk sausage. She also fixed a plate of biscuits and fresh sausage gravy. As she spooned his eggs onto a plate she hesitated and glanced at her father standing outside. Taking a small box off the top shelf of the cabinet she carefully examined the contents and looked at the bowl of gravy on the table.

"Your food is ready," she called.

Baxter stepped back inside and sat down at the table. He filled his plate with food and covered everything with a thick layer of white gravy.

Catherine watched.

"Where's your sister?" he asked as he took a sip of coffee.

"She's upstairs."

"Go get her," he demanded. "You both need to hear something."

As she turned toward the main living area, she heard a shout from outside.

"Boss! Boss, come quick," she heard someone shout. "We just seen that Riley boy."

Baxter jumped to his feet, grabbed a

biscuit, and hurried outside.

Catherine felt a sense of panic. Nelson Riley had planned to meet her on the ridge behind the barn later in the morning. Apparently, he'd been seen. She followed her father outside.

"Up there," pointed one of the hands. "On the ridge in those cottonwood trees."

"Get me my rifle." Then Baxter remembered his Winchester had exploded, killing Freeman. "No, get me any rifle. I'm going to kill that boy. I warned him."

As Baxter and two hands armed with rifles started up the hill, Catherine slipped into the barn and saddled her horse. She mounted and quietly rode out the barn's front door. She made for a place along the creek where she'd often met Nelson Riley before.

If he can get off that ridge unseen, he'll know where to meet me. She kicked her horse into a run.

Ruth also heard the shouting and looked outside her bedroom window. She saw everyone pointing up the hill and watched Catherine leave on horseback. The shaken woman went downstairs and found Baxter's uneaten food. She took some biscuits and covered them with now cold gravy. *With everything that's happened today, I guess I forgot to eat. Cold or not it tastes pretty good. I'm hungry.*

She felt better after eating and for several minutes watched through the kitchen window as the men searched for the young Riley. She could hear Baxter shouting at his men. With her hunger satisfied, she decided to take a plate of biscuits and gravy to Virginia, who had remained in her room upstairs. *Need to lie down. Not feeling so good. Maybe I ate too much too fast.*

She stopped by Virginia's room and found her daughter reading a copy of *Wuthering Heights*. "Aren't you hungry?" she asked. "Catherine fixed your father some food. I brought you a plate. He's out searching for that Riley boy. You might as well have some food."

"No thank you, Mother. I'm fine. I'm not hungry."

"Okay, I'm going to lie down for a few minutes. I'm feeling nauseous."

Ruth went to her room and fought the urge to throw up. Her heart beat faster. "Virginia," she whispered as a strong wave of nausea rolled over her. Her call went unheard. Weak, she stumbled toward her bed. She had trouble breathing. She slumped to the floor with the plate of biscuits and gravy falling beside her.

■ ■ ■ ■

Baxter and his men searched the area in all directions for almost two hours but found no sign of Nelson Riley.

"You ignorant idiot. You sure you saw someone?"

"Yes, boss. He was here, I swear."

"You men keep looking. I'm going to the house. I'm starved. Let me know if you see anyone."

Baxter entered the kitchen and found what remained of his cold food. The gravy bowl was empty and only two biscuits remained. In anger he swept his arm across the table pushing all dishes off the table, leaving it clean. He called, "Catherine. Virginia. One of you get out here and fix me some hot food."

Someone is going to pay for ignoring me. I'm starving.

Baxter glanced at the mess he'd created on the floor before turning to find himself a piece of sourdough bread. He located some honey and spread a heavy coating on the bread. Pouring himself some cold coffee he went outside. As he settled into a chair on the back porch he watched his men continue their search for Riley.

Time for a family meeting. Time for a come-uppance. I've had enough disrespect. They are going to rue this day.

Baxter went upstairs and first stopped by Virginia's room. "Where's your sister?"

"I don't know," answered Virginia looking up from her book. "I thought she was downstairs."

"Go find her and meet me in the kitchen. I'm going to get your mother."

Baxter found his wife's limp, lifeless body lying crumpled on the bedroom floor. Near her body he saw the broken plate of biscuits and gravy meant for Virginia. He bent over his wife and checked for a pulse. He made no effort to revive her. She was dead. Instead, he called for Virginia, "Get in here. Your mother isn't breathing."

He stared at the food on the bedroom floor and was hit with a revelation. *Oh my god, could it be Catherine tried poisoning me. My own daughter!* Taking a deep breath, he cautioned himself at jumping to any unfounded conclusions.

Virginia screamed at the sight of her mother's lifeless body. But when she turned back toward her father he was gone.

Baxter's rage consumed him. He felt his own heart racing. He removed a small bottle of nitroglycerin pills from his pocket and put two under his tongue to dissolve.

Meanwhile, Catherine rode into a clearing about two miles from home as her friend appeared on his own horse. "You gotta get outta here," exclaimed Catherine. "My father knows you're here. They're searching for you."

"I know. I saw them. Maybe it's time I face him. I'm tired of hiding and running from him."

"Not much longer," said Catherine, matter-of-factly. "I've taken care of him for good."

"How?" asked Nelson. "I just saw him."

"I put pieces of hemlock in his food. When he eats . . . and he will . . . he'll soon be dead. Nobody will be able to figure out how he died."

"Oh, my god, you poisoned him?" asked Nelson. "You murdered him? Your own father?"

"That's why I asked you to find me some hemlock."

"You told me you needed it to kill rats. Oh, my god."

"You don't want us together? I thought you wanted me."

"I do, but I never planned to murder him. I was going to confront him in a fair fight. Man to man . . . not just kill him. How could you?"

"You weren't doing anything so I did."

"But murder?"

"Don't you go righteous on me. I did what you didn't have the backbone to do."

"Maybe if you go back. Hurry back. Maybe he hasn't eaten yet," suggested Nelson.

"Are you serious? You can't be serious," she responded. "It's been more than two hours. He must have eaten by now."

"Yes, I'm serious. If you ride back now. There may still be a chance. Go!" he told her.

Confused, Catherine wheeled her horse and kicked him into a run toward home. She pulled up at the edge of some trees, and in the distance she could see her father standing on the back porch. She sighed with relief. *He hasn't eaten yet. There's still time.*

As she started out of the trees, she saw three men running toward the house. They were shouting something she couldn't understand.

Catherine rode closer and felt her father watching her. Then she heard one of the hands shout, "The lady is dead." Confused by the news her mother was dead, she again felt the icy stare of her father. Somehow, he knew the truth. Her mother not her father had been the one to die. She'd failed and her mother had died in the process. She felt her old life fly away as if a leaf on the Wyoming wind. The air rushed from her lungs. She felt the box of hemlock in her pocket, but her eyes were void of tears.

VIII

News of Ruth Baxter's death swept like a prairie fire throughout Chugwater and the surrounding area. Rumor was she'd committed suicide upon learning Austin Freeman had died in a gun accident. Baxter chose to play the role of grieving, heartbroken husband, although few believed him.

Too bad it wasn't that husband of hers. Gabriel Swanson still held a thinly veiled grudge against the rancher after their confrontation in the bank a few days earlier. *Someday that man will get his. There will be plenty of opportunities to get rid of him.*

Swanson's thoughts were interrupted when he saw Justin Riley and Thomas Douglas riding down the street in his direction. *Wonder what they want?* Through the bank's front window, he watched the two ranchers dismount in front of the bank and step onto the wood plank walkway.

"Gentlemen, welcome," he greeted the

269

two men as they came through the front door. He turned and told the young bank teller, "Davis, get these men some coffee.

"What brings you men out today?"

"Robert Baxter," said Riley.

Swanson glanced at Douglas, then back at Riley. "I don't understand. What's he got to do with me or the bank?"

"Everyone knows you and Baxter recently had a disagreement about something. You being his banker, we figure it had something involving money," said Riley.

"We know he's up to something," added Douglas. "We just don't know what."

"We figure you might have some idea," added Riley. "How about it?"

"Well, as much as I'd like to share my thoughts, you know I can't discuss the business of individual customers with anyone. It would be unethical. That's confidential information."

"We understand that," said Douglas. "We also know you aren't the most scrupulous person in these parts. We aren't asking for specific details but maybe some generalities."

"I'm not sure what you mean," said Swanson feigning offense by the comment.

"You aren't that naïve," said Riley.

"Save your pious and ethical garbage for

those who don't know you," added Douglas. "We need to talk."

The bank teller handed each of them a mug of hot coffee and returned to his station.

"Bring your coffee and let's go into my office," Swanson said, motioning toward the door. "Perhaps I might be able to share a few things."

Once seated behind the closed door of his office, Swanson told the ranchers about Baxter's plan to start fencing some of the open range country.

"Fence! Oh, my god, why would he do that?" asked Douglas.

"You'd need to ask him," explained Swanson. "He came to me for the money for barbed wire. I turned him down. That's why we argued."

"Figured it was something like that," noted Riley leaning back in his chair. "Don't suppose he told you where he plans to start fencing?"

"He told me up along Horse Creek over toward Lodgepole Creek."

"That's open range country all right. We all use that area. The cattlemen's association will never permit that. He just lost his wife and his foreman, but there won't be any sympathy if he starts fencing that country."

Swanson sighed and said, "That's not all. He plans to run Tellius Young and his sheep out of that valley up near Morton Pass. He's planning to get the cattlemen's association's help before he fences that valley with barbed wire for use by his T Bar 7."

"That's why he's been applying so much pressure," noted Douglas. "He even threatened me as president of the cattlemen's association to take action against the sheep owners up there, especially Tellius Young."

"Something's got to be done to stop him," said Riley. "He's out of control."

"You need to be careful, Justin," said Swanson. "After he confronted you and your son in town the other day, anything happens to him, you and your son will be the first everyone will suspect."

"You as well," added Riley. "We all heard that you two argued and Jake Summers was a witness."

"What if someone else had a reason? What if someone else could be blamed?" asked Douglas.

"What are you thinking?" asked Riley.

"Tellius Young. Baxter has made it clear he wants him and his sheep gone. He even threatened the use of force to make it happen. What if something happened to Baxter and it looked like Young or one of those other sheepherders like Victor Bennington or James Lincoln was involved? We might get rid of Baxter and a few wooly lovers at the same time."

"Mmmmm . . . interesting idea," said Riley.

"It can't look like we are involved in any way. One kills the other wouldn't matter much. The survivor could be accused and tried for murder. Either way our problems are solved," explained Douglas.

"How are we going to pull this off?" asked Swanson.

"Leave the details to me," said Douglas. "I'll send word to Baxter that I have a plan to get rid of Young. I'll invite him to come see me. He'll come."

"You realize, of course, if we are implicated in any way, it will be our necks getting stretched," said Riley.

"This will work. Leave the details to me," said Douglas.

The three men looked at each other and smiled. Miles away Robert Baxter, Tellius Young, and the other sheep owners went about their business unaware they were about to become pawns in a game of life and death.

IX

The burial of Ruth Baxter on the T Bar 7 Ranch took place on a cold, dark early spring day with the sky filled with a mixture of icy rain and wet snow. A small group of local friends attended with Jake and Sarah Summers among them. Even Tom and Molly Scott came from town to pay their respects.

Tragedy seemed to have taken up residence on the isolated ranch. Freeman had been buried on the ranch a day earlier without ceremony. Only a few ranch hands were in attendance. Baxter had come and gone not waiting to hear any words spoken over the body.

A preacher from Chugwater spoke over the plain pine box holding the body of Ruth Baxter. Her husband showed no emotion as he stood next to his daughters, Catherine and Virginia. The wind blew cold and relentless across the hillside chosen to hold her body for eternity. Clouds hid the sun cheating any promise of hope . . . instead offering only a solemn backdrop for mourning.

Jake noticed Baxter made no effort to console his girls on the loss of their mother. *What an insensitive jerk.* Jake watched the two girls weeping and supporting each other.

As Jake, Sarah, Molly, and Tom returned to Chugwater together, it was Jake who mentioned Baxter's lack of support for his girls. "The man seemed so cold, even heartless. Did you see how he acted around his girls?"

"I noticed that," observed Sarah. "Molly and I thought the same thing."

"Has anyone even asked how she died?" Sarah asked.

"The doctor checked her body," said Tom. "I asked him if she'd been shot or if there was any evidence of foul play. He concluded she'd apparently ingested some type of poison."

"Why was she found on her bedroom floor with leftover breakfast items scattered around? If she ate some poison she apparently didn't know it. If she committed suicide, why bother to eat breakfast?" asked Jake. "We saw her earlier that morning and she was clearly upset, but I wouldn't say suicidal."

Tom shrugged his shoulders and didn't immediately respond. "I wonder."

"You wonder what?" asked Jake as he urged the horses pulling their carriage to pick up the pace. The cold, drizzling rain had turned to a wintry mix of ice pellets and snow flurries.

"I stopped by the general store yesterday and Missy Fernsmith asked why someone would need hemlock. I told her I couldn't think of a reason unless someone was trying to kill something or someone."

"Hemlock! That stuff is extremely poisonous," noted Jake.

"When the Rileys were in town the other day and had that confrontation with Baxter, Nelson Riley apparently asked Missy if she had any hemlock. Told her he needed to get rid of some rats."

"Interesting," said Jake. "Did she have any?"

"No, apparently not."

"Didn't Baxter accuse that younger Riley boy of seeing his daughter Catherine behind his back?" asked Sarah.

"Yes, he did," answered Jake.

The four rode in silence for a while. Each deep in thought. Molly asked, "You don't suppose?"

"Makes you wonder, doesn't it?" said Tom.

Jake blurted out, "The rifle!"

"What rifle? What are you talking about?" asked Tom, somewhat confused by Jake's outburst.

"The rifle that blew up on Austin Freeman."

"What about it?"

"That rifle. We've all been assuming it was Freeman's rifle. He was obviously shooting at something."

"And —"

"That rifle was a Winchester Model 1873."

"That's right," said Tom.

"You mentioned the confrontation between Baxter and the Riley family in town the other day."

"Yes."

"I just remembered. Baxter was holding a Winchester Model 1873 rifle that day. Freeman held an old Henry breech-loading lever-action 1860 rifle. That's his rifle. I've seen him with it before. Suppose that Winchester belonged to Baxter? Why would Freeman be shooting Baxter's Winchester? What happened to his favorite rifle . . . that Henry?"

"Now that's interesting," said Tom. "And a damn good question."

The horses pulling the carriage had slowed but nobody seemed to notice as snow began collecting on the team's back and on those in the carriage.

Jake continued, "What if someone was trying to get rid of Baxter but wanted it to look like an accident? He or she plugs his rifle barrel. The first time he pulls the trigger it blows up. He's dead and it looks like an accident. But somehow Freeman ends up using Baxter's rifle and he's the one who dies by mistake."

"Okay, so that attempt to kill Baxter fails. So he or she puts hemlock in his food and tries to kill him that way. Only the wrong person eats the poisoned food and she dies by mistake."

"But who?" asked Sarah.

"I don't know but there are several people who would like to see the man dead. Not the least of which would be Catherine Baxter herself," Jake pointed out.

Conversation about Baxter ended when they reached town. They stopped in front of the sheriff's office. The kids, Cody Summers and Abigail Scott, had been left in the reluctant hands of Deputy Eli Black. "Wonder how Deputy Black got along with those two four-year-olds," laughed Molly.

As they entered the sheriff's office, they noticed it was quiet. Everything seemed in order. Eli Black was leaning back in a chair with his feet on the desk. He was reading a dime novel about Wild Bill Hickok.

Sarah exclaimed, "Where are the children?"

"In there," the deputy motioned toward the two jail cells. The cell doors were shut and there was a child inside each one. Both kids were asleep on the cell beds.

"Like herding cats," exclaimed the deputy. "Those two are a handful. We played prisoner and I locked them up for my own sanity and their safety. Those doors aren't really locked."

Tom looked at Jake and heard him mumble, "Tell us something we don't already know about herding cats."

X

Word reached Baxter the cattlemen's association had developed a plan to drive all sheep and their owners from the territory. Thomas Douglas wanted to see him to discuss details before sharing it with the other ranch owners. He invited Baxter to come to his ranch and talk.

Before riding to the Crazy Dutchman Ranch, Baxter warned his girls not to leave home under any circumstances. While he suspected Catherine had tried to poison him, he wasn't totally sure. *Virginia had also been in the kitchen or maybe Ruth really had committed suicide. Freeman and my cheating wife were lovers. She was distraught.*

Not knowing for sure, he hadn't mentioned his suspicions to anyone. Baxter decided to wait and see, but not trust anyone. His silence only confused and tortured Catherine. She was convinced he knew the truth. *So why hasn't he said anything?*

Once he rode away, ignoring her father's warning, she went to the barn and saddled her horse. She needed to see Nelson Riley. *He must be wondering what happened. He's probably concerned.*

"Father said stay home," Virginia reminded Catherine as she watched her sister mount her horse. "You're asking for trouble."

"Me . . . oh, my god. Talk about calling the kettle black."

"What do you mean by that?"

"You little hypocrite. You think father is upset about me and Nelson? Wait until he learns about you and your secret friend."

"What friend?"

"You and that Bennington boy. Your sheepherder boyfriend. The one you are so smitten with. Father will bust a gut when he finds out. Now get out of my way." She urged her horse forward, brushing past her younger sister and nearly knocking her down.

Baxter suspected his oldest daughter would try meeting Nelson Riley so he had waited in the trees. His patience was rewarded when he saw Catherine emerge on horseback from the barn.

Not realizing she was being followed, the young woman made no effort to hide her trail. Within an hour she rode into the Sybille Creek Ranch complex. Nelson Riley rushed to meet her.

Baxter pulled up within sight of the ranch buildings and looked around. He watched the two embrace and fought down the urge to ride down and confront them.

"You little tramp. Just like your mother. I'll come back for you both later. I've got sheep to worry about now, but soon . . . real soon, young lady," he said out loud.

With that proclamation, he set off to see Thomas Douglas, who was waiting on his Crazy Dutchman Ranch. South of Morton Pass he pulled up and gazed across a wide valley free of trees and covered with grass as far as he could see. Before riding on, he took a long draw of water from his canteen and wiped his mouth dry with the back of his right hand. Then he kicked his horse forward.

Within minutes he had a severe throbbing headache. He became confused, dizzy, and had trouble seeing. Baxter's heart beat faster and began pounding in his chest. His first thought was *heart attack.*

Need help. Still too far from the Douglas place. Maybe in the other direction. Tellius Young and his place. My nitroglycerin pills. Inside my coat pocket. Maybe I'm having a heart attack.

Reaching inside his coat he found the small bottle that held his nitroglycerin pills. He felt a sense of panic because when he looked there were only two pills. *I swear it was nearly full yesterday.* Baxter put the two pills under his tongue, then tossed the empty bottle on the ground. He turned his horse back down the trail.

Baxter felt the urge to vomit and felt faint. His headache grew worse and he struggled to stay in the saddle. He became fearful he might fall. The horse followed the main trail back in the direction from which they'd come. Once they reached Sybille Creek the horse without encouragement turned south back toward the T Bar 7, missing the trail toward the Young place.

Near the creek, Baxter could hear rushing water and voices. He started to call out but felt something around his neck yanking him backwards and from the saddle. Landing among some rocks he felt pain in his shoulder. He heard the bleating of sheep and he had the sensation of someone nearby.

Weakly, he called out, "Help me. Please help me."

"Drink this," he heard a familiar voice say. He felt something cool and wet like water against his lips. The same voice told him, "Chew on this. You'll feel much better."

The taste wasn't familiar but he had no choice but to trust whomever it was. He chewed on some type of plant.

Baxter tried seeing but couldn't, his vision all but gone. He heard someone say, "That should do it." The statement was followed by silence except the soft bleating of nearby sheep. He began to tremble and felt weak. He had no sense of time but soon the T Bar 7 owner felt his heart begin to flutter. He had trouble breathing. Death for the territory's most hated rancher came agonizingly slow.

XI

The death of Robert Baxter was cause for quiet celebration. The result of an often-predicted heart attack said some. Others blamed the fall from his horse and an apparent blow to his head. Nobody knew for sure and most didn't really care. The man was dead.

Tom Scott and Jake Summers sat in the sheriff's office reflecting on recent events. "The man won't be missed," noted Tom. "He wasn't liked much."

"All true," added Jake. "But I'm still bothered by some things like Freeman's death. Why wasn't he shooting his own rifle? Also, Ruth Baxter dying so sudden. Might have been suicide but maybe not. Word was she wasn't happy and with Freeman gone. I don't know."

"Neither do I," answered Tom. "But I do know members of the cattlemen's association are happy today. Baxter won't be fencing any open range country."

"Also a few sheep owners," said Jake. "Less pressure on them. People like Tellius Young and Victor Bennington must be downright giddy today at least for a day or two. Ranchers in this territory still don't like them much."

"Speaking of sheep. What about those sheep they found dead near Baxter's body?" asked Tom. "Seems mighty curious he'd be around sheep when he died, especially dead ones."

"I agree. Unless the sheepherders had something to do with his dying. Something doesn't add up," said Jake.

"What about Catherine Baxter? Wonder how she's holding up? And Nelson Riley?" asked Jake.

"Relieved most likely," said Tom.

"Maybe we should talk to Nelson Riley. Ask him about that hemlock he was trying to find," suggested Tom. "That's still troublesome to me."

"Let's go," said Jake as he started for the door.

Tom was close behind.

Jake and Tom rode into the Sybille Creek Ranch complex and headed straight for the house. A barking dog announced their arrival and he was soon joined by a second mongrel of questionable ancestry. The two men hesitated, not dismounting from their nervous horses.

Justin Riley stepped onto the front porch. "Men, what brings you out this way? Step down and join us for dinner. Barbara has some fried chicken. Don't mind the dogs. That brown one is afraid of his own shadow. And that other one is so old most of his teeth are gone."

"Fried chicken. Sounds great. I'm famished," said Tom, still watching the dogs.

"Thank you," said Jake as he dismounted and stepped onto the porch.

"We wanted to stop by and check on your

285

rat situation," explained Tom as they entered the kitchen.

Nelson, his brother, Vincent, and the Riley daughter, Elizabeth, were sitting at the table covered with food. Justin's wife, Barbara, was already getting extra plates for the two visitors.

"Rat situation," chuckled Justin as he returned to his chair at the head of the table. "Didn't know we had a rat situation. We may have a feral cat situation. They seem to keep any rats and mice we have under control. We have plenty of cats."

"That's interesting," said Tom as he put a piece of fried chicken on his plate.

Jake watched Nelson, who put his head down, his face turning red.

"Why do you say that?" asked the elder Riley.

"Well, unless I misunderstood, Missy Fernsmith at the general store in Chugwater told me your boy Nelson here was in her store a few days ago looking for some hemlock. Claimed it was to kill some rats."

"What?" said Riley turning toward Nelson. "That true? You were looking for hemlock?"

"Maybe," the boy whispered.

"Speak up, boy," demanded his agitated father. "Were you or not?"

Everyone at the table was waiting for the embarrassed Nelson to respond.

"Yes . . . yes."

"Why, on God's green earth, would you be searching for hemlock? For killing rats? That stuff is really poisonous."

"Not for us," stammered Nelson. "I was searching for a friend."

"Who?"

"A friend."

"I asked who," demanded his angry father.

"Catherine . . . Catherine Baxter."

"Why in hell would Catherine Baxter need hemlock?" He remembered Ruth Baxter committing suicide. "Was she getting it for her mother?"

"No . . . no."

"Then why?"

"Her father. She was tired of her father abusing them. She meant to use it on him but she couldn't do it. She decided she couldn't kill anyone much less her father."

Nelson trembled as he explained. "Her mother must have eaten it by mistake. It was an accident."

"Where did you find any hemlock?" asked the boy's father.

"I asked Missy Fernsmith in Chugwater but she didn't have any so I rode to Iron Mountain and found some there."

"Boy —" his father started.

"Ruth Baxter didn't commit suicide after all," said Tom. "She ate food tainted with poison meant for Robert Baxter."

"Yes . . . maybe," added Nelson. "Then again maybe she found the hemlock and took it knowing what it was. Maybe Catherine got it for her mother. Nobody knows for sure. Maybe Mrs. Baxter was going to poison him but decided to take the poison herself. Catherine didn't do it."

"And you knew about this all the time?" asked Riley shaking his head.

"Yes . . . I was afraid for Catherine."

"That girl has you under her thumb," shouted Riley. "She's a conniving little witch, you ask me. You always do what she wants?"

"Did Baxter, her father, know about the hemlock?" asked Jake. "Did he know his food had been mixed with hemlock?"

"I don't know."

"Did you discuss it with her after her mother died?" asked Jake.

As everyone listened, Nelson Riley explained, "Yes, the day her father was found dead she came to see me. She thought her father knew it was her that tried poisoning him but he apparently never said anything. She was scared."

"So Catherine was with you the day her father died?" asked Tom.

"Yes, but only for about an hour. She told me she had to get home so she left."

"Did she go home?" Tom asked.

"I don't know. She left in a hurry though."

"Did her sister Virginia know about the hemlock?" asked Jake.

"No. I don't think so. She might have."

Turning back to a stunned Justin Riley and the others, Tom stood up and apologized. "I'm sorry to spoil your dinner but we are looking for answers. We aren't convinced Baxter died of natural causes."

Jake and Tom left the kitchen followed by the elder Riley. "What happens next?" he asked, remembering the plan he'd developed with Swanson and Douglas to put the blame on Tellius Young for Baxter's death. "I thought Baxter died of a heart attack."

"We aren't so sure. Maybe," answered Tom.

"We find it strange Douglas found him dead where there were also dead sheep nearby," explained Jake. "He supposedly was going to meet Douglas so how did he end up dying among the very animals he hated so much? Doesn't add up."

Riley hesitated before asking, "You think them sheepherders might have been involved somehow? I mean everyone knows they hated each other."

"It's possible. Real possible I suppose," answered Tom. "We just don't know."

Riley couldn't help sigh with a degree of satisfaction and relief. The plan to get rid of Baxter and place the blame on the sheep owners was unfolding well. "Keep me posted," said Riley. "And if you need a posse to round up them wooly lovers, let me know. Me and my boys will ride with you."

"Thanks," said Tom. "But first we'll go talk to Catherine Baxter. See where that leads us."

As they rode from the ranch house, yet another cold spring rain began falling, forcing them to put on their rain slickers. Both knew, without saying, they had to visit the grieving Catherine Baxter and her sister. But they decided talking to Catherine could wait for another day. They rode straight for the Meadows Ranch rather than return to Chugwater. Thinking of a hot meal and warm, dry clothes, they kicked their horses into a short lope and raced the darkness for shelter.

XII

Icy rain fell in a steady cadence throughout the night. By the time Jake and Tom rode away the next morning, water stood in puddles everywhere, and the rain continued falling. They were soon wet again.

By midmorning they rode up to the Baxter home. The house no longer resembled the bright, whitewashed home of days earlier. There was a gray pall of sadness covering the entire building complex. An old dog met them, barking briefly before retreating back into the dry barn.

Catherine met them at the front door. "Come in. Please come in out of that rain. You must be soaked." She did her best to portray a refined hostess.

Virginia came downstairs and Catherine sent her for coffee. She hesitated, glaring at her sister for giving her orders before doing as instructed.

"Take off those wet slickers and come sit down. How can we help you? Is this about our father?"

Tom glanced at Jake and answered, "Yes, and your mother."

"Mother?" asked Virginia as she reentered the room carrying two mugs of hot coffee.

"Our mother?" said Catherine echoing her

sister's question.

"Girls, I'll get right to the point. Yesterday, we talked to Nelson Riley. He admitted he got some hemlock for you, Catherine. He didn't say where he got it and that doesn't much matter. Why would you need hemlock?"

"What . . . what do you mean he got it for me?" asked Catherine.

"That's what he said," answered Tom.

Jake watched Virginia's expression. She seemed irritated, although not totally surprised.

"Why did you get hemlock? That's so poisonous. Why?" asked Virginia.

"Shut up. You know why. And don't act so innocent, you knew about it," said Catherine as she turned back toward Jake and Tom. "He abused us. He was always yelling at us. And mother, he beat her down emotionally. I couldn't take it anymore."

"Did Mother know?" asked Virginia.

"No. I didn't tell her. She would never approve. You know that. As bad as things were she wouldn't agree to killing someone, even our abusive father."

"What happened, Catherine?" asked Tom.

The young woman stood and walked to the front window and stared out at the rain as she gathered her thoughts. "It was an accident — Mother dying. Yes, she was upset about Austin's death. But she'd never kill herself.

"Father asked me to fix him something to eat. I mixed the hemlock in his gravy. However, before he could eat, he got called away. Someone claimed they saw Nelson on the ridge. I was worried Father would catch him so I went to find him myself. While I was gone, I remembered the gravy and hemlock. I changed my mind. I couldn't kill anyone. I hurried back to clean it up before Father could eat anything. Mother must have eaten some. By the time I got back Mother was already dead. It was an accident."

"Oh, my god . . . you killed our mother," shouted a hysterical Virginia. "How could you?"

"Accident . . . it was an accident."

Virginia began to cry uncontrollably.

Jake asked, "Did your father know about your mother and Austin?"

"I don't know," said Catherine who also began crying. "I think he must have," she sobbed. "Everyone else did."

"Why was Austin using your father's Winchester rifle and not his own Henry the day he was killed?"

"What?" asked Catherine. "What do you mean?"

Virginia stopped crying and turned toward the group. Tom noticed her interest in what was being said had peaked. She stepped closer.

"The other day in town Austin had a Henry rifle. Your father had a Winchester. Freeman was killed when your father's Winchester blew up, not his Henry. And Austin's horse. Was he ever found? When I found Freeman's body, there was no horse."

"Austin's horse is here," said Catherine. "Father brought him home when he came back from Laramie. I never thought about his horse."

"Your father brought his horse home?" exclaimed Jake. "That means your father must have been there when Austin died or shortly afterward. May we go look at Austin's saddle and gear?" asked Jake.

"Why?" asked Virginia. "What purpose would that serve?"

"Curiosity. Just curious," answered Jake as he joined Tom in standing.

The four walked through the rain to the bunkhouse and found Freeman's saddle and gear. Still tied to the saddle was his rifle scabbard. Jake reached down and pulled a Henry Model 1860 from the scabbard.

"Here's Freeman's rifle. So why was he shooting your father's rifle?"

Both girls shook their heads as if unknowing.

"Your father's rifle was plugged by someone so it would blow up the first time your father pulled the trigger. Whoever plugged the rifle expected your father would do the shooting, not Austin. It was meant to kill your father, not Austin," explained Jake.

"You girls know anything about that?" Tom asked.

"Not me," said Catherine.

"Me either," added Virginia.

"Who had access to your father's rifle? Did your mother know how to use a rifle?"

"Just about everyone here on the ranch had access. He kept his saddle and gear along with his rifle in the bunkhouse most of the time," Catherine explained.

"Your mother . . . along with you and your sister," noted Jake before asking. "Could your mother use a rifle?"

"Yes," answered Virginia. "They often went coyote hunting together. She could really shoot."

"So it's likely she would know a plugged rifle barrel would blow up when fired?"

"Yes, I'm sure," said Catherine.

"That doesn't mean she plugged Father's

rifle. We all know a plugged rifle will blow up," said Virginia. "And we all know how to use a rifle. Father taught us."

"Still doesn't explain how Austin ended up with the rifle and how your father might have been involved," said Tom.

"Doesn't provide much insight on how Baxter actually died either," stated Jake.

"We were told it was probably a heart attack. Maybe he hit his head on a rock when he fell from his horse," said Catherine. "You don't believe that?"

Jake noticed Virginia had turned her back and was walking toward the bunkhouse door. "Virginia, is that what you understand as well?" he called after her.

She stopped and looked back . . . hesitated, then said, "Yes."

"How old are you?" asked Jake.

"I'm sixteen. Why?"

"Just curious. Ever have a boyfriend? One that might upset your father like your sister's friend, Nelson?"

"No . . . not like Catherine and Nelson."

"Did your father know you had a boyfriend?" asked Jake.

"Who says I do?"

Catherine rolled her eyes and shrugged but said nothing. However, the gesture was enough for Tom to notice.

"One more question. Did your father take medicine for his heart? We can ask the doctor in town but I figure you both would know."

"He took nitroglycerin pills. I think the doctor told him not to take more than four a day," said Virginia.

"Did he carry them with him?"

"Yes, in a small bottle usually in a pocket inside his coat," added Catherine.

"Any reason he might not carry them?"

"No, he always made sure he had them. Seems like he was fighting with someone all the time and that usually caused his heart to beat faster so he kept those pills handy."

"Okay, thank you. You ready to ride, Tom?"

"We'll be back in touch. I don't know what to do about the hemlock. Sounds like what eventually happened was an accident. Might also be a case of attempted murder. I'll ponder on it. Meanwhile don't go anywhere," said Tom.

Jake and Tom climbed on their horses, waved goodbye, and rode away. After riding a short distance, Jake spoke, "They aren't telling us everything."

"I feel the same," said Tom.

"And if Baxter always carried his heart pills how come none were found. No bottle . . . nothing."

They rode in silence for a while before Jake asked, "Baxter's horse, saddle, and gear? They still in town at the stable?"

"Yes, figured I'll send them back to the girls later this week."

"Don't just yet," said Jake. "I want to look them over, including his canteen, especially his canteen."

At that moment, the rain began falling in a torrent of moisture. "We'd better move these ponies along," Tom called out. "Let's ride."

XIII

Two of Chugwater's free range roosters began their morning call as Jake stepped through the stable doors. Jacob Helms, the livery owner, was haying horses in the back.

"What's up, Jake?" Helms called out. "You're up early. Almost before them fool roosters," he chuckled.

"Morning, Jacob. I'm curious about something. You still have Baxter's saddle and gear?"

"Sure, over there," Helms pointed toward a stall gate. "Tom told me Eli was taking it out to the Baxter place in a day or two. His horse, too, I guess."

"Mind if I take a look?" asked Jake.

"Help yourself. I gotta finish my chores."

Jake found the Baxter gear and carefully examined everything. He found nothing unusual, including the canteen, which was empty. "Say Jacob," he called out. "Was this canteen empty when you unsaddled Baxter's horse?"

"Funny you should ask," said the stable owner. "I thought it peculiar that he'd be off riding with an empty canteen. Unless of course he was extra thirsty and drank it dry while riding."

"Or it was emptied," suggested Jake.

"Why would he empty his canteen?" Helms asked, scratching his chaff-covered head. "That don't make no sense."

"It does if someone else did the emptying. Thanks, Jacob. I gotta go see Doc Collins. Talk to you later."

Helms watched Jake leave as a feral cat darted through the doorway. The stable owner was perplexed at Jake's comments but he shrugged his tired shoulders and went back to work.

As Jake entered the doctor's office, his senses were greeted by the strong smell of alcohol and other pungent chemicals. The doctor was with a patient in the back. "Be right with you," he called out.

"Take your time," answered Jake as he glanced around the room. The doctor's desk was covered with papers. Several medical books, most covered with dust, were on a shelf behind the desk. Inside a storage cabinet with glass doors, Jake saw bottles of laudanum, morphine tablets, carbolic acid, arsenic, ipecac, chloroform, and other herbal pills.

"Good morning, Jake," said the doctor as he came from the back. He was drying his hands on an old, ragged towel.

"Gotta couple questions about Baxter's death."

"Okay. I'll try to answer them. Want some coffee?" he asked while pouring a cup for himself.

"No thanks," said Jake. "Tom and I are curious about how Baxter died. Did you find anything unusual?"

"Not really. I checked him over pretty good. I decided he died of a heart attack compounded by a blow to his head probably when he fell from his horse."

"Could he have been struck in the head while standing on the ground and it just looked like he might have hit his head falling off his horse?"

"Well, yes, I suppose."

"The Baxter girls said he was taking nitroglycerin pills. Is that correct?"

"Yes, he's been having some chest pain issues so I gave him some nitro pills to relieve his angina. He carried them with him just in case."

"Doc, no pills were found on his body and I checked his equipment. There were no pills. Don't you think that's a little odd considering his concern about having a heart attack?"

"That's curious because I gave him a full bottle last week. He couldn't have possibly used them all by now . . . or I certainly hope not."

"What would happen if he took too many? Let's say a large number were dissolved in a canteen of water."

"They are meant to be dissolved under the tongue," explained the doctor.

"But what if?"

"Well, he'd probably get a severe throbbing headache with a fast or pounding heartbeat. He'd get confused and maybe have trouble breathing. He'd probably get dizzy, maybe faint or have a seizure."

"Enough to fall off his horse?" asked Jake.

"Yes, I suppose. But how could that happen? He'd been using them for several weeks. He knew not to take too many."

"What if someone wanted to poison him?"

"That would work I suppose. But who would do such a thing?"

"That's what Tom and I are trying to figure out. Thanks for your help," said Jake as he turned to leave.

As Jake reached the door, the doctor called to him, "Jake, I did find something I ignored until now."

"What's that?"

"I found traces of a plant under his tongue. They were small pieces like he'd been chewing on something. I assumed it was the remains of something he'd eaten earlier."

"Any idea what?"

"Strange as it sounds, my first thought was chokecherry leaves. I discounted the idea. He's a longtime rancher in these parts. He would definitely know not to eat chokecherry."

"I thought chokecherries were edible," said Jake.

"Only the fleshy part of the berries themselves," explained the doctor. "The rest releases toxins. Most parts are toxic to humans and livestock. Digestion of chokecherry seeds, leaves, twigs, and bark releases cyanide poisoning in the stomach.

"I've heard of cases where livestock like

cattle and sheep have eaten the stuff and died. Even wild animals like moose have died eating that stuff."

"What happens?"

"In humans you can have cardiac arrhythmia. Humans start trembling and feel weak. You may experience an increased heart rate, high blood pressure, and have difficulty breathing. That can lead to a coma, convulsions, and respiratory arrest. Humans will die within one to three hours."

"If someone who is already having heart problems starts having heart arrhythmia, wouldn't he be inclined to take more pills, maybe even more than recommended to control it?"

"He might."

"Thanks, Doc," said Jake.

"One more thing. I found several bruises around his neck like he'd been choked or something. Like something had been put around his neck and he was yanked from behind so hard it left bruises."

Back at the sheriff's office, Jake explained to Tom what he'd found out at the stable and from the doctor. "I'm more convinced than ever Baxter was killed."

"Who found him?"

"Thomas Douglas found him. Claimed Baxter was on his way to meet him. When he didn't show up, Douglas went looking for him."

"Why would he go looking for him? Why would he care if Baxter didn't show up for a meeting?"

"Good question. Morgan Davis, the teller over at the bank, told me Swanson, Riley, and Douglas were in there recently talking about Baxter and something to do with those sheepherders up there," said Tom. "Think I'll stop by and ask Swanson a few questions, pay him a friendly visit."

"Good idea," said Jake. "While you're at the bank, I think I'll ride out and talk to Douglas. He might be able to shine some light on all this. Remember Justin Riley started acting a little strange while we were talking to his son. Almost like he thought we'd come to talk to him, not Nelson."

"We may be on to something," said Tom.

"I'll stop by the T Bar 7 on my way to see Douglas and drop off Baxter's horse and equipment," offered Jake.

"Okay, maybe Riley, Douglas, and Swanson were planning something. Baxter had fought with all three recently," suggested Tom. "I'll see what Swanson has to say."

While Jake rode for the T Bar 7 leading Baxter's horse, Tom went to see Swanson. The banker admitted meeting with Riley and Douglas but claimed it was all about business. "We talked about Baxter but only in the context of him wanting to fence that open range country," said Swanson. "But honestly nobody is crying over his heart attack."

"Heart attack?" asked Tom.

"That's the rumor going around town. You believe it was something different?"

"Jake and I aren't exactly convinced."

"Maybe those sheepherders up there had something to do with him dying. After all, Baxter has been trying to run them off their land," suggested Swanson.

"Maybe," said Tom. "Maybe. But seems a little peculiar he'd die so close to sheep when he hated them so much. Kinda convenient if someone wanted to implicate those sheepherders in his death. Yep, mighty peculiar."

Jake left Baxter's horse with one of the hands before riding to the house. Both Baxter girls came onto the porch.

Still sitting on his horse, he asked, "Any reason you girls can think of why your dad's canteen would be empty?"

"Oh, my gosh no," said Virginia. "He was obsessed with having a full canteen. He didn't like drinking water from streams unless he knew they were spring fed. He was afraid some animal had peed or worse in the water upstream. Sometimes he even took two canteens so he had plenty of water."

"That true?" Jake asked Catherine.

"I suppose," she answered. "Maybe he was thirsty and ran out, or maybe he forgot to fill it before leaving. It happens."

"I don't know," said Virginia. "I can't imagine him forgetting. Extra thirsty maybe."

"One more thing," said Jake. "Doc Collins told me he gave your father a new bottle of nitro pills last week, yet none have been found. Any ideas?"

Both girls looked at each other and shook their heads no.

"Thanks," said Jake as he turned his horse toward Douglas and his Crazy Dutchman Ranch.

A barking dog signaled Jake's arrival as Douglas emerged from the barn.

"Jake, my friend. What brings you out to my place? Climb down and sit a spell. You still after my heifers for that cow herd of yours?"

"I'm helping Tom with the Baxter death."

"Baxter? I thought that was settled. He

died of a heart attack is what I heard."

"Not necessarily," answered Jake. "We aren't convinced . . . at least not yet. I understand you're the one who found him."

"That's right. He was lying on the ground near Sybille Creek. Lucky I stumbled onto him."

"I thought you were looking for him."

"I was. He failed to show up for a meeting. I got concerned. Not like him."

"You notice anything out of the ordinary up there?"

"Not really, except for a few dead sheep."

"Dead sheep?"

"That's right. Three or four of them lying dead about twenty yards or so from Baxter's body.

"Wait, I forgot," he continued. "I also found a shepherd's crook, a nice one. You don't suppose?"

"Suppose what?"

"Maybe those sheepherders had something to do with his death. I mean they didn't like him much."

"Interesting you'd mention them sheepherders as potential suspects," said Jake. "Justin Riley said much the same thing."

"He did? Might be worth considering. You never know."

"Word has it you met with Swanson at

the bank and Riley not long ago concerning Baxter, you remember that?" asked Jake.

Douglas hesitated, then said, "That's right. We wanted some clarification about Baxter wanting to put barbed wire up on that free range country near him."

"That all?"

"As president of the cattlemen's association I wanted to know more about his intentions. That was it."

"What happened to that shepherd's crook?"

"I've got it. Let me go find it." Douglas got up and disappeared into another room of his house. When he returned, he carried a wooden shepherd's crook. The long hand-made stick had unique markings.

"You found this near Baxter's dead body?"

"More or less. It was near the dead sheep not far away. I figured Baxter stumbled onto a small flock and started killing them. Whomever was watching them must have run off, dropping the stick. Baxter hated sheep, got excited, and had a heart attack. Everyone knew he had heart issues."

"Sounds plausible," said Jake.

After pausing for a few moments to gather his thoughts, Jake asked, "Was there much blood?"

"What? What blood?" asked Douglas.

"From the sheep. You said you figured Baxter was killing the sheep so there must have been blood."

"I don't know. I suppose. I didn't really notice. I was worried about Baxter."

"You said you found this shepherd's crook near the sheep, not Baxter's body. You noticed the stick lying on the ground but don't remember any blood."

"Wait a minute, Jake. What are you saying? Are you trying to imply something?"

"No . . . not at all. Just wondering."

"Well there must have been blood. I don't remember."

"How about chokecherries? Any of that poisonous stuff growing up there?"

"Might have been. It grows up here. I've seen moose that died from eating it."

"But you didn't notice any? Is that right?"

"Jake, I was concerned for Baxter and getting his body into town. I wasn't looking at the landscape . . . what plants were growing around there."

"Thanks, Thomas. I appreciate your time," said Jake as he stood to leave.

"Mind if I take the shepherd's crook with me?"

"Take it and go. I've got work to do."

Jake pulled up on a ridge a mile or so from the Crazy Dutchman Ranch house. He took his time rolling a cigarette and tried lighting a match. It took three attempts before he was successful. As smoke was caught on the wind, he examined the shepherd's crook closely. The intricately designed staff was covered with detail. Then he noticed what appeared to be some initials near the top.

XIV

The ride back to Chugwater gave Jake time to think about what he'd learned. Around him in the areas near town, spring grasses were starting to emerge. Streams were full with runoff from melting snow in the Laramie Mountains. The land was alive with promise.

I'm more convinced than ever that Baxter was killed. But who and why?

Once back in town, he rode to find Tom and share details of his day. "Let's start from the beginning," he told his friend. "Let's go over what we know.

"Austin Freeman died from using a rifle with a plugged barrel, but it's Baxter's Winchester not his own Henry. Somebody deliberately plugged the barrel figuring it would be Baxter eventually pulling the trigger. That attempt failed.

"Catherine Baxter admits she had Nelson

Riley get her some hemlock so she could poison her father. But she says at the last minute she had a change of heart and went back to stop him from eating the poisoned food. However, her mother apparently ate the contaminated food by mistake and she died, not Baxter. Unless of course, her mother knew about the hemlock and deliberately took some to commit suicide.

"We know Catherine wanted to kill him. We also know she knew how to plug a rifle barrel but so did her mother and sister.

"Doc Collins says Baxter was using nitroglycerin pills for his heart condition," continued Jake. "Who else would know that?"

"His wife and both girls," answered Tom.

"That's right. Something tells me those missing nitro pills were dissolved in the water inside Baxter's canteen. He might have been in a hurry to meet Douglas and couldn't find his pill bottle. He decides to leave home without them not knowing his canteen water was contaminated. Or he took some with him and when he started having heart issues used the remaining pills and tossed the bottle aside along the trail. I believe he overdosed on nitroglycerin pills from the canteen and any he had with him. That left him disoriented and confused. He got a major headache and his heart began beating rapidly.

"If he did have some pills with him he may have taken them trying to bring his pounding heart under control. That only added to his problem. Each time he takes another pill or takes a drink he unknowingly adds to his overdose. He begins to have trouble breathing and becomes dizzy . . . maybe even faints or has a seizure."

"But what happens to the pill bottle if he has some with him?" asked Tom.

"Like I said, he may have run out and thrown the bottle away, or whoever killed him finds him in distress and takes the bottle. They also empty his canteen of poisoned water to eliminate any evidence that nitroglycerin was ever mixed with his water."

"Then what?" asked Tom.

"Not aware he's already consumed enough nitroglycerin to kill himself, he's found barely alive. Determined to kill him, he or she forces him to chew some chokecherry leaves. Maybe he even knew his killer and trusted that person. He was convinced by chewing the chokecherry it would make him feel better. Within a couple hours he was dead."

"He would know chokecherry was poisonous. He would know not to eat that stuff," said Tom.

"Yes, unless he was so confused, he didn't know what he was chewing," explained Jake.

"Doc says he found plant material under Baxter's tongue that reminded him of chokecherry leaves."

"Okay, but we still don't know who did it," said Tom. "If your theory is correct, it could still be any number of people or maybe even a group of people."

"What do you mean?" Jake asked.

"Let's assume whoever doctored his water believes that's what killed him. Then someone totally different finds him hurt from the fall off his horse. That person doesn't know he's already dying from the overdose of nitro. But they see a chance to kill him so they convince him to chew the chokecherry leaves, which are growing nearby. Now that person or persons believes it was the chokecherry that killed him," suggested Tom. "Maybe Douglas with help from Riley."

"One more possibility," added Jake. "Suppose a third person or persons finds him still barely alive so they use the shepherd's crook around his neck and strangle him. Doc says there were marks around his neck as if he'd been choked. So, one of the sheepherders? Dead sheep were found nearby and Douglas said he found the stick near the sheep. Maybe it was chokecherry leaves that also killed those sheep."

"Or the same . . . one person . . . was so determined to see him dead they did all three things just to make sure he died," added Tom. "No more failures."

"That shepherd's stick has someone's initials carved into the wood. And I've got an idea whose. Care to take a ride?" asked Jake.

Three hours later Jake and Tom rode along Pole Creek and could hear the bleating of sheep in the distance. They rode through a stand of cottonwood and over a ridge into a small grass-covered high mountain valley. They could see Victor Bennington and his two sons, along with their dogs, moving their flock of Churros toward some buildings further down the valley.

The senior Bennington saw them coming and started in their direction. He called out a greeting while still several yards away. Both Tom and Jake pulled up their horses and waited, not wanting to frighten the flock.

"Afternoon, men," they heard Bennington shout as he waved at them. "What brings you up here?"

"Afternoon, Victor. We came to see your son."

"Which one?" he asked while gesturing toward the two young men in the distance.

"Your youngest, Samuel," said Jake.

"Samuel? Why Samuel?" Bennington asked.

Jake pulled the shepherd's crook from under a blanket in which it had been wrapped. "You recognize this?"

"Why, yes. Yes, of course, it belongs to Samuel. See the initials SB there on the top. He made it himself. Took him weeks. Where did you find it?"

"It was found over near Sybille Creek," said Tom.

"My goodness, wonder how it got way over there. Samuel told me he lost it. Thought he might have lost it searching for some ewes that strayed away from the flock. He will be excited to know it was found. He spent a lot of time carving that thing," Bennington smiled.

"Was he over that way recently? Maybe looking for some lost ewes?" asked Jake.

"He didn't say. We've had problems keeping them away from the chokecherry growing around here. Winter grazing gets kinda short this time of year. We've already lost several . . . four or five ewes and a couple

315

wethers. That stuff is really poisonous to livestock and wild animals. Found a dead moose the other day south of here."

"Mind if we talk to Samuel?" asked Tom.

"What's this about?" asked Bennington. "I'm guessing not about the return of a lost stick."

"This stick was reportedly found near Robert Baxter's body along with three dead ewes," said Jake. "Curious why it would be there."

A concerned Victor Bennington turned anxious. His eyes grew wide and he said, "You surely don't think —"

"We want to ask him a couple of questions is all," said Jake.

"Okay, he's down there," Bennington said, pointing toward the far side of the valley. "We can go see him."

Bennington waved at his sixteen-year-old son and the boy waved back. The boy started walking toward them. Nobody said anything as they neared each other.

"Boy, this is Jake Summers. He ranches down Sybille Creek on the old Meadows Ranch, and this is Tom Scott, sheriff in Chugwater. They have some questions about your stick here."

The young Bennington saw his shepherd's crook and started to reach for it. "You found it. I thought it was lost forever. Where did you find it?"

"Over near Sybille Creek along with three dead ewes," answered Jake.

"Really," said Samuel who appeared surprised. "Wonder how it got over there?"

"You don't know?" asked Jake.

"No," answered Samuel. "I lost it a couple weeks ago. I thought it was gone forever."

"Where did you think you'd lost it?" asked Tom.

"I really didn't know. I keep it either in the house or the lambing shed. I went out there a couple weeks ago and it was gone."

"Disappeared?" asked Tom.

"Yes, I made it myself. See my initials here on top? I had no clue where it was."

"Did you know Robert Baxter?" asked Jake.

"Not really. I know he's a rancher that doesn't like us much. He comes up here with his men from time to time and harasses us. Word is he's working with the cattlemen's association to run us out of the territory."

"What about his daughters?"

"I met the older one once. Chester knows them . . . both of them. He's met them a few times when out hunting and searching for strays. I think the younger one is named

Virginia. He calls her Ginny."

"What about the older one?" asked Jake.

"He calls her Cathy, I think," said Samuel. "He's talked to both of them several times. Chester's kinda sweet on that older one."

"Chester . . . your other son?" asked Tom.

"Yes, he's my eighteen-year-old son. He's over . . . now where is he? I don't see him. He was leading our bellwether when you rode up. I don't see him."

"Maybe we should go find him," suggested Jake.

"He may be down by the shearing shed and pens," said Bennington. "We start shearing tomorrow. That's why we are moving the flock."

A search for Chester Bennington turned up nothing. His father was befuddled and growing angry that his oldest son had abandoned his work.

"When he turns up, tell him we want to talk," said Tom. "We're going back into town."

"Okay. But he may not be in any condition to talk when I get through with him."

As Jake and Tom rode from the valley, Jake asked, "You thinking what I'm thinking?"

"Yes, I am. I believe we should go pay the Baxter girls another visit."

Two hours later as the shadows of late

afternoon grew longer, the two friends rode through a series of swales and then over a tree-covered rise. They could see the T Bar 7 ranch house and slowly rode in that direction.

The bullet of a rifle fired from too great a distance exploded into some rocks on the trail ahead of them. Pieces of shattered rock flew in several directions. Both men jumped from their horses and pulled their rifles. They sought cover as bullets continued to fly around them.

Jake pointed, "You go toward the bunkhouse and I'll circle around toward the barn. Whoever is shooting can't fire in two directions at the same time."

"Unless there are two of them," answered Tom as he ran.

Gunfire erupted from the house with both Jake and Tom under fire. *So much for thinking we could flank them.* Jake ran for cover in a shallow ravine. *Must be at least two of them . . . Catherine and Virginia.*

Jake and Tom both returned fire, then changed positions while moving closer to the house. Someone fired from an upstairs bedroom window and Jake returned fire.

Jake heard a scream. *One of the girls. Must have been hit.*

Now the only shooting came from the

kitchen window. While Tom provided cover, Jake burst through the front door and immediately found cover. He went up the stairs and found the room into which he was shooting earlier. Catherine was lying on the floor in a small pool of blood. She was hurt but would survive. *Was she the one shooting at me from up here?*

Jake decided the real danger was downstairs in the kitchen still shooting at Tom. He went back down the stairs and carefully stepped through the kitchen door. He spotted Virginia lying dead in a pool of blood on the floor. Shards of glass from the broken window lay across her body and covered the floor around her. Chester Bennington was shooting through the window at Tom.

Bennington heard Jake and turned away from the window. A shot from Jake's rifle exploded into the center of his chest. At the same time, he exposed himself in the window and Tom shot him in the back of his shoulder. Within seconds, the young sheepherder was dead.

Jake hurried back upstairs and began helping Catherine, who whispered, "They shot me."

XV

Two days later lying in one of Doc Collins's beds with her head and shoulder heavily bandaged, the only surviving Baxter tried explaining everything. She gazed out the window into the alley beyond, and struggled to find the words. Tom and Jake waited.

"My father was so mean to all of us but especially my mother. She tried protecting Virginia and me but was abused even more because she interfered. We all wanted him gone."

"What about the plugged rifle?" asked Tom.

"Virginia plugged it. I didn't know until after Austin was killed. She told me she thought it would look like an accident and none of us could be blamed. She took his rifle and filled the barrel with mud, then wiped it clean before putting it back in his scabbard.

"She figured Father would pull the trigger eventually. After Austin was killed, she was upset. Not about his dying but how her plan had failed. I kept warning her to stop trying to kill Father. I even suggested we come talk to Sheriff Scott about father's abuse but she refused."

"It never crossed your mind that one day

your father might use that rifle to shoot at your friend Nelson and he'd die trying?"

"No! No, of course not. It was Virginia."

"What about the hemlock?" Jake asked. "You tried to poison him."

"Yes and no," she replied. "Virginia blackmailed me into trying. She knew about Nelson and I so she threatened to tell Father about us if I didn't get some hemlock to poison him. But I changed my mind and went back to get rid of the food."

"Your father already knew about you and Riley. What difference did it make if Virginia merely confirmed what he already knew?"

"I don't know." Catherine feigned confusion.

"Why didn't you just throw the hemlock away?" asked Jake.

"I was going to but I didn't get a chance."

"What happened to your mother?"

"Virginia poisoned her. Just before she shot me, she told me Mother had found out about her seeing Chester Bennington. She was scared Mother would tell our father. He would have killed Chester for sure. After I went outside to follow Father, Virginia fed some of the poisoned food to Mother, who had come downstairs. But I didn't know so I felt responsible."

"Did you and your mother get along?"

interjected Tom.

Catherine hesitated, "I guess. She thought I was too young to be seeing anyone seriously. She didn't understand."

"Did you argue about it?" asked Jake.

"Sometimes."

"You felt she was wrong. You two had some big fights. Is that true?" asked Jake.

"Yes, I guess. She and Father had no right telling me who I could see."

"And the missing nitroglycerin pills," Jake continued.

"Virginia read somewhere about the dangers of taking too much medicine. She found his bottle of pills sitting on the dresser in his bedroom. She smashed them up into powder and put them in his canteen. Every drink of water pushed him one step closer to dying. She even left a few in the bottle so he wouldn't notice."

"She told you all this?" asked Jake. "Before she shot you."

"Yes!"

"Didn't you recently see Doc Collins in the general store and ask him what would happen if someone took too much heart medicine?"

"Yes, I asked him because Father wanted to know."

"Why do you think your sister wanted to

kill your father so badly that she kept trying?" asked Tom. "She was only sixteen."

Catherine took a sip of water from a cup on her bed stand. "She was afraid Father would find out about her liking a sheepherder. She was crazy. She met Chester while she was out riding one day. He was hunting those smelly animals. She got all googly-eyed telling me about meeting Chester . . . telling me how mature and handsome he was. It was sickening."

"You didn't approve?"

"He was a sheepherder! Oh, my god, just the idea makes me sick."

"Did you ever meet Chester Bennington?" asked Jake.

"No! Never! I wouldn't have anything to do with someone like that. I don't care how handsome he was."

"He was handsome? Thought you'd never met him?"

"Well, I never did. That's what Virginia told me."

"But your sister didn't care if he raised sheep. She was smitten. Is that right?"

"Yes, but I don't think Chester really liked her. He was playing her."

"How would you know that?" asked Tom.

"My god, who would really like my homely, freckle-faced sister? Had to be some kind of joke."

"That doesn't answer my question, why kill your father? Why would Chester get involved if he was playing your sister?" asked Jake.

"You know how Father hated sheep and anyone associated with them. Virginia obviously saw how Father forbid me to see Nelson and figured he would do the same for her and Chester. Can you imagine his rage if he learned one of his daughters was fraternizing with someone raising sheep? Oh, my god, that's disgusting thinking about it."

"Sounds like you were opposed to her seeing a sheep person as well. Is that right?" asked Jake.

"This is cattle country, Mr. Summers. You know that. We can't have those smelly animals ruining our grassland. Virginia should have known better. I tried to tell her. But, they were planning to run away together to California."

"Did it bother you she might be escaping from your father and his abuse and not you?" asked Jake.

"I don't know," she answered.

"Well, if they moved away, what difference would it have made to you or your father whether Chester was a sheepherder or not?"

"Just the idea of a Baxter involved with a sheep lover! Disgusting!"

"Do you know what happened the day your father died?" Jake asked.

"Not much. Apparently, the water in his canteen was poisoned with his nitroglycerin pills. She and Chester must have figured the overdose would be enough to kill him. But when they followed him to make sure he was dead, they found him still alive. He was confused and incoherent but alive. Chester used a shepherd's crook to grab Father by the neck and yank him from the saddle. Chester hit him with a large rock to make it look like he'd accidentally fallen from his horse and hit his head. They forced to him to chew on some chokeberry leaves that grow up there. A few sheep had already died eating the stuff."

"How do you know?" asked Jake.

"Know what?"

"How did you know there were dead sheep up there?"

"Virginia told me."

"Did your sister know chokecherry leaves were so poisonous?"

"I don't know. It was Chester's idea."

"She tell you that?"

Catherine hesitated before saying, "Yes, just before she shot me."

326

"That was a lot of effort to kill your father," noted Jake.

"Virginia was convinced something drastic had to be done. Every other attempt had failed."

"Seems like a lot of effort was made when your father didn't even know about Chester. Your sister must have really been worried what he'd do when he found out."

"He got what he deserved! And so did Virginia for being so naïve," exclaimed Catherine, growing angry. "Father didn't want us seeing anyone. He had no right!"

"Your father threatened to kill Nelson if he ever caught you two together. Is that right?"

"Yes. Yes, I was scared he would."

"What happened at the house before Jake and I arrived?" asked Tom.

"Chester came. He told Virginia that you and Mr. Summers were asking about the shepherd's crook. I guess they panicked thinking they were about to be caught. They were going to run. I tried stopping them. Virginia held her rifle on me. I reached out and she shot me. I don't remember much after that."

"What kind of rifle did Virginia shoot you with?"

"I don't know. I didn't notice."

"Doc Collins says the slug he took out of you was from a Winchester 1873 rifle. When I found Virginia, she was holding a Henry 1860. Don't you find that a contradiction?"

"Not really. She must have switched rifles when they started shooting at you and the sheriff."

"The Bennington boy was using a Winchester 1873 rifle but you said it was Virginia who shot you, not me. Is that right?" asked Jake.

"Yes. They must have switched rifles."

"Was your sister right-handed or left-handed?" asked Tom.

"Left-handed. Why do you ask?"

"Seems curious. She was holding that Henry in her right hand. Maybe it ended up there when she died," explained Tom.

"Young lady, you seem to remember a lot of details. Guess your sister shared a lot of information with you before she died," noted Jake, starting for the front door. "By the way, do you know how your sister was killed?"

"How would I know?" exclaimed an agitated Catherine.

"Guess you wouldn't know since you'd already been shot," said Jake. "But in case you were wondering, Doc says she'd been shot by a Henry rifle. Tom and I were both using Winchesters."

Tom looked at Jake and said, "I think that's all we need. Get some rest, Catherine."

As they started to leave, Nelson Riley entered the doctor's office with a rush. "Is she?"

Jake motioned toward the back room. "She's okay. Back there." Then he asked, "Nelson, do you know Chester Bennington?"

"Catherine introduced me to him once. But I never really knew him."

"You mean Virginia introduced you to him?"

"No, it was Catherine. I remember she and I were going to meet up on Pole Creek one afternoon and when I got there Chester and Catherine were there talking. He was up there looking for some lost sheep. She told me they had met a few times before."

"Did he find them? The sheep, that is?"

"I don't know. He didn't have any with him."

Outside, Tom glanced at Jake. "Something still eating at you?"

"Catherine knew Chester Bennington and lied about it. She was shot by a Winchester 1873 rifle like you and I were using, but the Bennington boy had one as well. And I know I hit someone in the house through the upstairs window."

"Did you find a rifle upstairs at that window?" asked Tom.

"No, but I found some .44 Henry cartridges."

"You think Catherine made up the whole story and is conveniently putting the blame on her dead sister. Maybe she had a second boyfriend?" asked Tom.

"Chester didn't come to the Baxter house to run away with Virginia. He came to get Catherine is what I believe," said Jake. "Maybe it was Virginia who tried stopping them. Maybe she was jealous. When you and I started shooting, maybe Virginia was merely in the way. She knew the truth. She was killed by either Catherine or Chester."

Jake looked toward the horizon and saw a flock of geese in their distinctive V formation flying north, signaling the end of winter. A shiver went up his back. Was it the laughter he heard from inside the doctor's office that made him shiver?

Catherine Baxter is a whole lot like her father. She's just lost her entire family and she's laughing. She's an attractive young lady who has become sole owner of the T Bar 7 Ranch. And as the late afternoon sunshine warmed his face, he whispered, "I wonder!"

ABOUT THE AUTHOR

Phil Mills, Jr. is the award-winning author of *Where a Good Wind Blows* and *Where the Wildflowers Dance.* He's also written three highly acclaimed children's books, *Bandit the Cow Dog, Mud Between My Toes,* and *Scooter: The Cow Dog.* In 2021, he was a WWA Spur Award Finalist winner for Best Storyteller/Illustrated Children's Book for *Bandit the Cow Dog* and was a WWA Spur Award Finalist in 2010 for Best Western Audiobook for *Where a Good Wind Blows.* Mills is a longtime member of the Western Writers of America (WWA) and currently serves as Vice President. He is also a member of the Montana Historical Society, the Oregon-California Trails Association (OCTA), and the Custer Battlefield Historical & Museum Association (CBHMA). His experiences include being a small-town newspaper editor, farm magazine editor, and work with two major advertising/public relations agencies. He lives in Texas.

■ ■ ■ ■

A SCRAP ELLIOTT MYSTERY

WIND IN HIS FACE

LARRY D. SWEAZY

■ ■ ■ ■

I

I tucked the official letter in the satchel that was strung across my ride's back. This horse was a chestnut mare, untested and new to me. I named her Mavis after a girl I knew down Brownsville way. I broke that girl's heart by not askin' her to marry me. I had tried to explain to her that I wasn't the marryin' kind and all, but she took my rejection of her undying love real hard. It wasn't the first time I'd made a girl cry, but I swore it'd be the last. When it came time to name a new horse, I remembered that swear and gave the mare the moniker of a broken heart so I'd remember to keep my distance from girls who had intentions that I didn't.

When I first started out with the Rangers in the Frontier Battalion, I rode with Captain Hiram Fikes, and he'd named his horse Fat Sally after a whore he'd been in love with. I figured if such a reason was good enough for the captain, then it was good enough for me. I picked Mavis because she was fast off the hoof, but not near as fast as my previous horse, a blue roan named Missy. That horse darned near broke *my* heart when it came time for me to put her down.

I needed a good horse for the mission I was on and Mavis was all I had. I hoped she was up to the task. The fella at the livery who sold her to me assured me that the sleek mare with the diamond on her nose had a knack for endurance ridin'. I 'spect I would be the judge of that, but the fella had a good reputation when it came to horses, so I took his word, and we'd exchanged an equitable amount of valuables to close the deal. I'd rather have a tooth pulled than go horse tradin'.

The sights and smells of Austin swirled around me so thick I couldn't wait to get on the trail. I don't know how folks tolerate city life all packed together so close with loads of horse shit in the streets and the river filled with excrements of all kinds. I wouldn't take a bath downstream of the city if I had to. I like stinky baths about as much as I like lovelorn girls.

Once I was sure the satchel was tucked in tight, I seated myself on my well-worn saddle, ready to ride out of town. I looked back at the state capitol building, one last time. I'd heard it called a giant corncrib with a pumpkin for a dome, and that's exactly what the building looked like to me. But I was in no mood to disparage the place. I was thrilled that a fella like me could come and go in the halls of power unnoticed and not judged poorly. Not bad for an orphaned boy from East Texas who didn't even complete the sixth grade. I kept my glee to myself, all things considered, since those of us who were Rangers still mourned the recent death of the adjunct general, John B. Jones. A set of first instructions to the company captains of the Rangers from the new general, Wilburn Hill King, was in my satchel. My charge was to deliver a letter to Captain Samuel "Soft Voice" McMurry, the commander of Company B. It was a two-hundred-mile ride almost due north, through Dallas, and on to Garland to make the delivery.

I was lightened by news of the journey to know that I would be able to stop at my Aunt Callie's boardin' house in Dallas. It would be nice to see a bit of family and rest my boots in a familiar place for an hour or two. If Mavis was the horse I thought she was, I'd be there in five days, six at the most.

I was as bereft as anybody else over the

loss of General Jones, but I did hold a slight grudge again' him. I'll admit I was tender as new buffalo grass when I took to bein' a Ranger back in '74. I couldn't grow a mustache like I got now unless I was standin' in the shade with a dirty lip. I had a lot of growin' and learnin' to do back then, but I wouldn't admit it. I served my time under another fine and deceased captain, Leander McNelly, and then I went on to ride with Captain George Baylor, and a whole lot of good fellas in between and beyond. I know some Rangers had bad reputations and I suppose some of them earned their stains, but I took a lot of lessons off the good ones. No matter how hard I tried, no matter how hard I worked, though, General Jones wouldn't give light to my earnest efforts. I could never gain the stripes to earn a promotion. Once I accepted my fate and digested the bitter truth that I would never become a captain, I went on to become a courier, a position that suited me like the good and worn saddle I sat on.

I took a slow trot at first as I turned away from the capitol, keepin' up with the traffic of horses, wagons, and buggies. The weather had been rainy of late, and the street was muddy, thick as a Mexican stew. I was in a hurry, but I wasn't about to risk the legs of my ride. I didn't know Mavis all that well, though she didn't seem to mind settin' her hooves to anything wet. The mare was sure-footed and carefree, which was a comfort as far as I was concerned, but I hoped she liked runnin' long distances like the livery man said. Boy, my Missy sure did.

A train whistled in the distance, comin' into the station. I wondered, as I made my way out of Austin, why I had been chosen for the task of delivery instead of sendin' another man on iron wheels and steam. Delivery of the letter would have been faster. A telegraph, too. But I didn't question the powers that be. I learned a long time ago to mind my mouth when it came to such things. Men in suits had their reasons for doin' what they did. I was the courier and nothin' more. Whatever the case, I was gonna deliver the letter to Captain McMurry no matter what. I was lookin' forward to gettin' on the trail and being by myself. I had been confined in the city for too long. Besides, bein' on the trail with Mavis would be a whole lot better than bein' stuck in a stinky train car with cryin' babies and grumpy old men to talk to.

It didn't take long to break free of the heavy traffic and the population that came with it. With Austin behind me, the trail became narrower and more compact. I felt like I could breathe again away from all the hubbub of the city. The hills were a welcome sight, and the springs bubbled so clear you could see twenty feet to the bottom. Best of all, I could give Mavis her head and let her run. That horse seemed happier than I'd seen her the whole time we'd spent together in Austin, which lightened my spirit as I settled in for the long ride ahead.

II

It took me two days to reach Waco. I rested Mavis a bit and poked around town, mindful to behave myself. I liked fun as much as the next fella, but my days in saloons and cattin' around were reserved for days off, not when I was on a mission. I'd learned the hard way that business and pleasure were somethin' I'm not good at muddlin' together. Folks get wind that you're a Ranger then all the sudden some fella bigger'n you are has somethin' to prove, then I have to go and show him why my nickname is Scrap. I might be a bit on the short and thin side, but that don't mean a tall boy should underestimate the hurt my knuckles can inflict. I've been fightin' for my way ever since I was old enough to stand. If somethin' knocked me down, I was too stubborn to stay on my butt. There have been times when I should have let things go, but those times were nothin' but lessons. I'll be the first one to admit I got a bit of a temper. Bein' on the ride like I am, like I have been since takin' up with the Rangers, I've gathered a collection of black eyes that's worthy of the finest art museum in Paris, France, if'n I say so myself.

I liked Waco well enough, but it was goin' through a growin' spurt and was on the verge of becomin' a big city. I heard tell that more than fifty thousand bales of cotton were bein' shipped through the town every year on the Waco and Northwestern railroads. I couldn't imagine such a thing, but the business and the railroads brought with them decent stables and a couple of fine hotels; one I was glad to lay my head in. The Harlow had a restaurant on the first floor, and a host of rooms to let on the second. All told there were twelve rooms in the hotel, with a bath and a barber across the street. It was fancier than the usual places I took a flop at, but I wasn't footin' this bill. This was bein' paid for by the Rangers. Who was I to argue about sleepin' on a clean featherbed instead of a mattress packed with straw?

After walkin' around town to work out the stiffness from the two-day ride, I headed back to the hotel for dinner. From there, I planned on risin' with the roosters and gettin' back on the trail to head north.

It was late in the evening when I got to the restaurant, and I was greeted by a short black man with hair so white it looked like every curl had come from the cotton field instead of growin' on his head naturally. He said his name was Clyde. His clothes were a lot nicer than mine and that set me on edge straightaway. Clyde wore a black wool suit free of any lint, a crisp starched white shirt, and a black string tied as perfect as it could be at the base of his throat. He held his shoulders square and his spine looked straight as the corner of a building. I thought he might be a little haughty actin', but I knew better than to say such a thing out loud. I learned the hard way not to offend no man in a restaurant, 'less they spit in your food when you wasn't lookin'.

"Dining alone this evening, sir?" Clyde said. We were both the same height. He looked me straight in the eyes knowin' full well what the answer to his question was before he asked it.

"Yes," I said.

"This way."

I followed Clyde like we was attached to each other by a chain. I felt out of place, and regretted that I hadn't visited the bath-house across the street and put on new duds before steppin' foot into the restaurant. Clyde pulled out my chair and I sat down feelin' like every eye in the place was on me. I'm no ill-mannered fella. I've been in fancy places before, so I've got a set of manners about me. But there was somethin' about this man and this restaurant that set my nerves on fire. It felt like he was lookin' down on me, to be honest, and I don't know a man who likes that kind of feelin' whether it's true or not.

"He won't be dining alone," a woman's voice said from behind me.

It was a familiar voice. I whipped my head around, shocked to see Mavis Lee Bowen standin' in the midst of the restaurant with every set of eyes focused square on her instead of me. There wasn't an empty table in the place. Folks liked a drama as much as they liked a good Delmonico steak, especially if it came free with their dinner.

"If the gentleman doesn't mind," Mavis continued, locking eyes with me.

Her eyes were blue as the jewels around her neck, sapphires, I think they were called. At one time, those eyes could make me melt like ice cream in the sun. Mavis Lee was a beauty. That beauty. The one from Brownsville that I named my horse after. She was stuffed in a lighter blue dress that showed all of her curves, which was in all the right places. Not in a trampy way, but in a sophisticated way. Her blond locks tumbled over her shoulder and reached halfway to her waist. Even with the muted lighting in the restaurant, her hair glowed like it had been dipped in pure gold. I was thinkin' I'd been a fool to let her slip through my fingers. I ain't seen a woman as beautiful since I left Brownsville. Could be 'cause I quit lookin', or it might be that none other existed. I was drownin' in a mud puddle full of regret.

It was easy to tell that somethin' had changed about Mavis Lee. She had always liked finer things, and that was one of the reasons why I had broke it off with her. I knew I couldn't keep her happy on the wages I made as a Ranger. I didn't know how to do anything else. I didn't want to do anything else. I was short a few head of cattle to say the least. I knew better than anyone that I wasn't the kind of man to keep her in the satin and ribbons she was used to. It wasn't like she had come from a whole lot of money herself. Her folks weren't wealthy by any means, but her pa had been a lawyer in Brownsville, so somebody was always tradin' a chicken or a dress for his services. It sure did look like she'd struck a vein of somethin' sparkly after her and I had parted ways, though. Those jewels around her neck looked like they would have cost me ten years' worth of wages.

My mouth went dry. "Of course, I don't mind," I said, standin' up.

Mavis Lee smiled, and Clyde seated her with a smirk on his smooth face. He hurried off as we sat down. I was glad of that. We still had everyone else's attention, though.

"Well, isn't this a surprise?" she said. "What are you doing in Waco, Robert Earl?"

Mavis Lee never called me Scrap. She'd always been too formal for that.

"Ranger business," I said. A waiter appeared out of the same door Clyde had disappeared into. He was a black fella, too, dressed the same way as Clyde, only a little taller and a little younger. His hair looked like black cotton shorn short to the skull. He filled our empty glasses with water without askin'. Everyone else in the restaurant went back to their business, talkin' low and responsible. It all sounded like chiggers hissin' to me. I knew they was talkin' about us. I'm not sure why that annoyed me, but it did.

"I assumed as much. Some things never change." Mavis Lee carried a hand purse, or a clutch, if that was what it was called. It sat in her lap and she stared at it longer than was normal.

"You're the last person I expected to see here, especially this far north. You're a long way from Brownsville, Mavis Lee. What brings you to Waco?" I said.

She sighed in a such way that it sounded like a little bird flutterin' away. It was like she was dyin' for me to ask her that question, so in a swift, calculated move, she placed her left hand on the table so the light from the candle would glint off the wedding ring on her left hand. "My husband has business here."

I suppose I should have expected her to find another man, to fall in love all over again, but I had imagined her never mendin' her broken heart over me, swoonin' like the girl left behind, an old maid in trainin'. Turns out I was the one pinin' for her instead of the other way around.

The Mavis Lee that sat before me was more mature, aged in a desirable way, even though she was ten years my junior. Just about everything about her had changed, and I wasn't sure that it was for the better. Whatever innocence she'd had about her had fallen off her like dried-up old skin. She had the eyes of an ambitious cat instead of the doe-eyed girl I had once knowed.

"Congratulations," I said. "Where's the lucky man this evenin'? I sure would like to meet him." I looked around the dining room, lookin' for her absent husband. I was in no hurry to lay my eyes on him, to be honest, but I didn't want Mavis Lee to know that.

She had taken a drink of water and sat her glass down next to mine. "He took ill upon our arrival. I hated to leave him in our room. He was sleeping, and between me and you, I'm glad of his lack of energy and sour stomach. I spied you from the balcony riding away from the hotel. I wasn't sure that it was you at first, but I went and asked the desk clerk, and he confirmed that my eyes had not failed me. I couldn't let the opportunity pass without saying hello to you, now could I? That would be rude."

"If you say so."

"I don't know that I believe you or not, Robert Earl."

"Well, I didn't know that I would ever see you again, Mavis Lee, and I sure wasn't expectin' to see you here."

She feigned standin' up. "I can leave if that's what you want."

"No, ma'am. Please sit back down. Of course, you're a sight for these tired eyes of mine. You look more beautiful than ever." I was tuned into the audience we had and was as embarrassed as much as I was unnerved.

Mavis Lee settled herself back in the chair and smiled at the compliment. She took a drink of water to wet her throat. She had picked up mine by mistake, but I didn't say nothin'.

"I wasn't expecting to see you, either," she said. "I thought of writing you to tell you of my good fortune, but I thought better of it. I didn't want to pour salt on the wound."

I scooted forward in my chair and was about to ask, what salt? I had broken it off with her, not the other way around. But I kept my mouth shut. I wasn't about to be cross with Mavis Lee in public. Or in private, for that matter. Not on purpose, anyways.

"Now," she said. "what kind of Ranger business brings you to Waco?"

"I'm passin' through."

"It must be important if you're staying *here*."

"I guess it is. I'm a courier for the adjunct general is all."

"I hoped you'd be a captain by now."

"I like my duties just fine. I rode with a company for a long time. Had me some real adventures. I sure did. I 'spect I've traveled this great state of Texas more than most men can brag about. I can't complain. And I don't want to. I like my life the way it is, Mavis Lee."

Without warning, she reached over and touched my hand. I didn't have the good sense to pull it away. "I didn't mean anything by it, Robert Earl. You don't have to get so defensive. I always thought you were captain material is all. A born leader of men. It was only by a stroke of bad timing that you weren't born early enough to show your skills in the War Between the States. I bet you would have been a captain. Maybe more. You charge into a situation and always come out of it with a win on your side. I always liked that about you. Once you get a hold of something you never let go. Perhaps you only needed a strong woman to prop you up when the need arose." Then she pulled her hand off of mine, sweeping the napkin in front of her off the table. Bein' the gentleman I aspired to be, I leaned down to pick it up.

Our eyes were hooked together so fierce when I settled back in my chair that the whole room had disappeared. It was like we was alone in a cave with only a candle between us. I knew we both could feel the heat. Sad thing was, we weren't payin' attention to anything else. Especially the man who had walked into the restaurant and parked himself right behind Mavis Lee.

"There you are," the man said. "I woke up to find you gone. Are you going to introduce me to this man, Mavis Lee, or must I make the introduction myself?"

III

Mavis Lee's face went as white as the napkin on the table. She looked over her shoulder to the man, then back to me. "This is my friend, Robert Earl Elliott. I was as surprised to see him here as he was to see me. I thought it would be rude not to say hello."

"Your friend?" the man said. He didn't believe her or like the looks of me from the tone in his voice. He wore a hateful look in his eye that I'd spied more times in my life than I cared to admit. A stink eye like that was usually followed up with the throw of a punch. I started gettin' myself ready for the inevitable.

I stood up, and said, "I'm assumin' you're Mavis Lee's new husband. Won't you join us so I can buy you dinner to celebrate your union?" I tried to sound as sophisticated as Mavis Lee and her new husband looked. I wasn't bein' generous, though. The last thing I needed was word to get back to Austin that I had caused a ruckus in Waco, that I went fist to fist with a man I didn't know. I still harbored hopes of a promotion to captain, if I said the truth aloud. Mavis Lee's belief in me had poked a sleepin' bear. She had always had a way of doin' that to me. I had tried to deny my ambitions to avoid any future disappointments. I guess there was no way around what I really wanted, even though I'd settled myself to bein' a lowly courier.

The man, who looked to be my age or older, didn't accept my offer right away. He stared at me, sizin' me up, lookin' for a reason not to believe me. I think he'd expected fisticuffs, too, discoverin' his wife sittin' with a stranger. I can't say I'd blame him, especially if a man was lucky enough to have a wife as purty as Mavis Lee.

"I mean you no trouble, friend," I said, aware that I was the center of attention again. Clyde the waiter stood at the entry of

351

the kitchen like a bobcat ready to pounce, or call for help if a fight broke out. I figured he might have a derringer of some kind tucked inside that uniform of his somewhere — if they let black folks carry guns in Waco. I didn't know, and I wasn't about to ask.

Mavis Lee sat with pursed lips and downcast eyes. She couldn't bear the stares or the commotion. I had to do whatever I could to make her obvious embarrassment go away.

I walked over to the man and extended my hand. He was taller than me and thin as a young oak tree. His eyes were set back a bit, and they was bloodshot, maps of a bender, or like Mavis Lee had said, a sickness of some kind showin' itself from the inside out. His face was the color of Clyde's hair, pale, drained white, and his skin was shiny with sweat. He smelled sour, and at that moment, I wasn't too concerned about the last time I took a bath.

I was relieved when he took my hand, shook it with as much strength as he could muster, then withdrew it with a weak sigh. "Harold Rockwell," he said. "Owner and originator of the Rockwell line of railcars." He wore a three-piece suit, the tie loose, and his shiny silver patterned vest unbuttoned. Put together I could see that Mavis

Lee's husband was a stern businessman, ridin' a modern tide of iron and steel toward wealth and fortune like I couldn't imagine. But Harold Rockwell was hardly put together. He was wrung out. I was surprised he could stand. Even his voice sounded like it was about to collapse. He was thrown together, or tore apart, I couldn't tell which.

"Nice to meet you, Harold," I said. "Why don't you sit yourself down and have a drink of water. Or somethin' stiffer. You sure look like you could use it." I went to pull out the chair I was sittin' in, and took my eyes off of him for a second. By the time I turned back to him, Harold Rockwell had started to wither to the floor like someone had come up and stole his backbone out from under his skin. He hit the floor like a snake dropped from a tree.

A woman screamed, and a squad of men stood up to help, to see what was happenin', all the while I was tryin' to reach Harold and save him from smashin' his head against the hardwood floor. I failed at my task, but from the looks of things, Harold didn't feel a thing when he hit the ground. His eyes were in the back of his head, and his tongue was sticking out the side of his mouth. He had bit his lip when his skull collided with the floor. Blood erupted out of the man with the force of vomit. Another woman screamed. I think she might have even fainted, because I could have swore I heard someone else thud to the floor. Or maybe I was hearin' things. It was all a mess of unexpected confusion.

"I'm a doctor," a man said as he pushed through the crowd toward Harold. I stood up to allow the mousy little man some room to help. I was hot, sweatin' myself, surrounded like I was by the mass of restaurant customers who stood around Harold tryin' to see what was going on.

The doctor went down on one knee and pulled out a bottle, popped it open at a distance from himself, and waved it under Harold's nose. "Smelling salts," he muttered. There was no reaction, so he closed the bottle, put it back in his pocket, and felt at Harold's neck. After a few attempts to find somethin' of value, he shook his head, then reached over and closed the man's eyes. "He's dead," he said.

A chorus of gasps echoed throughout the room. I withheld my own bout of shock. All I could think about was Mavis Lee. I turned to find her in the crowd, turned to try and offer her any comfort I could. But she was nowhere to be seen. There wasn't even a whiff of her toilet water left hangin' in the air. And no one seemed to be the least concerned that the dead man's wife had suddenly vanished. No one but me.

IV

I pushed my way through the crowd and ran out of the restaurant as fast as I could. The street was busy with the evenin's last bit of traffic. The boardwalk was full of people every way I looked. The light was dim, gray, and washed out. It was like the world was covered in shadows on purpose. I stopped in the middle of the street, not sure whether to run right or left. Neither way looked promisin'. There was no sight of Mavis Lee. My heart sank. I had expected to see her outside, in shock, gaspin' for fresh air, hopin' none of what had happened inside was real.

A heavy-duty wagon pulled by a team of Springfield mules about ran me over. The teamster hollered and cussed at me as he passed. He had a load of grain in the bed of the wagon, with most of it covered by a tarp. I wondered if Mavis Lee could have been hidin' in a wagon, escapin' Waco unseen? Then I wondered why she would do such a thing? How could I not? I felt bad about it, I sure did, but I couldn't make no sense of what had happened. Why would a newlywed woman rush out of a place if her husband fell ill, or lay dying on the floor? Wouldn't she rush to his side and profess her undying love for him as he departed this world? Those words would be what I would want to hear before I died. But that's not what happened. That's not what had happened at all. Mavis Lee had ran out, disappeared, fled like she was guilty of somethin' instead of lovin' someone enough to see it through to the end.

Clyde and the other waiter had ushered everyone out of the dining room by the time I returned inside the restaurant. Everyone but me and the doctor. As it turned out, we had a mutual acquaintance. This doctor, his name was Everett Reilly, knew Doc Tinker, one of the fellas who'd rode with Leander McNelly and his company of Rangers back when we all first started out with the Frontier Battalion. Doc Tinker never went to a medical school but had the gift of healin'. This fella, Doc Reilly, on the other hand, had gone to some fancy school back east in Boston. He had a thick accent like I ain't never heard before and a steel rod for a backbone. Him and a dowdy skunk had more in common than me and him did —

other than starin' at a dead man neither of us knew. Now that the room was clear, I figured I could ask him some questions while we waited for the sheriff and the undertaker to show up.

"How you think he died, Doc?" I had to tilt my head down when I asked the question. The man was about as tall as a broomstick, dressed in a natty blue checkered wool suit, and wore black store-bought shoes so shiny I could have shaved in the reflection.

"Well, it could be anything. His heart might have gave out or he might have been suffering from a long illness. Hard to say without information of some kind."

"Mavis Lee didn't say nothin' about him bein' sick for a long period. She said they was in town to do some business, and that he took ill when they'd arrived. They'd made a long trip up from Brownsville. It don't seem to me like a sick man would take on such a journey."

"Depends on what his business was."

"You could be right, but it still don't measure up to me."

"And you're passing through?"

I didn't like the tone of his question. "I'm on Ranger business."

"Texas Rangers?"

"What other kind of Rangers are there?"

357

"Arizona Rangers to start."

"Texas Rangers. I'm on business direct from the general. Why?"

"Just asking. That explains how you knew Verlyn Tinker. Fine man, he was. We crossed paths a few times, and I taught him some binding skills. Such a shame he never had any real training. He had talent."

"Doc Tinker sewed me up more than once, God rest his gentle soul."

"Yes, of course. Why do you have interest in this man's death? And who is this Mavis Lee you speak of?"

"You ask more questions than I do."

"That's no answer." The doc looked to the door, then took his gold pocket watch out and checked the time. Once he was assured of the hour, he knelt down and took a closer look at the deceased, Harold Rockwell. He put his nose almost directly over Harold's nose, hovered there for a long second, then looked up at me. "Did this man have anything to eat while he was here?"

I shook my head. "No, he walked in, saw me with Mavis Lee, introduced himself after a tense moment, then collapsed. He didn't have time to stick a bite of food in his mouth. He didn't even sit down at the table."

"That's odd," the doc said. "He smells of garlic."

I shrugged. I didn't know what that meant.

Doc Reilly stood up and looked to the door again. "This Mavis Lee wouldn't be his wife, would she?"

"Yes, she is. They are newlyweds from what I was told."

"And how did you know this woman?"

"We, uh, um, were fond of each other in Brownsville, but that's been broke off for a while. Neither of us knew the other was here in Waco. Our dinner meetin' was a coincidence. I didn't even know she was married, or within a hundred miles of here for that matter."

"You'll need to tell that to the sheriff. About you and this Mavis Lee, I mean. I hope you can prove what you just said. Where is she, by the way?"

"I don't know. Once you said this man was dead, I looked for her and she was gone. I have no idea what happened to her. I think she might be distraught."

"Or on the run."

"Why would you say a thing like that?"

"Because I believe this man has been poisoned. That's why. He smells of garlic, which might be arsenic."

V

Sheriff Harper J. MacDonald flew into the restaurant like an annoyed wasp. His portly face was as red as his hair — once he took off his hat at the sight of the dead man — and his manner of dress was disheveled; crooked, one button off a hole, like he'd had to put on his shirt and badge in a hurry. "What the hell happened here?" he said to the doc.

"Man fell over dead is what happened," Doc Reilly said. "And I have reason to believe he was poisoned."

"On purpose?" The sheriff looked past Doc to me, and said, "Who are you?"

"Scrap Elliott. Robert Earl Elliott."

"Says he's a Texas Ranger," Doc said.

"That true, Scrap Robert Earl Elliott?" Harper MacDonald looked me over like he was sizin' up a piece of beef to buy and eat. "What the hell kind of name is that?"

"Yes, sir, it sure is. Been a Ranger since the start. Rode with McNelly and a few other fine captains. I'm a courier for the new general, Wilburn Hill King. My friends call me Scrap, is all. It's my nickname, and Robert Earl is my given name. I'm on a special mission."

"Are you now?" MacDonald said. "And

what kind of mission is that?"

"What does that have to do with this dead man, here?" I wished I wouldn't have said it, but I did.

"I'm the one askin' questions, now, aren't I?" the sheriff said.

"Yes, you are. My apologies. I'm a little upset is all. I didn't mean nothin' by it." The last thing I wanted to do was get the sheriff all riled up at me and put off on his bad side. I already had the feelin' that the doc didn't believe that I was tellin' him everything I knew. It wouldn't take much for them two to get together and pull me head and foot into their sights. Somebody had to be held accountable for poisonin' Harold Rockwell if the doc was right about that, and there wasn't no one in close proximity to blame but me. "I'm to deliver a special letter to Captain McMurry of the Texas Rangers up Garland way," I said, standin' up as straight as I could. "The letter's from the general himself. So, I'm on a courier mission, Sheriff. I'm passin' through Waco, nothin' more. I happened to stay here and see this man come to grief, I'm sorry to say."

Before either of us could say another word, the doc jumped into the conversation. "He knew this man's wife. Had a previous dalliance with her."

"I did not say that," I protested. "I did not dalliance with Mavis Lee one time."

The sheriff shuffled between me and the doc. "I don't think you understand what the doc means. Maybe you and I should step outside so you can tell me everything you know about this dead man and his wife." Harper MacDonald looked around the empty dining room, then said, "Where is this woman?"

"She disappeared," I said. "Ran off. I think she's distraught."

"So that's what you call it," he said.

"Call what?"

"Killin' someone. Distraught ain't the right word, is it? Sounds like guilty of somethin' if I do say so myself."

"The Mavis I knowed is kind, and beautiful, and I ain't never seen her harm any living thing."

"Would you stake your life on that?" the sheriff said.

I knew what he meant. I wasn't that slow upstairs. He wanted to know if I was willin' to hang based on my assumption that Mavis Lee was innocent. "Well, sir," I finally said, "now that you put it that way, I can't say that I would."

"All right, boy," he said as he grabbed me

by the sleeve and started to pull me toward the door, "I think we need to have us a long talk."

"Who are you callin' boy?" I said. My words fell on deaf ears, and before I knew it, I was standin' outside again.

The night had gone on without me, waxin' toward true darkness as the hour grew late without my reckoning. The traffic had slowed, and the tinkle of piano keys comin' from the nearest saloon, a place called the Happy Spur, floated on the air like they belonged next to the raindrops that had started to fall. A fresh scent washed away the dust and horse smells I had noticed earlier.

"I'm gonna send a telegraph to the capitol, boy, and you better be tellin' me the straight story. You understand me?" the sheriff said.

I yanked my arm away from the man's pinch, and said, "I wish to hell you'd stop callin' me boy. I ain't one of them waiters workin' at the restaurant, and it's been a long time since I wore peach fuzz on my lip. I ain't no boy. I'm a Texas Ranger, and I damn well expect to be treated like one. I ain't got no reason to lie to you."

Harper MacDonald smirked as he judged the mustache I wore on my face. I'll admit it wasn't no hedge, but with some wax I could make it as stylish and curved as the next man's. "You sure do get riled easy enough. You really want to make an enemy out of me before we get to know one another? I call everybody boy. It's a habit. I don't mean nothin' by it. Now are we gonna get square or am I gonna have to hightail you down to the jail and have an official conversation about this situation you done found yourself involved in?" The man's face relaxed and the wisdom of his wrinkles shined through, even in the dim light of the rainy evening.

We stood under a flimsy overhang, protected from the weather, but still in sight of those who passed by. Rain streamed off the roof and splashed mud onto the boardwalk. I followed suit and relaxed a bit myself. "I swear to you I had no idea Mavis Lee was in town. I ain't spoke a word to her since I left her standin' on her pa's doorstep, in tears, in Brownsville."

"You broke her heart, then."

"I thought I did."

"That ain't nothin' to be proud of, boy."

I still winced at bein' called a boy, but I let it slide by me. "I ain't proud now, and I wasn't then. I was countin' my time with Mavis Lee as a mistake. If I didn't get out of Brownsville, I was gonna end up on the wrong end of a preacher's sermon about devotion and true love, and I wasn't ready for that. Besides, Mavis Lee went off and married a rich man in my absence. I knew that was what she wanted all along. I was never gonna be a man who was comfortable in a vested suit. Just the thought of it makes me want to choke."

"So," the sheriff said, rubbin' his chin, "you left out of Brownsville and never heard a word from this Mavis Lee again? No letters, no nothin'?"

"That's right. Nothin' until I heard her voice as I sat down for my dinner this evenin'. I 'bout swallowed my tongue and quit breathin' at the sight of her."

"Why's that?"

"She was always purty, but she was dressed in fine clothes and her hair was different. I hardly recognized her. I told you, her new husband was a businessman, wealthy from the looks of it, owned a railcar company is what he told me in the last minutes of his life. That takes more dough than I can imagine in one place. Anyways, Mavis Lee, she looked like she'd done graduated from a girl to a woman if you know what I mean."

"I do."

"She sat down with me and talked low

and looked me in the eye the way she never did before. Then her husband came in and withered to the floor and died. I scrambled to help him, but I think he was dead before he hit the floor. When I looked up, Mavis Lee was gone. Disappeared. Vanished. I ran out to the street to see if I could find her, hopin' she was just gettin' a breath of fresh air, and there was no sign of her at all. I don't know what happened to her. It doesn't make no sense to me that she isn't here."

"Doc Reilly says he thinks the man was poisoned."

"I know what he said."

"This doesn't look good for your friend, Mavis Lee."

"I don't suppose it does."

"Or for you, either." Sheriff Harper Mac-Donald looked up the street, and I followed his gaze to an ornate hearse strugglin' toward us in the mud, pulled by two giant draft horses as black as the devil's soul. "That'll be Hiram Coldstone come to collect the body."

"This ain't how I expected my evenin' to go," I said.

"Well, boy, do us both a favor and don't leave town until I get to the bottom of this."

"But I'm on a mission. I can't stop my ride. I got orders. I have a letter to deliver, no ifs, ands, or buts."

"You step one foot out of Waco city limits and I'll haul your ass to jail and lock you up for as long as I can. Do I make myself clear? I don't care who you say you are, or who it is that gives you orders, I'm tellin' you not to leave this town."

I hung my head low and accepted my fate as much as I could. What other choice did I have?

VI

I didn't stick around to see the undertaker haul out Harold Rockwell's body. I skulked around town searchin' the shadows for any sign of Mavis Lee. I thought maybe she'd got spooked like a horse, you know, after hearin' a big boom of some kind. I've seen skittish creatures take a run for their life at the exposure to somethin' unexpected, so it wasn't out of the question that a woman in Mavis Lee's situation would do the same thing. I hoped she was somewhere close by, gatherin' herself so she could face the loss of her husband without showin' the world how upset she was. I didn't catch one glimpse of her. No matter where I looked, there was no sign of Mavis Lee.

I headed back to the Harlow House, not

sure of what else to do. I didn't know where else to look for Mavis Lee. I knew I had to find her. If she was innocent, I could help save her. If she was guilty of murder, then I'd have no other choice but to see her to justice.

By the time I arrived, the lobby of the hotel was as quiet as a saloon on a Sunday morning. The desk clerk looked up at my arrival, then looked back down to whatever he was readin'. I almost walked past him and went up to my room, but I remembered that Mavis Lee had asked if I was stayin' there after seein' me ride off down the street.

"Hey, friend," I said to the middle-aged man. Flecks of gray had started to sprout on his sideburns and had worked their way into his full black beard. It cascaded off his chin and onto his barrel chest. He was well-groomed, wore a white shirt, and looked at me with mild annoyance through wire-rimmed glasses.

"Good evening, sir, is there something I can do for you?" He had an accent I recognized as Scottish.

I'd rode with a man called Brian Fraser in the time of McNelly. Fraser had the temper of a bull with a thorn permanently stuck in his side. I remembered to caution myself.

The last thing I needed at the moment was to get charged by an angry Scotsman. "I was wonderin'," I said, "if you know if Mrs. Rockwell had returned to her room, this evenin'?"

"And what business of it is yours if she has?" The clerk stood up straight and closed the book he had been reading. A novel of some kind by an author, Thomas Hardy, that I had never heard of and knew nothing about. Books for readin' pleasure were expensive, and usually reserved for high-falutin' people. I admired the man for bet-terin' himself, but I didn't really like the tone he took with me. He looked at me like I was up to something nefarious, which was not the truth at all.

"I'm a friend," I said, and that was no lie.

"There was some trouble in the restaurant earlier," the man said. I knew nothing of his name. He hadn't introduced himself and there was no badge anywhere to be seen on his uniform offerin' that information.

"I was there," I said. "Sittin' with Mrs. Rockwell herself."

The Scotsman looked at me closer, then nodded. "You are the Ranger, Elliott, that she asked about earlier in the day?"

"One and the same." Now we were gettin' somewhere.

"I was on duty when the disturbance occurred." He spoke softly, but his voice rose up to the two-story ceiling without regard to his effort to quell it. He leaned forward. "The missus ran up to her room and she hasn't been seen since."

"Does Sheriff MacDonald know this?"

"Of course, he does. When they went up to the room, Mrs. Rockwell was nowhere to be found." The man looked around as if he wanted to make sure no one was listenin' to our conversation. "But he don't know about this," he said as he pulled out an envelope and handed it to me.

I hesitated before I took the envelope. It felt like I was in the middle of a secret, and I didn't like that at all. It has always been my job to be honest, uphold the law, set an example if that was possible. Bein' a Texas Ranger meant somethin' to me. I liked it when people showed respect to those of us who'd earned it by ridin' on the right rails. But I couldn't help myself. I recognized Mavis Lee's swirling, perfect script straightaway. She'd left me a note. "How come you didn't tell the sheriff about this?" I said as I took the envelope and stuck it in my pocket.

"Mrs. Rockwell paid me a handsome fee not to, and I keep my word."

"When did she give you this note?" I said,

starin' the Scotsman direct in the face, lookin' for any indication that I was bein' fooled with.

"That last time I saw her. She rushed in, stopped here, asked for an envelope and paper, which I provided, then made me an offer after she had finished her quick correspondence to you."

"Okay," I said. "Thank you." I started to walk away but stopped a few feet from the stairs. "What room was the Rockwells stayin' in?"

"Number one at the end of the hall. The presidential suite," the man said.

"All right." I still felt uncomfortable, but somehow, I was a little more at ease knowin' that Mavis Lee had left me a message of some kind. I was curious what that message was, but I wasn't gonna read it until I was in private. "Thank you for keepin' your word," I said as I hurried away.

The second floor was quiet as I topped the landing. The floor was covered with fancy rugs that were thick as a winter sheep's coat, patterned in brown and red squares. My boots made no sound when I walked on them and the light was dim. The hallway was lit with low-burnin' candles in sconces set between each room door. There were no windows that looked outside, so time stood still, and the shadows didn't change. There was no place to hide, no alcove to tuck into, no closet to wait out the sheriff, so Mavis Lee must of gone out some other way. I'd figure that out once I read the letter she left me.

I took out the brass skeleton key to my room and went in slow-like. I didn't figure anyone was waitin' to do me any harm, but all things considered, a fella can't take any chances. The room was just like I left it, everything still in its place, includin' my satchel that held the general's letter. I closed the door behind me and took a deep gulp of stale hotel room air and let it out slow to relax myself.

I stared at the letter before openin' it. A voice in my head said I should take it straight to Sheriff MacDonald and be done with it, not get involved. And I would have if this would have concerned anybody else. But it was Mavis Lee, and I didn't like the things I was thinkin' about her. Not one bit. I couldn't imagine her bein' a cold-blooded killer, someone who would poison her husband, but that sure was the way it looked to me — and the sheriff.

It was dark in the room, so I struck a match and lit a hurricane lamp that sat on the dry sink next to the bed. The curtains was pulled, but I could hear the rain still dribblin' down outside. I got a sudden chill, then went ahead and opened the letter.

Dearest Robert Earl,
    Please don't try and find me. I will be fine. I wish you a fine adieu and hope with all of my heart that you have a good life. Never forget that I loved you in Brownsville.
                                    Sincerely,
                        Mavis Lee Rockwell

I stuffed the letter back in the envelope and returned it to my pocket for safe-keepin'. Mavis Lee's words confused me even more than I already was. She was askin' me to not chase after her.

"What have you gone and got yourself into, Mavis Lee?"

This whole day had left me confounded and troubled. I didn't have an answer to my own question, but I knew one thing. The letter, written on the fly, was meant to stop me from lookin' for her. I was sure of that — and nothing else.

VII

I poked my head out the door to make sure the hallway was clear. Once I was certain no one was about, I made my way to the door of the presidential suite at the end of the hall. First thing I did was try and open the door. It was locked like I feared it would be. Next, I took out my skinnin' knife with the narrow blade and started to rattle the innards of the lock the best I could. The good thing about skeleton key locks is they are pretty darn easy to line up and pop open if you know what you're a doin'. The bad thing is that it is a noisy proposition. I didn't see that I had much choice in the matter. I figured if I was gonna go lookin' for Mavis Lee, then the best place to start was in her room. It was the last place that I knew she was at, so that was my starter. Waco's a big place and gettin' bigger every day, and I didn't know my way around, to boot. Mavis Lee could be anywhere.

I felt a little bad about not goin' to the sheriff and lettin' him know about the letter, but there really wasn't nothin' in it that would help him. It actually might make things worse for Mavis Lee the way I looked at it. She knew somethin', I just didn't know what that somethin' was. I also knew that the sheriff had told me not to leave town, which complicated my mission with the Rangers. If I didn't show up with that letter to Captain McMurry when I was expected, then my reputation as a courier would be lost. I couldn't be trusted, no matter the cause of my delay. But if I was able to find Mavis Lee and get her to tell the sheriff what she knew or confess, then maybe I'd be set free to go about my business. My motivation was partly selfish, there was no denyin' that, but I wanted to help Mavis Lee out of this mess, too. That is, if she was innocent, if she had nothin' to do with Harold Rockwell's death. There *was* a dead man to consider. A wealthy dead man from the looks of things, and that would bring problems and questions of its own. Mavis Lee was a widow, and perhaps, the inheritor of all of the man's riches. Or not. There was no way to know the legalities of their relationship. But it sure seemed odd to me that she would be the one to kill him if she expected any money to come her way after everything was settled. That didn't make sense even to a man such as me. I ain't never been around much money and wealth, so what did I know of such things? Not much, only that I knew there was a way the world of finance worked, and it seemed to me that a dead man's wife was entitled to a share of his fortune, no matter how long they had been married.

Armed with even more purpose, I jiggled

the knife and pressed on the lock with as much might as I could, and the door popped open. The hinges eeked, complainin' for oil, and I turned around to look down the hall to make sure that I was still alone, that I hadn't alerted anyone of the unlawful intrusion to the room I was makin'. No one had poked their heads out of their rooms, so I was in the clear. I slid into the suite, closed the door, and locked it behind me, as quick and quiet as I could.

The room was three times larger than where I was layin' my head and ten times fancier. The rugs were thick and the furniture heavy and hand-carved. Faces of old bearded men were chiseled into the walnut mantel, and brass lamps adorned the place. Thick red draperies hung up against the windows, which overlooked the main street. I imagined Mavis Lee seein' me ride off, squintin' to make sure it was really me. I wondered where Harold was then. His suitcase lay open on the unmade bed with the contents strewn about; ties, shirts, socks scattered as if somebody had been searchin' for somethin'. A hurricane lantern burned with whale oil on the dresser across from the bed, castin' light across the room. The flame danced a bit when I walked by, which I thought odd until I realized one of the windows was open behind the drapes. A draft climbed up my leg, and with it came the sound of rain falling steadily on the muddy street outside.

I made my way to the window with my knife still in my hand. I was figurin' it was the way Mavis Lee had escaped, but I wasn't gonna assume nothin'. Someone had saw fit to poison a man, hard tellin' what else they might be willin' to attempt.

I moved the heavy fabric, holdin' my breath at the same time, not knowin' what to expect. To my relief there was no one there, just an open window that led out to a fire escape. For some reason, Mavis Lee must of felt it was the best way to leave the hotel instead of going out through the lobby. I wondered why she would do that? Was she afraid of bein' seen? Or was someone comin' after her, and she needed a quick escape? Either way was troublin' and didn't shed any new light on her innocence or guilt. If anything, the open window made me question her even more.

Unsettled, I closed the window and moved outside of the drapes. The room was cavernous, and the bed was as big as I'd ever seen. Six people could have slept in it with comfort. I looked underneath it to make sure no one — including Mavis Lee — was hidin' there. It was void of anything but clumps of dust. From there, I went over to the suitcase and looked there, hopin' to find something that would give me some new information of some kind. I found nothing but clothes. No papers, no diary, nothin' that could tell me any more about Harold Rockwell than I already knew, which was that he liked fine clothes. Everything looked store-bought and tailored.

There was no sign of Mavis Lee anywhere in the room. No clothes, no toilet water bottles, nothin' that would suggest that there was ever a woman in the room. I had to assume she had a suitcase of her own and she took it with her when she escaped out the window. That would slow her down if it was heavy, if she had planned on a long trip. It was a curious discovery findin' nothin'.

I slid my knife back in its sheath, fixin' to give up when my eye caught a glint of glass on the floor opposite me. The flame had calmed so there were no shadows dancin' on the walls; a steady glow of calm light warmed the empty room. I moved across the room and was about to reach down when I heard someone tamperin' with the door. I had locked the door, so I had a second or two but not much more if it was the sheriff come to search the room like I had.

I found the glass — it was a small bottle without a cap on it — stuffed it in my pants pocket and disappeared under the bed. It was the only thing I knew to do, that and pull out my six-shooter and cock it just in case I needed to defend myself.

The door creaked open after a long minute and a man with heavy boots eased into the room as soft and quiet as he could. The only thing that told on him was the door closing behind him. I didn't recognize the boots, but then again I didn't pay much attention to Sheriff MacDonald's footwear when I was explainin' myself to him. These boots looked like they'd fit a shorter man. They were brief, the leather worn with the heels angled at the side and coated with mud from the street. No spurs jangled off them, so that told me he wasn't a long rider, but most likely from town. One thing that I was certain of was that the boots didn't belong to the desk clerk. Everything about that man was clean and shiny; no mud allowed.

The man walked around the room almost followin' the same track that I had. He inspected the contents of the suitcase, then went and poked his head behind the drapes, and took a long look outside. Satisfied, he came back and opened all of the drawers. I hadn't got there yet. I could see his shadow on the wall, and that told me that my assumption had been right. He was a small, bony man, unfamiliar to me. He didn't find anything in the drawers and went on to look in the small closet, then did something odd. He left. Slipped out of the room as quietly as he could without looking under the bed, which was a good thing for me. It seemed like he was lookin' for somethin' specific, a thing, not a person. If I was right, then I had to wonder what that thing was? I had to wonder if the empty bottle I'd snatched up and put in my pocket was what the man was lookin' for — and didn't find. If I was right about that, then I had more questions than I knew what to do with — and there was no one I felt like I could trust to talk things over with. Not even the sheriff.

VIII

I needed to find Mavis Lee as quick as I could, so I followed the path I assumed she'd took out of the hotel room. Instead of goin' out of the suite the way I came in, I eased out the window, and made my way down the rickety fire escape. The night was dark and soupy, what with the rain still drippin' down from the sky and all. There was no one around to be seen. The streets were vacant of traffic, and the boardwalk was like carpet rolled up and tucked away for the morrow. There was no piano tinkerin' late into the hour, nor were there laughs and cheers to accompany the absent tunes. Once darkness had fallen and the foul weather had settled overhead, the town of Waco had hunkered down for the night. I hoped that meant Mavis Lee was still in town.

I considered the timetable of events as I knew them, walked myself through the day as carefully as I could. I figured by the time Mavis Lee had run out of the restaurant, made her way to the desk clerk, wrote the note to me, then headed up to her room and escaped out of the window, it had to be near dark. The last train would have already pulled out of the station, and there wasn't a stagecoach line in the country that would schedule a drive straight into the night, rainy or otherwise. So, I had to figure that Mavis Lee was still in Waco somewhere. That was a lot of territory to cover, and to be honest, I didn't know where to start lookin'. I didn't know my way around Waco any more than I knew my way around Paris. I'd passed through the town more than once, but like I said, it was changin', growin' like a sprout of corn in the spring.

I stood next to Harlow House contem-platin' my next move, doin' my best to stay out of sight. I didn't know if the man who'd stole into the presidential suite was lurkin' around, keepin' an eye out for Mavis Lee, or anyone else for that matter. The thing was, I didn't know whose side the man was on. If he worked for the sheriff, was a deputy on a task, or if he was up to no good. I wasn't about to ask questions and give myself away. I had to think that the man in the room was lookin' for somethin' to clean up the mess that had been made. Somehow, he'd figured out that he'd left somethin' behind — and he was right. I had that somethin' — that bottle — safe in my pocket in case I was right.

At that thought, I took out the bottle, brought it up close to my eyes, and exam-ined it. The thing looked like any bottle a woman might have. It was made of dark blue glass with fancy ribs and edges. But it wasn't like any other bottle, at least that I had ever seen. I wasn't takin' no chances that it was poison, so I stuck the bottle back in my pocket and wiped my hands on my pants.

I had distracted myself from my aim, and that was tryin' to figure out where Mavis

Lee might of ran off to. I looked up and down the street, and couldn't come up with nothin', so I started thinkin' about what I knew about Mavis Lee. It only took me a second to knock my hand against my forehead. Mavis Lee's daddy had been a lawyer in Brownsville, and she'd been brought up around the law. If she was in trouble — and she sure seemed to be — then maybe the first place she'd go was to another lawyer, someone who could help her. Or maybe she would go to the telegraph office and send a telegraph to her daddy and see if he knew any lawyers in Waco.

I was proud of myself for that kind of thinkin'. Now I figured the telegraph office was a stretch because Mavis Lee would have to have a place for a telegraph to be delivered to — unless she already had a place to hide. But that might be a place to start lookin', to start askin' questions. If I came up empty there, then I'd poke around the courthouse. Lawyers gathered their offices around courts like birds built nests in cliffs overlookin' a river.

At least I had a plan. Now all I had to do was find the telegraph office.

I headed for the nearest saloon — it was the only thing that I knew would be open this late. But as I started off, I walked straight into an oncoming fist. I had been so deep in my thinkin' that I wasn't payin' attention to my surroundings. A bad habit that has cost me more than one punch in the nose.

I stumbled back from the shock of the blow and found myself flat against the wall of the hotel. Now, there ain't nothin' that gets me more riled than bein' punched in the face unawares, but there wasn't time to shake off the hit. My attacker came at me with another swing. I expected that. I staggered. I didn't fall. If I was going to attack, I had to keep on comin', which is what this feller did. I ducked in time to miss the blow. That threw his balance off some, givin' me enough time to counter with an undercut on the inside. I caught him under the chin and his teeth slammed together unexpected like. I think he bit his tongue, but I didn't wait around to find out. I hit him again with the other fist. That punch knocked the man off the boardwalk, into the street.

Rain peppered down like we was under a waterfall, gushin' from the sky unhinged. On top of the rain, it was like a black cloud had settled down to the earth, making it hard to see anything clear at all. I couldn't make out the man's features. He wore a cloak with a hood pulled up over his head.

I don't think the man figured me for a threat. He stood straight up, rubbed his cheek, and said, "You move another inch and you're a dead man." He was short, as tall as a fence post, if that. I assumed he was the man who was inside Mavis Lee's room.

I heard the cock of a gun, and since I ain't no fool, I did exactly what the man told me to do. My hand was already at my side, and it wouldn't take much for me to match his move and pull my own gun on him. But I didn't have to. A burst of wind whooshed up the street hard enough to blow the rain sideways. For a second, I lost sight of the man. And then when I was able to see clear enough, he was gone, like he'd never been there before.

I heard a horse take off at a run not too far away, and I figured that was my attacker, makin' a go of it while he had a chance. The last thing I was gonna do was chase after a stranger who'd jumped me. If he had a message to give, well, I heard it loud and clear. Somebody was after me, didn't want me out and about. That didn't take much to figure. Still, I made my way back under the overhang of the hotel to gather myself. I wasn't gonna make myself an easy target, and I had to consider that the man might be a killer. If that was the case, then that might have meant that Mavis Lee was innocent.

No one but the barkeep was in the saloon. He was a thin old guy with a scraggly gray beard and a bald head. He wore a dingy white apron over an even dingier white shirt. He scowled at me when I pushed through the batwings.

"We're closed." He might as well of told me to skedaddle, I wasn't welcome there, but I didn't interrupt my purposeful stride up to the bar. That only made the scowl deeper. That old man had a talent for holdin' hate in his eyes, I'll tell you that.

"I ain't here for a beer," I said.

He straightened up. "This ain't that kind of place."

I didn't know what the heck he was talkin' about at first, then it dawned on me that he thought I was lookin' for a woman. I chuckled, and that made the man even madder.

"What the hell is so funny about that?" he said.

"You don't make friends out of strangers easy, do you, mister?"

A rag had been draped over his shoulder, but he ripped it down like he was gonna swing it at me and crack me upside the head. I stepped back. My jaw, and my pride, was still hurt from gettin' jumped outside the Harlow House. I wasn't in no mood to take a whuppin' from this old fella. I raised my hands in surrender and he stopped whatever it was he was gonna do. He glared at me like an old bear who'd been woke up early from a winter nap. "What the hell do you want? I got things to do," he said.

"All I need to know is where the telegraph office is," I said.

"That all?"

"I ain't fool enough to ask for anything else."

"By the look of your face you might be in need of a doctor."

"Doc Reilly? No, I don't need him."

"Who's that?" the man said, puzzled by the name. "I ain't never heard of no Doc Reilly."

"There's probably a lot of doctors in this town." I rubbed my jaw, and it felt sore. Must have been marked red, or bruisin' up since the barkeep made a note of my face. It was a familiar condition for me.

"I know all of the doctors in this town. All four of them," the barkeep said. "And as far as I know, there ain't one named Reilly. Ain't gonna be a whole lot of folks have much faith in an Irishman tendin' to their ills. Except maybe the Irish themselves, but they keep pretty much to themselves. Maybe they got a Doc Reilly, I don't know."

"Short, mousy man," I said. "A fancy dresser who takes charge easy."

The barkeep shrugged and shook his head. "Don't know 'im."

I was startin' to get confused. I was sure as I was standin' in a saloon that the man in the restaurant had said he was a doctor. He sure did act like one. Looked like it, too. "Well," I said, "maybe this Doc Reilly was passin' through. I met him at the Harlow Hotel."

"Anything is possible." The barkeep studied me a little closer, then said, "The telegraph office is around the corner, two blocks down on the right. Cole Haymer is the operator. You best get down there, but he might have already left for the night, considerin' the weather and all."

"You're sure you ain't never heard of this Doc Reilly?"

"Why would I lie to you, boy?"

Why in the hell did everybody have to go and call me boy? I grew this danged mustache so folks would take me serious-like, see me as older and more mature, but it sure wasn't workin'. I guessed I was gonna have to grow a beard. One way or the other,

I was gonna have to do somethin' so people respected my age. I couldn't help it if I looked younger than I was.

I swallowed my anger and my pride again and nodded. "Thank you, then. I best get to the telegraph office." I spun around and headed for the door, uncertain about what I'd heard, but considerin' everythin' that had happened since Harold Rockwell had taken a nosedive at dinner, I had to consider there was somethin' goin' on that went beyond Mavis Lee. Someone had come into her room lookin' for somethin', then I'd been jumped outside the hotel, and now I learned that the doctor who said he was a doctor might not be a doctor at all. If I didn't care for Mavis Lee like I did, I'd have lit out on my horse, got on with my mission, and never looked back.

IX

The lamps were still burnin' in the telegraph office. I ran inside in a rush and gave the man behind the counter a start that caused him to jump and reach for whatever it was he had hid to defend himself.

"I'm sorry, I'm sorry," I said, puttin' my hands in the air so he could see them plain and without threat. "I don't mean you no

389

harm." The last thing I wanted to do was get cut in half by a scattergun.

The agent looked me up and down and must have figured I was tellin' the truth because he stood up straight and relaxed. He was a middle-aged man with wiry hair under his cap startin' to go gray, and he had easygoin' blue eyes that suggested he had a decent demeanor about him. But his reaction told me he had a set of nerves that could spur him to action, if needed. Must have been robbed at one time or another, and not taken it well. That happens to some men. I would have to be cautious and gentle-like with this one.

"I'm about to close up," the man said. He reached down, picked up a piece of paper and a pencil, and handed both of them toward me, assuming I wanted to send somethin'. "Here you go."

I shook my head. "I ain't here to send no message. Not tonight, anyways."

"What can I do for you then?" He put the paper back where he got it from.

"I have a couple of questions is all." I walked toward the counter, wet as a cat thrown out in the rain to fend for itself, and just as uncomfortable. There wasn't a part of me that was dry, and my face had started to swell. I could feel the tightness in my skin pullin' again' my face like leather shrinkin' in the sun. It felt like everythin' inside my cheek was tryin' to pop out from inside of me. I knew the feelin' all too well. I must of looked a sight by the expression on the man's face once he settled down and trusted I wasn't there to cause him any trouble.

"I'm not sure I can help you," he said.

I stopped opposite him and we stared at each with the counter between us. "Did a woman with gold locks of hair, wearin' a blue dress and jewels the same color around her neck, come in here this evenin' and send a message to Brownsville?"

"I can't tell you that."

"Would it help if I told you I was a Ranger, a Texas Ranger — since there seems to be Arizona Rangers, too — and I'm on a mission to figure out who killed a man at the Harlow House?"

"Ain't never heard of a Ranger doin' law work other than quellin' feuds," the man said, "and running the Comanche out of the state, thank you very much. Sheriff MacDonald tends to all those kinds of incidents from what I understand."

He had me stripped bare of the truth before I could even get started. I figured this was gonna be tricky, findin' out if Mavis Lee had sent a message to someone. "It would be a great help to me, and to the Rangers, if you would answer my question. I've been ridin' with the Rangers for a long time. Served under McNelly, faced down the Kiowa, too, in the early days. I was there at the start with the Frontier Battalion." The telegraph man seemed to appreciate the Rangers, unlike some folks, and I needed every edge I could get. He wasn't buyin' that I had any right to investigate a killin', and he was right about that. I was supposed to be in my hotel room, restin' up for my ride north to deliver the letter to Captain McMurry. I wasn't supposed to be knee-deep in mud, traipsin' after Mavis Lee, tryin' to prove her innocence or guilt, one or the other. But that's what I was doin'. Whether it was right or wrong, I couldn't say for sure. My gut told me that Mavis Lee needed my help, and that's all it took for me. "Now," I went on, "I ain't gonna beg you to tell me if this lovely lady came in here, but I'm bettin' if she did, you'd remember her. She's about the purtiest thing I've ever seen."

The man looked past me to the door, then out the window, into the rain, darkness, and empty street. "I could lose my job."

"I won't tell a soul. I promise," I said. "All you have to do is tell me whether or not you saw her."

The man sighed and shook his head. Maybe he took pity on me, I don't know, but he gave me the answer I was lookin' for. "You're right," he whispered, leaning forward, "she was awful pretty."

"I knew it." I about jumped out of my skin. "This evenin' right? Around dinnertime"

"Yes, sir, that'd be about right."

"And she sent a message."

"Yes, sir, she did, but I can't tell you what it said, no matter what. You surely understand that." His expression begged me not to press him anymore. Fear and discomfort joined together in a bead of sweat on his upper lip. It looked like a single, tiny drop of rain had fallen from the ceiling and landed on his lip, on purpose.

"I do," I said as I sighed, disappointed. "Can you tell me if she asked for a response? If so, where is that message supposed to be delivered?"

"If anyone found out I told you that, Western Union would drive me out of town on the rails and I'd never work again. I got a family to feed, mister. I done told you more than I should have anyway." The single bead multiplied to two.

"I need to know where I can find her. See

this face?" I pointed to my throbbin' cheek. "I think she's in serious trouble. I think there's people lookin' for her for some reason, and these ain't nice people. You get what I mean? I would hate to think what they'd do to a purty thing like that woman, all alone, who can't defend herself like I can. I got a few punches in. Drove the man that jumped me off. She ain't gonna be so lucky."

The telegraph man lowered his head so I couldn't see his eyes. "I understand." Then he looked up at me, and said, "She wasn't alone."

I wasn't expectin' that. I imagined Mavis Lee runnin' in and sendin' a telegraph home to her pa, tellin' him what had happened, that she needed help, then runnin' back to wherever it was she was hidin' out. "Who was she with?"

"Another woman."

"Do you know the name of this woman?"

"I do. Marie Ledder Lord. Her brother is part owner of the Waco and Northwestern railroad. They're the big to-do in town recently."

My mind swirled a bit. I ain't never heard of no Marie Ledder Lord, but I had heard of the Waco and Northwestern railroad. I knew it was makin' headway in Waco, and I also knew Harold Rockwell said he owned a business that made railcars; there was a connection there. Mavis Lee had found refuge with someone of her own ilk, or at least, Harold's. But that made everything clear as the mud stuck to my boots, even though it gave me comfort to know that she wasn't out in the world on her own.

"Where's this woman live?" I said.

"I can't tell you that, but the Ledder Lord House is the biggest house on Austin Avenue. You shouldn't have too hard of a time a findin' it."

"One more thing," I said. "Has anyone else come in askin' after this woman?"

"No, sir, I can say for sure they haven't. You're the first one."

"Thanks for your help, mister, I really appreciate it." I thought about shakin' his hand, but time was wastin'. I ran to the door, excited by the news, but skidded to a quick stop before I was all the way outside. "Which way to Austin Avenue?" I said through the open door.

"That way." He pointed north, and I had to take his word for it that he was tellin' me the truth.

The weather had gotten worse, not better, since I was inside the Western Union office.

Rain hammered down from the sky and blackness surrounded me like a cold, wet blanket. I would have been more confident on a nicer night, but I was hopin' that whoever had jumped me outside the Harlow was tucked in some place dry, givin' up on the chase — if that's what it was. I was heartened to know that Mavis Lee was all right. At least she had been all right enough to send a telegraph and have a friend along with her. Now I just had to hope that whoever it was that was in her room pokin' around hadn't tracked her down like I had. I hurried my pace at the thought.

I skirted up against the buildings as close as I could, keepin' to the shadows and stayin' out of the downpour as much as possible. Rain still peppered my bare skin, hitting me in the face like someone was throwin' pebbles at me. I wasn't slowed, though. The hard thing was keepin' my head up so I could see my way in front of me, see if anyone was about, or comin' after me. I had plenty of reason to worry about such a thing.

It didn't take long before the business district gave way to houses and I lost the protection of overhangs and awnings. I didn't mind. I was gettin' used to bein' wet as a duck's belly. I was glad it wasn't too late into the night, and folks weren't takin' to sleepin'. Every house I passed was lit up like it was Christmas. Candles burnin' in the windows, and all. Some folks even had lamplights that lined the walks up to their porches, casting a safe, easy pace to the front door. The wind had died down, but the flames still flittered about in the lamps doin' their best not to die out. Shadows waltzed about me everywhere I looked. Trees were a hundred feet tall, and others were so short I couldn't tell if they were men or ghosts. I didn't stop to find out.

The hard thing was gaugin' which house was bigger than the next in the darkness. They all looked the same to me; huge as mountains, mostly. Bein' a simple man, a cabin on some land has always been my dream of a house. I couldn't imagine the wealth or need for a house so massive. I saw the same thing in Austin. It seemed wherever there was money, men had to have plenty of room to roam around in. Libraries, kitchens, and such. I guess that kind of livin' was somethin' I would never understand. Most nights I was lucky to have a roof over my head.

X

The Ledder Lord House was easy enough to find. It was almost twice as big as the rest of the houses on Austin Avenue, and that was sayin' somethin'. This house stood three stories tall with turrets posted on each corner. A broad porch wrapped around the left side, and ended with a walk that led to a four-stall carriage house. I couldn't tell what color the house was, or if the house was in good repair, I could only assume that it was. Unlike all of the other houses I had passed, the Ledder Lord House was almost dark. Only the lamplight in the front yard glowed, doin' a swish again' the wind along with a dim light in the front parlor that looked unvitin' and distant. The only way I could tell the house was the largest one on the street was that it sat on a corner lot, with light cast through the rain and gray murkiness from other houses around it. On any other day I would of marveled at such a residence, but on this night, my only inter-est was findin' Mavis Lee, and makin' sure I got my questions answered. Like why she ran out of the restaurant at the Harlow House in the first place.

I stood at the closed wrought-iron gate and pondered my next move. It made perfect sense to me to walk up to the front door, knock on it, and ask to speak to Mavis Lee. But I was hesitant. If she was hidin', then she might not want to talk to me. I had to ask myself why that would be, why she would be hidin' from anything, and I couldn't think of an answer, so I opened the gate and stepped toward the door. I figured there was only half a chance that somebody was gonna answer my knock since it didn't look like no one was home.

I stepped on the porch to look around to make sure I hadn't been followed. It was a relief to be out of the rain. The weather didn't look to be slowin' down any time soon. Rain fell from the sky in steady buckets. The ground was soaked with water snakin' away every which way it could. Mud got muddier, makin' the streets impassible. A wagon would get stuck up to the axle in two seconds; there hadn't been any traffic on the road since I left the Western Union office. I figured the trail leadin' out of Waco was in the same shape. I had hoped to be able to stop at my Aunt Callie's in Dallas on the way north, but I hadn't planned on gettin' held up in Waco. Maybe I could stop on the way back from deliverin' the letter to Captain McMurry. I still had a job to do, after all — though at the moment, findin'

Mavis Lee felt more important to me. Time was tickin' on the back of my neck whether I liked it or not. I had to ride out in the mornin', no matter the weather or the state of Mavis Lee's being — as long as the sheriff said I could. That was the other thing. If I found Mavis Lee and found out what was going on, I could be on with my mission.

With that thought and the fragile certainty that I hadn't been followed — as certain as I could be considerin' the murky weather — I stepped to the door and pressed the buzzer for a long dash. After the harsh sound stopped, I cocked my ear to the door, tryin' to detect any kind of life inside the house. There was nothin' to indicate any movement at all. The house was quiet as a mausoleum.

I sighed out loud and felt a creep of doubt twitch into the front of my mind. I supposed it was a silly thing, standin' on a stranger's doorstep in the middle of a rainstorm, lookin' for a woman whose husband had been poisoned. Ten minutes before it all happened, I would have said such a thing wasn't possible. All I had wanted was a nice steak dinner, which I didn't get, and a good night's sleep. All I'd had time for was a glass of water, and I didn't even get to take a drink of that. My chance encounter with Mavis Lee changed everythin'.

I pressed the buzzer again, only this time I was more impatient with the button and stabbed it with my stiff, wet, finger three times, holding each push for a long time. If someone was avoidin' the door, I was gonna annoy them the best I could. At least I would know I had tried if no one answered, because beyond that, at the moment, I didn't have much of a plan.

After I let off the buzzer the last time, I stood back, readying myself to pack it in. But I stopped movin' when I heard footsteps thumpin' toward the door. I steeled myself for whatever was comin' my way. I knew I looked a sight, and I was out of my element among the fancy houses more than I was at the restaurant in the Harlow House.

The front door of the house swung open in one swift pull. The sudden movement was accompanied by a burst of bright light contained by a large hurricane lamp, which was unexpected, to my eyes at least, blinding me for a second.

"Who are you, and what do you want?" It was a female's voice. There was no mistakin' the cadence of a black woman in her words, or the ferocity and annoyance of her mood.

I cleared my eyes to make sure I wasn't

starin' down the barrel of a scattergun. That's how it felt. The woman sure didn't use no welcomin' tone.

"My name's Scrap Elliott." I stopped and corrected myself. "Robert Earl Elliott. I'm lookin' for Mavis Lee Bowen. Well, I mean, Mavis Lee Rockwell. The wife of the late Harold Rockwell."

"You got a problem keepin' names straight, don't ya?"

I could see clearly now. The woman was as wide as she was tall, with a round, suspicious face, bright white eyes, and a broom in her left hand like she intended to scat a stray cat. Her right hand held the lamp, and she completely blocked the doorway like she was a wall made of flesh and bone. I wondered how she had opened the door, but I didn't say as much. It puzzled me, though.

"Mavis Lee calls me Robert Earl. My friends call me Scrap. I guess I call myself that, too. Mavis Lee done went and got married since the last time I saw her, and now she's a widow, so all I'm tryin' to do is keep up with her."

"I'm havin' a hard time keepin' up with you, mister. Why you standin' on Mr. Lord's front step? It's late and ain't no one but a fool or a man up to no good be out on a night like this."

"I ain't up to no good. I'm tryin' to help Mavis Lee."

"You're a fool then."

"Could be, but my aim is true."

"I ain't never heard of no Mavis Lee Bowen. Or what you say, Rockwell?"

"That's right, Rockwell." I stood my ground, too. I knew I looked like somethin' somebody dropped off unwanted and unannounced, but I had to find Mavis Lee. The telegraph man was confident that she was in the office earlier. I didn't think he was tellin' me a tall tale, but he might have been. "Could I speak to your missus, then? Mrs. Ledder Lord? I was told she was at the telegraph office with Mavis Lee earlier this evenin'."

"She ain't here. Who tol' you she was at the Western Union?"

I about blurted out the telegraph man, but I didn't want to betray him, so I just stared at the woman with the same kind of judgin' look she was givin' me. "Was she there?"

"That ain't no answer. You get snippy with me, I'll take this broom to you." She thrust it forward and scowled at me, forcin' as much of a mean look on her face as she could.

403

The wind rose up, kickin' the sides of my jacket aside enough to expose my sidearms and knife sheath. I didn't do anything to hide my weapons. The weather had cooperated to make us equal. Now, I had to wonder who was afraid of who?

"I think you best jus' leave now," the woman said.

I shook my head. "Mavis Lee is in trouble. Look at this face." I pointed to my black and blues without any pride at all. "Some man jumped me when I went lookin' for her. Now, the way I see it, if that man was smart enough to know I was with Mavis Lee, then he might be able to figure out where she's hidin' out like I did. Or at least that I came here. I promise you that fella's gonna cause a lot more trouble than I am. I only want to make sure Mavis Lee is all right, that she's safe. She's had enough trouble for one night."

The door creaked open a bit more, and a shadowy figure stepped out from behind it. I could tell it was another woman. Not Mavis Lee, another stranger I didn't know.

"You go on now, Loretta," a calm female voice said. "I'll talk to Mr. Elliott."

"You shore?" the woman at the door said.

"Yes, I'm sure. I believe what he says."

"All right then." Loretta stepped back,

taking the light with her, stopping about five feet behind the door so I could see the other woman a little better. "But I ain't goin' far, you hear? I'll be ready with this broom if he gets smart with you."

The woman walked to where Loretta had been standing and stopped. "I am Marie Ledder Lord, Mr. Elliott. I've been expecting you."

I wanted to ask why she was expectin' me, but I didn't. If she was a friend of Mavis Lee's that might explain it, but I wasn't sure. Mavis Lee would have told her about meetin' with me in the restaurant, and what had happened to Harold. Or maybe there was another reason. How could I know?

Marie Ledder Lord was older than Mavis Lee by about ten years, which made her around my age. She was a spritely woman with her hair piled upward, which was the fashion. She wore a long green velvet dress that bundled at the floor. A thick mane of brunette hair flowed over her shoulders, and she had eyes that sparkled in the dim light. She carried herself with confidence, and I could tell that in full light there was some beauty about her, different from Mavis Lee, and without my heart attached to it in any way.

"If you knowed I was comin', then you

know of the troubles that Mavis Lee has faced on this day."

"It's a tragedy."

I couldn't restrain myself. "Is she here? I'd like to speak with her."

"I'm sorry that's not possible." She might as well of added, "and don't argue with me," but she didn't.

"She's in danger."

"She's not here."

"Where's she gone to."

"You assume she was here."

"I do. How about I talk to your brother, Mr. Ledder Lord?"

"Thomas is not here, either."

I was able to still see Loretta standin' behind Marie Ledder Lord. The light reflected off her face, and she kept lookin' back and forth, away from us, then back to us with a nervousness that hadn't been there when she stood blockin' the door. I stared back to the woman who stood before me, took in her stance, her slow answers, and the tension she held in her cheeks, and I realized that she was stallin' me.

"Well, your assumption is wrong, Mr. Elliott."

"My friends call me Scrap." I stepped back from the door. Even over the pour of rain, I thought I heard a door open in the distance.

"We're not friends, Mr. Elliott."

A horse whinnied and I knew I had been right about the door, about bein' stalled. "No, we're not," I said, tearing to the side of the porch so I could get a good look at the carriage house.

A dim light glared from inside the barn-like buildin', and I could see a one-horse buggy bustin' out the door. A lone woman was drivin' it. Even in the poor light, in the downpour of rain, I could tell it was Mavis Lee with the reins in her hands.

I broke into a run, leavin' the protection and occupants of the house behind me. On any other day, I wouldn't have been a sprintin' match for any horse. But this wasn't no ordinary day. It was wet and muddy as could be. Mavis Lee wasn't going to get too far.

XI

My boots went out from under me as soon as I hit wet ground. My rear end slammed into the cold, soggy yard that wasn't nothin' but a pen full of mud. It was a soft landin', sounded like a baby gettin' its first swat, but the thickness of the slick mud made it hard to scramble to my feet. I stumbled and fell a few times before I righted myself and got my balance. When I was able to finally stand up, I heard Loretta stampedin' toward me. A quick glance over my shoulder showed me she intended on usin' that broom to do more than smack me with it. By the fierce look in the whites of her eyes, and the rage set in her jaw, I could tell she meant to hobble me, slow me down the best she could.

"You stop!" Loretta hollered. "You stop right there!"

There was no sign of her missus, Marie Ledder Lord, but truth be told, I wasn't worried about neither of them women. Mavis Lee was gettin' away quicker than I thought she would. The buggy was already out into the street. The crack of a whip echoed backward to me, cuttin' through the rain with the force of determination of a woman doin' her best to escape a bad situation.

I ran after the buggy, dodgin' puddles, dancin' across the yard in zigs and zags, doin' my best to cause Loretta to take a tumble. I was afraid of what I would step in, of breakin' my ankle or somethin' worse. That was the last thing I needed.

I tried to keep my eyes on the buggy, but somethin' else captured my attention: A man standin' in the open stall of the carriage house. A hurricane lamp lit him from behind, showin' me that he was of about the same stature as Marie Ledder Lord; short, spritely, and proportioned with narrow bones and a common thinness. Just like the man who had jumped me outside of the Harlow House. I had to wonder if he was one and the same, if the man who attacked me was Thomas Ledder Lord, Marie's brother. But I didn't have time to wonder too long. He saw me at the same time that I saw him.

I had no choice but to pull my six-shooter to protect myself. I had trouble comin' for me from both directions. It sure would have been nice to have had a partner at my side, a man that I could trust with my life. I rode with such a fella for a long time, Josiah Wolfe was his name. We're still good friends, but my ambitions took me to bein' a courier, and his, well, from time to time he still rides with a Ranger company, but he's more inclined to be a family man these days rather than put himself in harm's way. His tolerance for ambition is far less than mine. I could have used Wolfe's presence, his forethought and dependable marksmanship, but sad as it was, I was on my own, and I had to figure my way out of the mess I'd got myself into.

Just to get everyone's attention, I fired off a round into the air. The man in the carriage house stopped just inside the door. He had produced a pitchfork in his hand, leavin' me to hope that he didn't have a gun on him, or nearby anywheres. Loretta stopped behind me, too. Another quick glance over my shoulder allowed me to see the mountain of a woman had slid into a statue position, holdin' her broom with less enthusiasm than she had been now that she knew I'd use my gun if I had to. And I would have. I didn't have no clue who these people were or what they were capable of.

"I only want to talk to Mavis Lee," I shouted at the man. The rain hammered my head, dumpin' buckets of cold rainwater between us. He shimmered in a fuzzy way and I couldn't tell if he'd heard me or not. All I could hear was water pourin' from the black sky. I was so wet I feared I'd never dry out. The bones in my toes shivered.

"Leave her alone," the man called back.

"I can't do that," I said, then broke into a run toward the street, toward the last place I'd seen the buggy before it had disappeared from my sight.

I was bettin' that Loretta and Thomas, if that's who the man was, wouldn't take me on, at least right away, until they was able to arm themselves and come after me. I had a head start and I planned on makin' the most of it.

I dodged puddles again, skirted the carriage house, and landed square on the muddy street after some tricky strides. I was ten yards down the street, away from the Ledder Lord House, before I heard a horse strugglin' to pull a buggy; it had to be Mavis Lee. I could see it stuck up ahead and hear the switch of the whip as it slapped wet horsehair and muscle with more desperation than I thought a woman like Mavis Lee could ever muster.

I couldn't imagine why she was tryin' so hard to get away from me. Why she had ran from the restaurant when Harold had died, and now, from the Ledder Lord House in weather so unhospitable that an alligator would have scurried for cover and stayed there until the storm passed. Unless, of course, she had reason to fear me — or the questions I had to ask her. I had almost convinced myself that she was innocent of havin' anything to do with Harold's death until that very second. I slowed my pace, reconsiderin' if I wanted to talk to Mavis Lee after all. I knew, though, no matter the cause, I had no choice even if she had somethin' to say I didn't want to hear.

I pushed through the mud, put away my concern about what was behind me, gripped my six-shooter tight, and came up on the buggy faster than I'd expected.

The poor horse, black as the clouds over my head, was strugglin' to move an inch a minute in the mud. Mavis Lee was panicked, doin' her best to make the beast run, slappin' the whip across the beast's ass with equal parts of frustration and fear.

A look of resignation crossed her face as soon as she saw me. She let the whip drop from her hand, and the horse, bein' a smart one, surrendered its effort and stopped, pantin' on the edge of collapse.

The rain hadn't let up and neither had the darkness. I could barely see Mavis Lee; she was all covered up in a black slicker, covered head to toe like a Confederate spy tryin' to sneak across a border of one kind or another. She looked nothin' like the girl I first met in Brownsville, or the young woman who had glided into the restaurant, capturin' everybody's attention, includin' mine.

"I'm stuck," she whispered, then lowered her head, resigned to her fate. "I'll never get away."

I climbed up on the seat and slid in next

to her, tuckin' my gun at my side, not holstering it, in case I needed it to fend anyone off us. "Your friends'll be here in a second. I don't want to have to hurt them."

"They won't harm you, Robert Earl. They're trying to protect me is all."

"Why?" I was finally able to ask. "Why are you runnin' from me? Why did you leave Harold when he died? What in the heck is goin' on here, Mavis Lee?"

"It wasn't supposed to turn out like this." She was starin' forward, down the road, her eyes fixed between the horse's two pointed black ears.

"What are you talkin' about?"

Mavis Lee turned to me with her eyes wet with tears and rain, tainted with a twisted emotion I didn't understand. "Have you ever been in love, Robert Earl? Truly in love? With someone so deep that when you first saw them your heart jumped to your throat and you lost your breath? A person you needed and wanted so much that you would do anything to be with them?"

I shook my head, and started to answer, started to tell her that I thought I was in love with her once upon a time, but the first utterance of my words was interrupted by the voice of a man from behind us.

"You need to step to the ground, Elliott."

I didn't recognize the voice, but a quick look told me it was the man that I had assumed was Thomas Ledder Lord. He had a scattergun pointed at my back. "Don't test me, now. Drop your gun, climb down from there, and leave Mavis Lee alone. This has nothing to do with you, even though you think it does."

Loretta and Marie Ledder Lord came runnin' up behind Thomas and stopped. It was three against one. A broom and scattergun against a six-shooter. None of what was happenin' made a lick of sense to me.

I looked to Mavis Lee and ignored the fella with the scattergun. A risky thing to do, but he didn't look — or sound — like no killer to me. He had a quiver in his voice as deep as a South Texas canyon.

"Call 'em, off," I said. It was more a request than a command. I didn't know how much currency I carried with Mavis Lee, but I didn't want to show my power and pull my gun up from my side unless I had to.

She sat there, still as a widow starin' at her husband's coffin, unmovin', uninterested in anything around us. "I loved him right away, you know. I couldn't help myself."

I assumed she was talkin' about Harold

Rockwell, tellin' me about what had happened after we'd parted ways in Brownsville.

"You don't have to tell him anything," Thomas said. His voice competed with the rain, with the wind that swirled around us. It almost got lost in the darkness, but I heard what he said, and saw Mavis Lee flinch. It was like he had snapped her out of a trance.

Mavis Lee looked at me like a she'd found a fierceness in her soul that hadn't existed there before. I didn't recognize her. "I won't let you come between us, Robert Earl. I won't let anyone come between us. Not now," she said. "After everything that's happened."

It was then that I realized the man she had been talkin' about, the love she had been talkin' about, was Thomas Ledder Lord, not Harold Rockwell.

She rustled her hands inside the slicker, out of sight, as a deep rage grew on her face. I had no choice but to trust my gut, to stand up and defend myself. If I didn't, I might end up dead. If I was wrong, I'd apologize for makin' a fool out of myself for pullin' a gun on a lady.

I pointed my Colt at Mavis Lee, and yelled, "Stop. Don't move. You hear. Don't move an inch, Mavis Lee."

"Don't shoot her," Marie Ledder Lord said as loud as she could, tryin' to overcome the rain and the wind. The night was as unforgivin' as I had seen in a long time.

I was sideways and could see them all, Thomas, Loretta, and Marie frozen in shock, in recognition of somethin' I couldn't figure out. Thankfully, Mavis Lee complied with my order. The movement under the slicker stopped, and she angled her face upward, so we were lookin' at each other eye to eye.

"See, Robert Earl, I was right, wasn't I? You get on something and you never stop. You just keep going until you win, until you figure it all out. You would have made a great captain. I'm sure of it. You're just like Thomas, only you weren't lucky enough to be born into a family of wealth and ambition. I've always been attracted to men like you and Thomas. I failed with Harold, weak as he was, no spine at all. I thought all was lost to me until I met Thomas. I thought I was doomed to a miserable, intolerable life, but we had our moment, didn't we, Thomas?" She looked away from me to the man she clearly loved.

Thomas Ledder Lord looked beat. The barrel of the scattergun was pointed to the ground, no threat to me. "Stop, Mavis Lee," he said. "You don't owe anyone an explanation for anything."

"But I do. I can see the horror on Robert Earl's face."

I kept the gun trained on her, though I was tempted to drop it. "You killed Harold, didn't you?" I said. "You poisoned him so you could be with Thomas. Is that right? Or is my thinkin' crashin' into somethin' else? Please tell me I'm wrong, Mavis Lee. Please tell me I'm wrong." The tip of my Colt trembled with uncertainty.

"Oh, what you must think of me. That's what will separate us, Thomas, what people think. That was always the risk. That our love wouldn't be accepted. I'll take that with me, then. Our love. No one can have that," Mavis Lee said, followed by a pop that startled me, unexpected. A brief firecracker sparkled from inside the slicker, erupting out of the neck of the cover. With that, Mavis Lee gasped and toppled over. A small caliber handgun slipped from her hand as Marie Ledder Lord let out a scream that joined the thunder and wind overhead.

Mavis Lee was dead and for the second time in a day, there was nothin' I could do to save her.

XII

Once things got settled down and someone sent for help, Thomas Ledder Lord told me and Sheriff MacDonald everything he knew. He sat in a grand chair carved from mahogany wood, just inside the parlor, drippin' wet, with his head hung down, exhausted in defeat and grief. The sheriff and I stood across from the man, shoulder to shoulder. I was doin' my best not to be overcome by the show of wealth around me. Everthin' around me looked like it'd been dipped in silver and gold.

"Harold, of course," Thomas said with a weak voice, "was anxious to do business with us, with the Waco and Northwestern railroad. He has been calling on us for some time, but once he brought Mavis Lee with him, in hopes, I think, to charm us, the visits and business calls became more frequent."

"Charm you, you mean," I said.

Sheriff MacDonald glared at me but didn't say anything.

"I suppose you could assume that," Thomas said, lookin' at me, rubbin his bruised jaw tenderly. I'd given him a hefty undercut earlier in the night outside the hotel, and he hadn't forgot it. "I am usually immune to such feminine pressures, but

Mavis Lee was persistent."

"But she was married," I said.

"Yes, that was a problem," Thomas answered.

The sheriff shifted uncomfortably. "You sure you don't want a lawyer here, sir," he said in a tone that sounded like he worked for the man instead of bein' the law.

"I didn't do anything wrong," Thomas said.

The sheriff acted like he wanted to say somethin', but restrained himself. Me, too, as far as that went. I figured the best thing to do was let the man tell his story. I wanted to hear what he had to say.

"I had no idea about Mavis Lee's plans," Thomas continued, "Harold and I were to meet tomorrow and complete a deal that would see his company suppling railcars to our railroad for some time to come. I know he planned on a long celebratory voyage around the world afterward. It must have been the fear of that trip, of being away from here, that set her in motion to stop it."

"You mean bein' away from you," I said, not able to stop the words comin' from my mouth.

Thomas Ledder Lord looked up and glared at me. "Your jealousies are not welcome here, sir."

Sheriff MacDonald jabbed me in the side with his elbow. I suppose I could take a hint, but I didn't. "I ain't jealous. Just curious is all," I said.

"About what?" Thomas said.

"What you was doin' in Mavis Lee's hotel room if you didn't have nothin' to do with all of this? Was you lookin' for somethin'? Like this?" I said, as I pulled out the small blue bottle I'd been carryin' in my pocket.

If Thomas Ledder Lord was pale and defeated before, his face went white as Loretta's eyes once he fixed his gaze on the evidence I held before him. He started to get up, looked to the door, but I stepped in between him and any thought of exitin' the house.

"What is this about?" Sheriff MacDonald said.

"I went into Mavis Lee's room to see what I could find out, and a man came inside. One that had ridin' boots on that, now that I take them in, are the same as this fella's here. He was lookin' for somethin', but I already had it my possession. I suspect it held the poison that did Harold Rockwell in. Seems to me that Mr. Ledder Lord here knew what Mavis Lee was up to. Or maybe it was what he was up to. Isn't that right, Mr. Ledder Lord? It was you that jumped me outside the hotel, and it was me that gave you the black and blue stretch on your face."

All of the air escaped from Thomas's lungs and he collapsed into the chair. "She said you were going to be a problem," he said.

"That's why she found me at dinner," I said, realizin' that Mavis Lee wasn't payin' me no social call. "She was there to get rid of me, too. Ain't that right?"

"You best tell the truth, sir," Sheriff Mac-Donald said. "Is what Ranger Elliott is sayin' true? This was the plan between the two of you?"

Thomas looked at me with eyes empty of feelin', and said, "Be glad you didn't take a drink of water."

Sheriff MacDonald stood outside the Harlow House the next mornin' with a satisfied look on his face. The sun was up, and the rain had moved on, leaving the sky blue, without a cloud to be seen. Mud was ankle-deep in the street, but it was navigable since most of the water had run off it. I hoped the trail ahead would offer an easy ride, but I had my suspicions that it would be treacherous and slow goin'. After everythin' that had happened, I was still on schedule to deliver the letter to the company headquarters in Garland.

"That's a fine-lookin' horse you got there, Elliott," the sheriff said.

"She's new to me. Me and . . ." I stopped. I couldn't say the horse's name. I didn't want to remember Mavis Lee or the hurt she'd caused me and everyone else anymore. No beast deserved a moniker that evoked a killer. This mare had been dependable, a perfect shinin' example of what I had hoped she would be. I looked down the road and my eyes focused on the closest saloon, the Happy Spur. "Me and Happy," I stuttered, "are gettin' to know each other. I 'spect we'll ride a lot of miles together." I finished cinchin' up the saddle, and joined the sheriff on the boardwalk.

"I owe you an apology, Elliott," he said.

"Why's that?"

"I didn't know who you were or what you were up to when this calamity we found ourselves in broke out. I wasn't sure what was goin' on."

"I didn't pay it no mind. I knew I didn't do nothin' wrong. I can leave town now, can't I?"

MacDonald smiled. "Of course. My troubles are just gettin' started, though."

"How do you figure?"

"The townsfolk are mad as flies shut out from the kitchen that Thomas Ledder Lord is in jail, and I think the trial is gonna be a big ol' circus. I ain't lookin' forward to it, I'll tell you that."

"I'll ride through on my way back to Austin."

"I'd appreciate that. You'll be needed to tell your side of the story." The sheriff hesitated, then said, "I sent a message to General King in Austin and told him of your exploits here."

"I sure do hope that's not a bad thing." I didn't know what an exploit was.

"I told him your talents are bein' wasted as a courier."

I understood that. I suppose you couldn't have wiped the smile off my face with a brick. I nodded, stuck out my hand, shook the sheriff's, then climbed on my horse, Happy, and settled into my saddle. I sure did hope I didn't run into any more trouble before I got where I was a goin'.

"Come on, Happy, let's ride." Then I urged the mare on, takin' it slow and safe until I knew I could let her run. She didn't object to her new name in any way that I could tell. We ran as fast as we could with the wind in my face, leavin' Waco, and all that had happened, behind us. I bet I wore that silly smile that Sheriff MacDonald gave me for a hundred miles.

ABOUT THE AUTHOR

Larry D. Sweazy is a multiple-award-winning author of eighteen western and mystery novels, and over eighty nonfiction articles and short stories. Larry lives in Indiana with his wife, Rose, where he is hard at work on his next novel. More information can be found at www.larryd sweazy.com.

he genre to enjoy. She has been reading the
genre for more than five decades.

ABOUT THE EDITOR

Hazel Rumney has lived most of her life in Maine, although she also spent a number of years in Spain and California while her husband was in the military. She has worked in the publishing business for almost thirty years. Retiring in 2011, she and her husband traveled throughout the United States visiting many famous and not-so-famous western sites before returning to Thorndike, Maine, where they now live. In 2012, Hazel reentered the publishing world as an editor for Five Star Publishing, a part of Cengage Learning. During her tenure with Five Star, she has developed and delivered titles that have won Western Fictioneers Peacemaker Awards, Will Rogers Medallion Awards, and Western Writers of America Spur Awards, including the double Spur Award–winning novel *Wild Ran the Rivers* by James D. Crownover. Western fiction is Hazel's favorite genre to enjoy. She has been reading the genre for more than five decades.

The employees of Thorndike Press hope you have enjoyed this Large Print book. All our Thorndike, Wheeler, and Kennebec Large Print titles are designed for easy reading, and all our books are made to last. Other Thorndike Press Large Print books are available at your library, through selected bookstores, or directly from us.

For information about titles, please call:
  (800) 223-1244

or visit our website at:
  gale.com/thorndike

To share your comments, please write:
  Publisher
  Thorndike Press
  10 Water St., Suite 310
  Waterville, ME 04901